CAMP HOPE

Dangerous Sanctuary

LOIS RICHER

HEART QUEST

Romance fiction from
Tyndale House Publishers, Inc., Wheaton, Illinois

www.heartquest.com

Visit Tyndale's exciting Web site at www.tyndale.com

Check out the latest about HeartQuest books at www.heartquest.com

HeartQuest is a registered trademark of Tyndale House Publishers, Inc.

Edited by Lorie Popp

Designed by Ron Kaufmann

Published in association with the literary agency of Janet Kobobel Grant, Books & Such, 4788 Carissa Ave., Santa Rosa, CA 95405.

Some Scripture quotations are taken from the *Holy Bible,* New Living Translation, copyright © 1996. Used by permission of Tyndale House Publishers, Inc., Wheaton, Illinois 60189. All rights reserved.

Some Scripture quotations are taken from the *Holy Bible,* New International Version®. NIV®. Copyright © 1973, 1978, 1984 by International Bible Society. Used by permission of Zondervan Publishing House. All rights reserved.

Some Scripture quotations are taken from *The Living Bible* copyright © 1971. Used by permission of Tyndale House Publishers, Inc., Wheaton, Illinois 60189. All rights reserved.

Some Scripture quotations are taken from the *Holy Bible,* King James Version.

Some Scripture quotations are taken from the New King James Version. Copyright © 1979, 1980, 1982 by Thomas Nelson, Inc. Used by permission. All rights reserved.

Library of Congress Cataloging-in-Publication Data

Richer, Lois.
   Dangerous sanctuary / Lois Richer.
      p. cm. — (Camp Hope series ; #1) (Heartquest)

   ISBN 0-8423-6436-6 (sc)
   1. Canada, Northern—Fiction. 2. Stalking victims—Fiction. 3. Women cooks—Fiction.
4. Nurses—Fiction. I. Title.
PR9199.4.R53D36 2004
823'.92—dc22   2003023253

Printed in the United States of America

09 08 07 06 05 04
9   8   7   6   5   4   3   2   1

People often ask where my story ideas come from.
Dangerous Sanctuary began to germinate several summers ago
during the sizzling July heat when I cooked at a local summer camp.
For the past fifty years, Torch Trail Bible Camp has accepted kids
from every situation and endeavored to show them
more about God and His love.

I would like to gratefully acknowledge Ken Leonard for allowing me
a peek inside the life of a camp director. Rarely does his dedication to his
work receive public affirmation, nor would he want it. But how often,
I wonder, does his personal sacrifice of time, sleep, and sheer effort
permit another soul to enter the kingdom?

No one can know the circumstances behind anyone's arrival
at Torch Trail, but God continues to use Ken and his family to meet
the needs of those who need this ministry.

This book is lovingly dedicated to all those who keep
Torch burning for God. He knows.

ACKNOWLEDGMENTS

Many contributors add their own spices to the soup of ideas that becomes a story. I would like to thank Torch Trail Bible Camp, Canadian Sunday School Mission, Ken and Louise Leonard, a host of campers, counselors, and helpers unnamed who never knew they'd be providing perspective for a writer. I've appreciated the support, friendship, and prayers of Aven Paetkau, Lyn Cote, and Linda Tangjerd through the past year of ups and downs. Many in my home church have kept me focused and on track, so thank you, Nipawin Alliance.

To the many Tyndale blessings: Anne Goldsmith, who caught my vision and let me write it; Lorie Popp, who polished my words to a pearly sheen; cover designer Ron Kaufmann, who captures ideas so well; and to those whose names I never knew but who put their all into this project—thank you! You are a talented, dedicated group determined to give your best, and I cherish your efforts.

To Janet Kobobel Grant, agent invaluable, who graciously handles all the niggling details and always listens, I stand in awe of your abilities. To my husband, Barry, who is the personification of the word *patience*, I love you. To my two sons, who have accepted that their mom forgets a lot of good stuff, I apologize and promise we will have pie again, one day.

Most of all I want to say thank You to the Father who sees all, knows all, and hears all. He is Lord.

PROLOGUE

Tiny sparks, fanned by the wind and boosted by an unseen accelerant, burst into devouring flames. Mutely ominous, they crept across the gable end of the house in a silent quest for more, then bit into the scrolling gingerbread trim with malicious delight.

Once savored, their appetite became insatiable.

They licked across the roof, hungry, flickering orange tongues, dazzling against the inky blackness of midnight. Barely minutes later the upper story of the house blazed in the night shadows as the crackling inferno consumed in a mad, voracious anger.

It was a fitting end.

Now, let her feel the same pain he carried in his soul—poker hot. Searing.

No one noticed the skeleton of a smile lift his thin, angry mouth. No neighbor saw him walk to the bus stop on the corner, linger there, waiting under a pine tree for Calgary's firemen to arrive.

Come. He ached to shout it, to tell the world. *It doesn't matter now. You're too late to tame the beast I've let loose.*

Grim satisfaction eased his fury when the whining cry of a fire engine moaned around the corner, howled to a halt. Firemen poured onto the street, then gaped in horror. Where to start?

Still, he waited in the shadows—and the hoses spurted their puny stream over his inferno.

Ashes to ashes, dust to dust.

Bitter gall soured his stomach, accentuating the void. As he turned to leave, a car plummeted through the barricade, squealed to a stop. A woman fell out, screaming her grief in mournful wails as she tried to break free of a firefighter's restraining hold.

Her!

He swore at the futility of it. All that planning and he'd missed his target. The unexpected again. He hated chance, hated having his plans disrupted. And yet, wasn't that exactly why he was here?

She'd ruined it all. Utterly destroyed everything. Now, for the second time, she had escaped justice. For that he would exact payment—in full.

With a curse of disgust, he turned, slipped into the denseness of a smoky gloom that allowed him to leave without arousing suspicion. He walked a long time, pausing to check over his shoulder every so often. No one followed.

A single thought brightened the darkness of his soul. Perhaps tonight wasn't a waste but merely another step along the path of retribution she deserved. For months he'd waited . . . watched. He could afford to wait longer. Meanwhile, she would suffer.

This was just the start of the battle, the first assault.

But he wouldn't lose. She *would* pay his price.

Justine demanded no less.

CHAPTER ONE

You're leaving? To go where?"

He frowned, which Georgia interpreted as a reminder that she stay in touch.

"I don't know where, Doug. Not yet. I just know I've wept for too long. Nothing will bring them back. Nothing. It's been nearly two years. It's time I figured out how to live the rest of my life." A pause, a break in her voice as she fought for control. "Please understand. I have to learn to move on."

"Yes. But move on where? To what? Back to nursing?" He watched her carefully.

"No." That much was certain. "I'll always be 'that' nurse. People will always wonder if I did it deliberately, if I knew." Georgia shook her head. "I can't go back. I have to go ahead."

"And that means leaving the city?"

"For now."

"Okay. Where?" Worry lines carved his forehead.

"I haven't decided for certain, but I thought perhaps I'd visit the bush country Dad always talked about. I need some place where I can think."

"Sounds lonely. And then?"

"I don't know about the future, Doug. I can't think that far ahead. I'm not booking hotels or anything. I'll just drive, take things one day at a time."

"Why not stop at that camp I told you about? The one the youth group has decided to raise funds for. Our church supported a student who worked as a counselor there last summer, remember? Apparently it's in the boonies, very much back to nature, which you claim is what you want."

Doug's eyes flashed with an excitement she remembered from long ago. "It might be good, Georgia. Anyone who's been there says the rustic peace of the place restores them. In fact, if you're traveling north to your dad's old stomping ground, you'll drive right past it."

"It's a children's camp, isn't it?" In her mind rang an echo of toddler laughter, the sound of pure joy abruptly silenced. "A summer camp. There probably isn't anyone there yet. What did you say it's called?"

"Camp Hope. And I think someone lives there year-round. Why not check it out? You can always leave if it's not what you want."

Camp Hope.

"Good name." She leaned forward, hugged him. "I'll think about it. Bye, Doug."

"I'll be praying," he whispered.

Hadn't he always?

———≫◆≪———

The Northern Canadian Woods

Georgia MacGregor huddled in the back pew of the old country church and asked herself why she bothered now that Evan wasn't here to share with her. Why keep up their Sunday morning tradition? Why torture herself with a dream that would never live again?

"God's very nature is love. Pure, honest, intense love that never changes."

She didn't want to hear it. But in spite of her efforts to block them, the words of the sermon slipped through her consciousness, pierced through to her very soul.

"He may discipline us. He may send us people or allow events that we don't understand or appreciate, but the truth of who He is never changes. God personifies love."

No! She wouldn't listen anymore.

Georgia reached for the trifold bulletin and scanned it with mounting desperation, searching for something—anything—that would keep her mind off questions no one could answer. Baby- and wedding-shower announcements sprinkled through the list of dates to remember. A ninetieth birthday, two retirement parties, a funeral notice. A picnic for the church family and a church cleaning. There was plenty going on in this small rural assembly, even though it was hidden away from the hubbub of the city. Proof that life went on?

She smiled at the list of special dates marking weeks and months that lay in the future, every important milestone lovingly remembered by friends, families, and neighbors who cared.

Once Georgia had considered remembering a good thing. But in the end, the memories had almost consumed her—until she'd run away, determined to find a new life.

Yet she could not forget. She would never do that. Just to stop hurting, that's all she craved. And hadn't found. Not in six weeks of endless traveling.

It was time to go back.

> *Camp Hope needs a head cook for the summer. Our first camp begins soon! The situation is critical. Please contact the camp office if you can help out.*

Doug's camp. Georgia flipped the paper closed, her mind swinging back to her childhood. The few times she'd been allowed to attend summer camp she'd loved it. Did kids today do the same silly things she'd done? Toilet paper the cabins, stash candy from the tuck shop for evening parties conducted after weary counselors finally fell asleep?

She opened the bulletin to the back page, reread the ad. Sounded like they were desperate.

"Miss MacGregor, it's lovely to see you back with us again."

The minister! Georgia jumped to her feet, only then realizing she'd somehow missed the closing hymn and the benediction.

"Th-thank you," she stammered, her hand limp in the pastor's firm grip. She wouldn't correct him—he didn't need to know. Besides, technically she wasn't a Mrs. any longer, was she?

"It seems you stayed a little longer than you intended." The pastor's blue eyes twinkled, as if to remind her of her insistence that she couldn't possibly remain for their brunch last weekend.

"Actually I did," she murmured, drawing her hand from his. "I traveled up to the lakes last week. With all the road construction, I had to return this way."

"Ah." His intent gaze probed the curtain of reserve she tried to draw between them. "And did you enjoy your trip to the north?"

"Oh yes. It's a beautiful area. I hadn't realized so much wild country still remained out here." She searched for a way to escape. But the woman on the other side of her was deep in conversation with a petulant child. Both of them blocked her only exit. There was no way out.

Georgia gave up and faced the garrulous pastor.

"I suppose you've had a chance to see Camp Hope then." He grinned. "It's our pride and joy. Thirty years ago that place was nothing but bush. Now it houses camps all summer long. Even a few in the winter."

Georgia followed his gaze to the bulletin in her hands. "I'm afraid I didn't go there. In fact, I've only just read their announcement in here."

"Yes, the cook." He shook his head, his smile disintegrating. "It's a serious situation, I'm afraid. Normally they've long since filled their staff vacancies. But after all the rumors . . ." He sighed. "Well, we've been praying for Kent."

She didn't really care about the camp, but what was this about rumors?

"Kent?" she asked, hoping he would take the bait and offer some illumination on his unusual comments.

"Kent Anderson. He's the camp director. He was here this morning. I'll introduce you, if you like. Just let me look." The pastor glanced around the sanctuary but didn't find the person he sought. His gaze moved to outside the window behind her. "Yes, there he is." He chuckled. "I might have known."

"Known?"

"Look over there, with the Murdock sisters. Funny hats," he added when she didn't immediately see where he was pointing. He laughed. "To that boy, those ladies are the equivalent of twin grandmothers—double everything!"

"That's nice." Georgia wondered if she dared nudge the woman who blocked her exit, but when the child began to wail anew, she declined, concentrated on what the pastor was saying.

"They must have asked him for lunch. I can tell from the way he's helping Miss Emily into her car instead of teasing her about her hat that she's offered him food."

Georgia glanced out the window again. A man stood with his back to them, carefully assisting a tiny white-haired woman from her walker into the passenger seat of the oldest car Georgia had ever seen. The feathery nest trembling atop Miss Emily's white head demanded attention. Georgia stifled her giggles. She didn't blame the man for his gingerly help or the smile that flickered at the edge of his mouth. That hat threatened to topple with the tiniest gust of wind.

She focused on the man. He was good-looking, his face a blend of rugged angles and tanned lines that told the tale of his outdoor life. Tall and muscular, he wore faded corduroy pants, a checkered shirt, and battered brown loafers with an air of elegant grace. All in all,

Kent Anderson looked very comfortable standing there waiting, as a car older than he rumbled away.

"He's not going with them. Isn't the Murdocks' a good place to lunch?" she asked absently, still watching.

Kent covered the smile on his face with one hand while the car rounded the corner in a series of backfires. He turned, only then becoming aware of the attention several giggling teenage girls were paying him. He grinned, then pretended to doff his hat at them, bowing from the waist. They giggled even more.

"Good afternoon, ladies," he called. "Got your registrations in for teen camp?"

"Not yet," one of them said. "We weren't sure whether—"

"You'd better hurry." He cut across the rest of their sentence, his voice betraying a hint of strain. "Things are filling up. Teen camp is always a good one."

They nodded.

He seemed to want to say more but apparently changed his mind and instead jumped upward in time to snatch a bright red Frisbee, which he tossed back to a little boy. "Good one, Jeffry. You're getting better."

Jeffry grinned with delight at Kent's praise, and Kent grinned back.

Georgia watched him amble across the lawn in a long-legged stride that carried him toward a van on which *Camp Hope* had been painted in large, if not precise, dark blue letters. The Frisbee landed at his feet. He stopped, then crouched down. Jeffry raced over to speak to him. Georgia couldn't help smiling at the bent heads and serious gestures, imagining a manly discussion on Frisbee throwing.

"That man purely loves kids. And don't let him fool you. He's going for lunch all right," the pastor assured her. "The Murdock sisters' is the best place in the world for a bachelor. Delicious food and plenty of it. By the look on Kent's face they're serving chicken and dumplings today."

Kent ruffled the boy's hair, laughing as the child walked backward to grab his dad's hand.

Georgia turned to the pastor. "Dumplings. Oh." She hid her smile. "How can you tell?"

"See the way he licks his lips?" The pastor performed a gesture that Kent immediately copied before he climbed into his van. "See?"

Georgia blinked in surprise. "How did you know?"

"Kent loves dumplings." The pastor's eyes hinted that he wished he were going to attend a feast at the Murdock sisters' too.

"'Course, right about now Kent loves almost anything somebody else prepares. He's acting as chief cook and bottle washer at Camp Hope, but if he's going to the Murdocks', he must have got a reprieve." A faint look of distaste crossed his face. "His cooking—it's not a good thing, Miss MacGregor. Not with them trying to rebuild."

He stopped, thought a moment, then began again. "Next week the school groups start coming in. I can't imagine how he'll manage then, even if he wheedles a stack of baking from those two ladies."

"I see." She didn't, not really. Rebuild what?

All at once Pastor Benjamin's faded eyes opened wide. "Say, you don't happen to know anything about cooking for big groups, do you?"

"Uh . . . well . . ." Georgia gulped, searched for a denial that wouldn't come. "A little," she admitted at last. "But not enough for what they want, I'm sure."

"What they want is someone who can make pots of spaghetti, dozens of grilled-cheese sandwiches, and gallons of juice. Those are about all the qualifications you need to feed kids at camp." He tipped backward on his heels, his eyes narrowing. "Might give you a break from all this traveling you've been doing, Miss MacGregor. Something new to focus on."

Georgia blanched. He couldn't know. He couldn't possibly have guessed how much she wished to bury herself in something— anything—that would take her mind off the past and the brooding questions. He couldn't know that she didn't want to go back home, not until she'd found some of the answers she sought. All she needed was a reason not to return, but he couldn't know that either.

"Then again, there's plenty of busywork." His speculative gaze assessed her scraped-back hair, her thin face with its camouflage makeup meant to hide the circles under her eyes. "Wouldn't want you to overtax yourself."

Georgia *was* tired, but it was a mental weariness that dragged at her spirit. Busywork was exactly what her doctor had ordered, something to focus on so she wouldn't have time to think about her future. But cooking for children?

"I couldn't possibly spend the entire summer there." The old fear erupted like molten lava. In a place like this, gossip would spread fast. Once they found out, people would talk, stare. Maybe she'd even give the camp a bad name. If she hung around that long. Georgia swallowed, hard. "Not possibly."

The minister nodded. "Of course not. No one expects that. But maybe a few days? a week? Be nice to give Kent a break before the big camps get going. He's got an awful lot to do out there." He rubbed his stomach ruefully. "Believe me, cooking just isn't his forte. And I should know. I ate his stuff last Friday. I'm still swallowing heartburn medication."

She didn't need to ask—his puckered face conveyed his meaning in vivid detail.

"There's only one person to run the place?" It didn't sound like much of a camp to Georgia, nothing like she'd pictured from Doug's description. Anyway, why was she even discussing this? She'd left home for solitude, to forget.

"Oh no, Kent won't be the only one! Not by a long shot." Pastor Ben shook his head, big grin firmly in place. "Fred and Ralna Jones are there already. Fred tries to manage the maintenance work the camp needs, though it's getting to be a bit much for him. Ralna handles the office stuff, helps out in the kitchen when she can, and generally acts as the camp grandmother to the kids. They've been there forever."

He stopped for a moment, his mind obviously somewhere else. Then he smiled at her. "I wander out myself now and then. Makes me feel young."

He rambled on, painting a vivid picture of boisterous camp life that attracted Georgia in spite of herself. Suddenly she longed to be needed, to listen to the laughter of exuberant children, to relish the freedom of living among people who didn't care about her past, hadn't heard the rumors and innuendos, and were too busy to care.

"Well, I can see I'm putting you to sleep." Pastor Ben chuckled. He waggled his fingers in front of her nose, drawing her attention back to him. "I'm sorry, Miss MacGregor. I do tend to get carried away when it comes to Camp Hope. They do such good work. I hate to see the place suffer just because no one will commit to cook a few meals."

"It sounds like a lot of meals to me." Georgia picked up her purse, anxious not to give herself away. Not yet. In spite of her misgivings, in spite of the little warning voice in her head and the prickles of nervousness that flickered over her, she was interested in Camp Hope. Maybe looking after someone else's needs would help her forget—for a while. At least she wouldn't have to go home yet.

Home—where was home?

"Will we see you next week?"

"I'm not sure." Georgia stepped out from the pew and into the aisle, glad to be free of the constricting space, when the woman beside her finally moved. "I don't plan too far ahead. Not anymore." What was the point?

Pastor Ben nodded, his face grave. "Sometimes that's best, isn't it? Then the Lord can step in and turn us around more easily." He reached out, folded her hand in his, and patted it gently. "Well, take care, Miss MacGregor. Trust in God; He'll lead you."

Her feet faltered as her mind absorbed the words: *trust in God?* Her mouth pinched tight. The pastor wasn't at fault. He wouldn't understand, and she couldn't explain that God had left her alone two years ago to face a future she didn't want.

Georgia nodded good-bye, then strode toward the door, her advantage in height allowing her to negotiate a clear path through the small group of folks who remained behind to chat, only then remembering that she hadn't learned what the rumors he'd mentioned were. But what did that matter? She had firsthand experience of just how little truth rumors contained and how damaging they could be.

Perhaps she was being foolish, but she thought she might take a drive out to this camp. Just to look.

CHAPTER TWO

Since the Murdock sisters hadn't invited Georgia for lunch, she had to find her own, preferably something that didn't include dumplings, which she loathed. The sun, the delicate breeze, and a tiny park she'd glimpsed earlier that morning all decided her. She'd picnic.

Funny how an ordinary burger and a few fries could taste like filet mignon in the fresh air. She reached for another fry and blinked, surprised to find the carton empty. For the first time in weeks she'd been hungry.

Georgia swallowed the last of her lemonade, dumped everything in a garbage container, then wandered across the park, reveling in the brush of air against her skin, the budding leaves with that fresh tint of spring green that would darken as summer progressed. She stopped to admire a bed of daffodils and tulips wavering in the breeze. In Calgary, thanks to the numerous chinooks, the spring bulbs would be finished, but here on the prairie they were in full bloom.

But no matter how hard she tried to focus on the beauty around her, her mind kept going back to him.

Kent Anderson. Had he enjoyed his chicken and dumplings? Was he back at the camp yet? Would he hire her without knowing the details of her past?

At ten past two, Georgia couldn't procrastinate any longer. She'd go out there, see the place, and then decide. She dug inside her purse for her cell phone, then dialed the number on the bulletin.

"Camp Hope. Kent speaking."

The low male voice sounded frazzled, as if he were juggling this phone call with several other duties. What would he be doing at a summer camp on a Sunday afternoon in May?

"Hello? Is anyone there?"

"Oh, I'm sorry." Georgia shook off her nervousness and plunged ahead. "I'm . . . er . . . I wonder if I could get directions to your camp."

"We'd be happy to show you our facilities," he said, just the slightest hint of reserve in his tone. He rattled off the directions. "Be prepared for a gravel road and lots of dust. We're tucked away, but I'm sure you'll see the sign. Is your child a boy or a girl?"

"No. That is, the . . . uh . . . cook's position? Is it still open?"

A moment of silence.

"You're a cook?" His voice dropped, as if he couldn't believe it.

"I have cooked," she corrected. "Not recently, but my parents owned a restaurant and catering business. I helped them out a lot." All at once it seemed vitally important that he not write her off yet. "I've had all the food-safe courses. My parents insisted that everyone who worked for them had the proper training."

"I see." Some type of buzzer rang in the background. "Oh no! It's burnt."

Georgia waited a moment, lips twitching as she remembered the pastor's words about Mr. Kent Anderson's cooking ability. "Hello?"

"Sorry. I . . . uh . . . had a little problem. With a cake." His voice mourned the loss, then grew resigned. "I'll be glad to show you around, even gladder if we can offer you the job. Feel free to come on out. But I'm afraid I've got to go now." He stopped. "Something's . . . come up."

The high-pitched whine of a smoke detector transmitted clearly across the airwaves, cutting across his harried voice.

"Yes, I can hear that." Georgia wondered if this wasn't the biggest mistake she'd made in months. She heard him call something to someone else; then he was back on the line. "I'm really sorry. Was there anything else?" he asked. A loud bang punctuated that sentence.

"No. I won't keep you. I'll see you later. Good-bye." Georgia clicked her phone off, her mind sorting through the task she'd just set for herself. "I don't have to do it," she muttered. "This is only a preliminary check. I can still change my mind."

A way out. She shook her head but knew it was true. She'd become adept at avoiding commitments. It wasn't that she didn't enjoy people—or hadn't, once. It was just that nothing seemed to hold her interest anymore. But something about this camp sparked a curiosity she hadn't felt in months. Whether or not that spark was strong enough to hold her at Camp Hope for more than a visit remained to be seen.

One thing was perfectly clear. She wasn't ready to go home.

———◆———

Safe.

It was the only word Georgia could come up with to describe the awning of peace that enveloped her when she turned left at the sign and followed the sandy road down a dusty, rutted trail that twisted back and forth, light fading as the forest canopy sifted the brilliant sunlight into shade.

She drove slowly, probing the feathery shadows that beckoned her farther and farther into the soft green embrace of this woodland hideaway. Here and there, little log cabins poked their heads out

between ferny boughs of spruce and pine, red roofs half covered in
a thick dusting of golden brown pine needles.

So lovely. So . . . secure.

A dog raced in front of her, jerking her attention back to the
road. Her foot slipped off the gas as she emerged from the trees into
a clearing. She pressed the brake with a sigh of pure delight, barely
aware that her car had shuddered to a halt.

It lay in front of her like a mirage in the desert—a swimming
pool, shimmering a rich Mediterranean blue in the blazing sun.
Olympic-sized, she guessed as she pulled to the edge of the open
space. Though nearby horses grazed on tender blades of lush new
grass, even they couldn't distract her from the glory of it.

Memories swamped her as she clambered out of the car, mesmerized by the oasis she'd discovered in the middle of this wild sanctuary.
Provincial swim meets, national races, shiny gold cups, glittering
medallions, and friends cheering her on.

She walked steadily forward, drawn inexorably closer to the one
place she'd always felt truly at home. The pool. It lay east to west,
offering the swimmer a stunningly different panorama in each direction.

She took a moment to check out the view. To the north, the
main camp buildings were visible beyond the attached shower
complex. To the east, the parking lot, several cabins, the bare outlines
of a barn, and the pasture—complete with six placid horses. For
several miles to the south, Georgia savored an unobstructed sight of
newly green fields with crops sprouting above the black loam. West-
ward, the trickle of a creek, a grove of trees—a place of shadowy cool.
A niche to hide.

Her gaze slipped back to the pool and the metal fence protecting it. At least six feet high, she judged, and chain link. A not-so-
subtle hint to keep out? But then, why was the gate open, inviting?

Georgia glanced around, but there was no one to ask permission.
After a moment's deliberation, she stepped through onto the smooth

gray cement apron that skirted the water. At once the aromatic pungency of chlorine drenched her in memories of her teenage years and the hours she'd spent honing her diving skills. She'd never made the Olympics, but she'd come close.

On the drive into camp, Georgia had considered some of the buildings worn and dilapidated, almost beyond repair. But as she studied the pool, she realized that it, at least, looked in perfect condition, calm and shimmering its welcome, not a breeze rippling the smooth azure water. Broad steps led down into the shallow end nearest her. Behind that, a three-foot cement wall blocked the paddling pool from the deeper water, or perhaps it was a resting spot for weary swimmers.

There were any number of balls, water guns, fins, masks, and other equipment piled into a wire basket with wheels that sat perched in the corner, as if awaiting an influx of children. At the far end, a diving board beckoned the more adventurous. High on either side, guards' chairs floated atop white metal ladders, offering a bird's-eye view of the water and everything around it.

For one brief moment she was ten again, a rush of anticipation bubbling inside before she pushed off the tower.

Georgia sank down onto the edge of the pool, removed her sandals, and dipped her feet into the shallow end. It was heated! Surely the kids must love this camp, run-down though it might be. She sat there, lost in daydreams of children racing through the water, shrieking with delight as they splashed and played in a place where reality disappeared.

"I'm sorry, but I'll have to ask you to leave. I'm afraid the pool is closed."

She jolted awake, her head tilting back to get a better look at the owner of that quietly amused voice. It was the man from the church, the one with the van. Kent Anderson. Only then did she realize how tall he was. Probably taller than her, which was saying something since Georgia stood five feet ten in her bare feet. Thick brown hair curled up at his neck, defying the slicked-back hairstyle he'd tried to impose. Whipcord lean, his biceps bulged from the short sleeves of his faded T-shirt.

Now she could see that his eyes were the same rich green as the moss she'd noticed growing on the north side of the shaggy pines. He looked as if the outdoors were his natural habitat.

"Miss?"

"Sorry." She blinked to get the sun out of her eyes, slightly unnerved by his sudden presence. "Did you say something?"

"Uh-huh." His green eyes twinkled. "Zoned out, did you?"

"I was . . . thinking." She blushed at the knowing look. "I was."

"Of course you were. Well, thinking's not a bad thing. You just can't do it here."

She watched his eyes change color. Not really fading. It was more like a light switched on behind them, made them sparkle to match his smile.

"I can't?" Georgia looked away, tried to pretend her nerves weren't skittering. What was it about him that made her so jittery?

"Nope. You can't. Not inside the pool area." He motioned over his shoulder. "It's closed to the public right now."

"Oh. Yes, of course." She yanked her feet out of the water and struggled to stand up, slipping and sliding on the concrete as her toes sought a firm purchase on the wet surface. She'd almost made it when a flutter of awareness in her stomach made her glance upward. One look at him and she overbalanced; her feet began to slide from under her.

"Allow me." He stretched out one hand and grabbed her, fingers strong and sure as they held her arm until she was in control of her limbs. Then he let his hand drop down to his side. "The deck is a little slippery."

"Yes." Embarrassed, Georgia stepped back. "Thanks very much. That was clumsy of me."

"I doubt if you're ever clumsy." He grinned, sunlight dancing through his hair. "But I'm afraid you will have to leave."

"Of course. I wasn't trying to break any rules. I just wanted to get a closer look at the pool." Embarrassment surged through her when he walked to the gate, waited, obviously impatient for her to leave. "I didn't mean to trespass."

"It's my fault. I shouldn't have left the gate open, but I got called away and since there were no kids—" He shrugged, his rugged face tightened. "It doesn't matter. I should have known better. Especially now."

Red dots of color appeared on the jut of his cheekbone. He was angry. With her?

"No, it was my fault. I don't want to keep you." She hurried through the gate to the grassy verge on the other side.

"No problem." His tone was cool, the smile gone. He placed a large silver padlock on the gate and snapped it closed.

Georgia searched for a way to reassure him. "I didn't touch anything. Just paddled my feet for a few minutes. It's been a long time since I've been in a pool like that. I used to dive. I entered my first meet at a camp something like this."

"Really?" He squinted at her, then turned at the sound of a whinny, his eyes examining the horses who'd moved to graze nearer the fence. Several moments passed before he nodded, apparently satisfied that all was well with them. He turned his attention back to her. "I'm sorry the camp isn't open yet, but later on we will be having public swimming nights. Perhaps you'd like to try out our pool then."

She shook her head. "I don't think so."

"Oh. You're not from around here? Well, I'm sorry." His confusion couldn't be masked. "Did you take a wrong turn? Perhaps you didn't notice where you were going?"

Georgia almost laughed. He was trying to be kind, but even he didn't believe that excuse. She'd have to be brain-dead and legally blind to have missed the ten-foot sign at the entry gate that proclaimed this Camp Hope.

"I know where I am," she assured him, amused by the tilt of his quirked eyebrow. "I followed your directions. And I did read the sign. 'Camp Hope—Where Nothing Is Impossible with God.'"

Something akin to relief flashed across his face. "You're the cook."

"I don't know if I'd go that far."

"Please, don't say that."

He sounded so forlorn. She laughed at his groan. "I *can* cook," she corrected. "I just haven't done it for a while. I phoned you earlier."

"Yes, I remember. I was in the midst of—oh, never mind. I didn't think you'd show up." His eyes moved from the top of her head and the curls she'd left loose, past her wrinkled white sundress, to the soles of her still-bare feet. "Anyone qualified to work in the kitchen seems determined to steer clear of us this year."

"I don't have any papers or anything, but I understood cordon bleu wasn't part of your requirements." She glanced around, saw the long building in the middle of the compound that could only be the dining hall. "This is a kids' camp?"

"Yes, but—" He cut off whatever words should have come next. One hand raked through his groomed hair, leaving behind a riot of freed curls. He kept staring at her, obviously sifting through whatever he'd been about to say.

Georgia shuffled her bare toes on the thick swatch of grass and wondered why she was so anxious to have this job. It wasn't that she needed the money. It certainly wasn't part of her plans. But now that she was here, something about this place beckoned, promised revitalization. An unspoken voice in the corner of her heart whispered that by remaining here she might begin to find her life again, start over.

Camp Hope indeed. Suddenly she *wanted* to stay, to find out if the place lived up to its name.

"Do you have references?"

References? "It's been a while since I worked in the kitchen," she admitted at last, frustrated that she hadn't foreseen this request.

"Oh." The eyebrow quirked again. "Why was that?"

"College. Studying. Life."

His soft, gentle probing annoyed her. She didn't want to go back; she wanted to go forward. Still, it was a camp for children. He had to have some confirmation of her suitability. But she didn't want to answer any personal questions that would give rise to the memories she'd tried so hard to erase.

"So you wouldn't be able to give me the names of the places you worked for?" Defeat dragged at his broad shoulders.

"I can give it to you, but it wouldn't do any good." She shook her head. "I'm afraid it—they've gone out of business."

"Not due to your cooking, I hope."

It should have been a joke, but Georgia winced at the memories. "It was my parents' restaurant. They passed away a few years ago." And now she was alone. As usual, her fragile emotions seesawed, bringing a tear to her eye. She ducked her head, then peeked up at him. "Maybe this wasn't a good idea."

"Oh, don't give up yet," he murmured, that spark of fun glinting through his mossy eyes once more. "After all, you've come this far."

"You want me to prove myself?" She couldn't decipher his expression.

"It isn't that." His voice softened; the harsh lines of his face eased. "I'm sure what you say is true, but you can understand that I must require some references. I'm responsible for a lot of kids. I can't risk anything at Camp Hope." He paused, thought a moment. "Look, Miss—I don't even know your name." He blinked, his entire face a question.

"I should have introduced myself. Sorry. Georgia MacGregor. Originally from Calgary. I read your notice in your church bulletin." She told him the particulars of her visit. "The pastor thought maybe I could help out. Just for a little while. I'm actually a nurse, but I've taken a leave of absence. I needed . . . a break." She substituted the word for *escape*, which was what she'd been going to say. He didn't need to know that.

"A nurse?"

"Yes." Georgia frowned. Why the shock? "I'm fully qualified for that. I have my registration card in my wallet in the car, if you want to see it." She relished a certain smugness at his surprise as she told him where she'd earned her degree. "I prefer pediatrics but . . ." There it was again, the past, pushing its way into everything. She let the words die away, unwilling to explain further.

"A cook *and* a nurse. A pediatric nurse, no less." He gave her a strange look. "Imagine."

"I beg your pardon?" She stepped backward when a huge grin pasted itself across his face. "Is . . . uh, everything all right, Mr. Anderson?"

"It might be," he mumbled. "It just might be." The smile disappeared. A frown drew little crinkles at the corners of his mercurial eyes. "How did you know my name?"

"Your name?" She thought a minute. "Oh. The pastor."

"What else did he say?"

It was an odd question spoken in a rushed tone. His eyes veered away from hers, as if afraid he'd asked too much.

Georgia shrugged. "Well, I know about the Murdock sisters and the dumplings, if that's what you mean."

Kent Anderson burst out laughing. "He's a jealous man, our Pastor Ben. Envies me a lot." His chest puffed up a little.

"I don't think it was you. I think his envy had more to do with the chicken dinner you were treated to." She saw his surprise and grinned. "He knows more than you think. But other than a discussion about your lunch, he didn't say a lot. He mentioned that you have a handyman and his wife here, that there might also be some program staff, and that you were trying to manage the kitchen on your own. Are you a good cook, Mr. Anderson?"

"He's horrible." The laughing voice emerged from a diminutive woman with white hair and sparkling blue eyes who walked up behind Kent. "Burns everything he touches, or else we eat it raw. Gives us indigestion most of the time; that's why we need a nurse on staff. I'm Ralna."

"Hi, Ralna. Georgia MacGregor." They shook hands. "I'm . . . um . . . interested in cooking here."

"Wonderful! Anything you can do has to be better than his half-cooked, three-pepper scrambled eggs and salsa." She patted her stomach. "Took a mouthful of antacids to clear that up this morning, and me already sporting a weak heart."

"Ahem! I think you've tarnished my reputation enough, Ralna." Kent turned to Georgia. "To get back to our discussion . . . is there someone who would vouch for you? A pastor from your home church, a former boss?"

"Sure. Do you want a list of them now?" A bubble of hope rose. Maybe staying here, just for a few days, wasn't impossible.

"If you don't mind."

"I don't mind at all, but—" she held up her hands—"I need something to write with."

Ralna held out the yellow pad and pen she carried, her face wreathed in smiles.

Georgia accepted them, scribbled down names and phone numbers as quickly as they came to mind, placing Doug first on the list. "You can call any one of these if you'd like. Or all of them." She handed him the pad. "I'm sure they'll tell you what you need to know."

She only hoped no one launched into the sad story of her past.

Ralna teetered on tiptoes, peeking over Kent's arm. "I know Ed Maguire. Worst sense of humor God ever gave a man. Dreadful tease. He's your pastor?"

"Was." Georgia swallowed hard. "We . . . I . . . moved. I attended First Avenue Church in Calgary, but it's so big, I doubt the pastor there would remember me specifically." She used her index finger to point to another name. "Mary Anne might though. We . . . I am . . . was in a growth group with her once. She works in the church office."

"I've been to that church. It's massive." Ralna grinned, her eyes glinting with fun. "I got lost trying to find the ladies' room and missed the entire morning service."

A spurt of warmth touched Georgia's heart. Here was a woman who wouldn't dig for information but could be counted on in a pinch. A friend.

"What kind of meals did your family's restaurant prepare?" Kent tore off the sheet of paper, folded it, and tucked it into his shirt pocket. He would have done the same with the pen, but Ralna stopped him by the simple expedient of holding out her hand.

"We had a regular menu—burgers, fries, hot sandwiches. Normal stuff." Georgia smiled as memories of those hectic years returned. "Catering for weddings, reunions, parties. The standard fare—roast beef, chicken, mashed potatoes, gravy—that kind of thing."

He licked his lips, but his forehead pleated in a frown. "Not exactly kids' fare."

"True. But the last two years in high school, a friend and I started a little sideline in the basement of the restaurant. We catered to kids' birthdays on Saturdays. He's still a friend of mine. Doug Henderson's name is the first one on your list. He could tell you some of the most popular concoctions we came up with." She chuckled at the memory. "I think I could produce whatever you need."

Why was she trying to impress Kent? Georgia didn't know the answer to that, but she wasn't prepared to give up yet.

"I'm sure you could manage very well, Miss MacGregor." His eyes held hers, his voice gentle. "Please don't think I'm questioning your ability. But I will have to check out the names you've given me. It's policy."

"I understand. I think it's great that you're concerned about the kids. Their parents must appreciate that." After watching him with Jeffry, Georgia had a hunch the kids would always come first with this man.

"Well, go make your calls, Kent. I'm starved and I'm not looking forward to the dinner you'll create." Ralna ignored his huff of disgust. "God gives everyone talents. Unfortunately, when it comes to food, your talent lies in eating it."

"Are you here just to ruin my reputation, or was there something special you wanted, Ralna?" Kent winked at Georgia, then glared at the older woman, a twinkle in his eye ruining his pseudofierce look.

"Your *reputation* with food died last week when you killed our lovely roast turkey." Ralna giggled at his shamefaced protest. Then her face grew solemn. "Actually, I came because—" she cast a quick glance at Georgia—"that is, you're needed at the big house, Kent."

Georgia watched him pale, saw worry and grim fear meld together on his face.

He frowned, gave Georgia one more look, then nodded. "Okay. Ralna, I hope you won't mind if I change your schedule this afternoon."

"Change is good," Ralna chirped, grinning up at him.

"So you keep telling me." Kent patted her shoulder. "Thanks." He turned toward Georgia. "What did you have in mind for the rest of your afternoon, Miss MacGregor?"

"Not a thing. Actually I'm on holiday."

"If you're willing, I'd appreciate your help with the evening meal."

"I'm willing."

"Great." Relief flooded his face. "Ralna, I'd like you to show Miss MacGregor the kitchen, give her a tour of the facilities. Between the two of you, dinner should be a snap. I left some stew meat thawing in the cooler."

"I don't mind chipping in, but, Kent, Miss MacGregor isn't here to spend her afternoon in some kind of cooking audition." Ralna's slight reproof stopped him.

"You're right. As usual. Thanks." He shook his head. "Forgive me, Miss MacGregor. I don't want to impose on your afternoon. And you mustn't feel compelled to stay just because I asked. There aren't any kids here yet, only the staff. We could manage."

Behind his back, Ralna stuck her finger into her mouth in a gagging motion.

Georgia smiled. "I'd like to stay. To help out, if I can." She had no desire to return to the city. Not yet anyway. "If you want the truth, being here reminds me of my own childhood. I—" she wondered how much to say—"I'd like to be of some use. At the moment, I'm a little bored with my own company."

"As long as you're sure it won't be too much." He scanned her white sundress, forest gaze darkening with concern.

"I'll be fine. I'm tougher than I look. Besides, I had nothing planned for the rest of the afternoon." Wasn't that the truth? She had nothing planned for the rest of her life, except dragging herself from one day to the next. Wasn't that why she'd left Calgary—to find hope for the future? That had proven elusive until she'd come here. Now something tugged at her heart, urged her to stay at Camp Hope.

"Okay, it's a deal. You go on now, honey." Ralna patted Kent's shoulder. "I'll stick with Georgia. Don't worry so much. I don't think it's anything serious."

"I hope not." With a heavy sigh, Kent stalked over to the ATV he'd left parked under a huge spruce tree, hopped on, revved the motor, and tore across the compound.

In a second both man and bike disappeared behind the dining hall. All Georgia could hear was the faint rumble of the motor as it revved twice, then died away.

"I hope everything's all right," she murmured, glancing at the older woman. "Has there been an accident or something?"

"No, nothing like that. Just . . . um . . . camp business." She turned away. "Come on; let's check out the kitchen." Ralna led the way down a graveled path toward the main building.

Georgia followed her, busily noting basketball hoops, volleyball nets, a swing, children's climbing sets, and a horseshoe pit. On the right, a long white building rested in the shade of towering pine trees. Its sloping roof supported a plain white cross that barely cleared the trees' lobstick tops as they swayed in the light breeze. This had to be the chapel.

To the left, a small log building crouched under the ferny arms of a tamarack. Office, the sign read. To the right of that, two large trampolines waited in a half-assembled state.

"This is the dining hall. The kitchen's at the other end." Ralna bustled up to the big metal door and tugged it open, waiting for Georgia to precede her inside.

The dining hall boasted a huge stone fireplace. A number of old-fashioned kettles and memorabilia were displayed on shelves throughout the room. Horizontal blinds covered the south windows, turned closed to keep out the sun. The air felt warm, clammy on her bare arms. In the dimness Georgia glimpsed a grouping of long tables on which benches now lay upside down. On the north side of the room, a serving hatch offered a limited view of the camp kitchen.

"I'm afraid it's pretty stuffy in here." Ralna walked through a set of swinging doors into a long narrow room and began pointing out the equipment. "Stove, ovens, grill, toaster, microwave, small cooler, walk-in cooler, pantry, and freezer. There are two more freezers downstairs."

Stuffy wasn't the word for it. The room was stifling hot. And this was only May! July would be deadly.

Georgia stopped before a towering silver monstrosity almost hidden behind the dishwashing area. "Pizza ovens?" She pulled open one of three doors to peer inside.

"Someone donated them. They're old but lovely to bake in. Very even."

"My parents had ovens like these in their restaurant." The words slipped out in a wash of memories.

Ralna seemed not to have heard. "*Oven* is kind of a touchy word around here. These pizza ovens take an hour to heat up, which makes the kitchen awfully hot, but the stove ovens will take you extra baking time. Don't ever believe that by setting them at four hundred you're actually cooking at that temperature." She shook her head. "I'm afraid they need calibrating, and we haven't yet found a plumber willing or able to travel way out here for our price—free."

Ralna chuckled at her own joke as she dragged open the walk-in cooler door.

"Careful!" Georgia reached out to grab it before it could close.

"Don't worry," Ralna called over her shoulder. "This thing is specially rigged so you can't get locked inside." She studied the shelves.

Georgia wondered what was so fascinating.

"Ah, yes. Here it is. The meat for dinner." Her tiny hands grappled with a huge roaster.

"Let me. I'm sure no one with a heart condition is supposed to lift something as heavy as this." Georgia carried the pan to the counter, lifted the lid, and peeked inside. "Wow! Just how many people will there be for dinner?"

Ralna giggled. "He's a little out on his proportions sometimes. Not more than twenty-five, I'd guess. The staff are away now, but they'll be back for dinner."

"But this is enough for eighty! And it's still frozen." She glanced at the clock. Three-twenty. "What time is dinner?"

"Each of the camps has a different time for meals, but at the moment we're just staff, so we've been eating around six. Later if Kent gets caught up in something and forgets. Last night we had our last meal at 10:30—P.M." She laughed at Georgia's surprise. "Every day's an experience at Camp Hope."

"I see. Well, there simply isn't enough time to cook this for dinner at six. And it's frozen in such a huge lump, there's no way I can pry it apart to thaw it in the microwave either." Georgia plunked the lid back on and looked at Ralna. "Any ideas?"

"I don't think *what* we eat matters very much. We'll all be happy if it's edible." She shrugged. "Whatever you'd like to make will be just fine."

Georgia glanced into the cooler, then the freezer, mentally ticking off ingredients. After considering a moment, she asked tentatively, "Lasagna?"

"They'd love it. So would I."

"Lasagna it is." She grabbed two packages of ground beef from the freezer, placed the roaster of unthawed stewing beef inside the frigid cavern, and slammed the door. While the microwave zapped the beef into a malleable state, she put two pots of water on to boil, then checked the pantry for the croutons she'd need for a Caesar salad. Three shelves were loaded with boxes of powdered orangeade—surely more than enough orange drink for the entire summer?

Ralna moved toward the cooler, then stopped and reversed direction until she'd retrieved the cordless phone and set it on the counter. "I work in the office across the way. We're beginning to get phone calls to fill up our camps, and I don't want to miss even one so I'm going to have to answer this when it rings. Okay?" She waited for Georgia's nod, then grinned. "I can hardly wait for dinner." She chuckled. "How can I help?"

"Just give me a minute to think." In her mind, Georgia organized the details in precise order. If Kent Anderson thought she didn't know what she was doing with lasagna, he was in for a surprise. Everyone, including Evan, always said her lasagna beat anything for miles around. She went back to the cooler, grabbed the mozzarella.

"You could grate this," she said, plunking the block down on the counter. "I'll get some lettuce cleaned and crisping."

"Okay." Ralna set to work.

"Someone must have a thing for orange drink," Georgia said as she cored and washed the lettuce heads. "You've got a year's supply in there."

"Oh, that's Kent." Ralna rolled her eyes. "He always buys stuff that's on sale. Someone was selling out of that drink mix, and he claimed it was a good deal."

"I hope it was." Georgia made a face. "Because he's going to be drinking it for a long time."

"You don't like orangeade?" Ralna asked.

Georgia grinned. "Most orange things don't like me. I think I'll stick to water."

"Coffee's my poison."

It took a minute to find the salad dressing on a back shelf in the cooler, but when she did, Georgia couldn't help noticing the box of less-than-perfect apples. The idea popped into her mind and took root immediately.

She'd love to whip out some apple pies for dessert. It was a bit heavy to go with lasagna, and ordinarily she wouldn't have pushed herself so hard, but suddenly she longed to prove that she could manage whatever she took on—if only to herself.

As a job, cooking at Camp Hope might be kind of fun. She hadn't worked in a kitchen like this for years.

Once the ground beef was sizzling on the grill and the noodles immersed in hot water, Georgia measured out flour and shortening.

Ralna finished her grating, covered the bowl, and set it in the cooler. She watched Georgia for a few moments, her eyes wide. "Apple pie?" she asked in disbelief.

"If I can manage it. How do you feel about peeling apples?"

"Pretty good, actually." Ralna grinned, seizing a knife. She began to pare long strips of red off the fruit. "In fact, I'm feeling more hopeful by the moment. To think I had no idea God would answer our prayers for a cook so quickly."

"God?" Georgia froze, her hands covered with flour. "You think God sent me?"

"Who else?" Ralna shrugged. "'Before they call I will answer,' the Bible says. I'd say He answered big time." She tilted up on her tiptoes to stare out the window. "Now I wonder who that is."

Georgia glanced through the window, saw a brown compact car pull into the sandy clearing in front of the office. Someone sat inside, a baseball cap shielding the face.

"I'll be right back."

But as soon as Ralna opened the dining-room door and called out, the driver took one look at her, reversed the car, and roared away, leaving a trail of dust behind. Georgia watched Ralna frown, scratch her nose, shrug, then return to the kitchen.

"That's funny," the older woman mused, resuming her peeling. "They never even said what they wanted."

"Maybe they were lost." Georgia rolled thin sheets of pastry, then flopped them into oversized pans.

"Then why not ask directions?" She shook her head. "No, and I don't think it was a parent either. They didn't stop to look at the pool."

"Why would they look at the pool?"

Ralna's face tightened; her blue eyes lost their sparkle. "Everyone does. Since the accident, people think they have to check things out. As if we allowed it to happen."

Accident?

"Allowed what?" Georgia didn't understand what made the woman so sad. "Is something the matter with the pool?"

"No." Ralna visibly drew herself together, dredged up a smile. Even so, she couldn't quite disguise the cloud of tension that now filled the room. "If you don't mind, Georgia, I can't talk about it. Anyway, it's Kent's story, not mine. He'll tell you if he wants you to know. Now, these apples are finished. Shall I make some garlic butter? We can use those loaves of Texas toast in the freezer for garlic bread."

"That would be great. Thanks." Georgia kept working and gradually her mind drifted back to the pool. Thoughts of that blessedly refreshing water helped her forget the curious visitor, the simmering heat, and the strange look she'd glimpsed on Kent Anderson's face when he'd learned she was a nurse.

Could he have heard something?

Georgia chastised her overactive imagination. *Stop feeling so guilty. You never did anything wrong!*

The hospital administrator's voice whispered from a corner of her mind, the sting of it barely dulled even two years later. *"It's the perception of wrong, Georgia. That's what we're concerned with. That's why we're suspending you. It's just a temporary measure."*

But in the end, she'd never gone back.

———≫·◆·≪———

She was here!

He drove several more miles, glad for the cover of dust that the gravel road provided. Eventually the gravel gave way to pavement, and he turned into the tiny campsite someone had carved out of a bluff of trees. Satisfied only when he'd checked to ensure that his vehicle wasn't visible from the highway, he slipped a can of orange soda from his pocket, popped the lid, and took a deep draft.

Justine had introduced him to orange soda way back in junior high. He used to drink it to please her. Now he drank it to remember her by, to renew his pledge to her and their—no! He wouldn't think about that now. He needed a clear head. *Concentrate.*

There must be two roads into that camp; otherwise he'd have

passed *her* vehicle on the way in. As it was, on his way out he'd almost missed seeing the sooty black car roof hidden by the trees.

What was she doing at a kids' camp? That puzzled him a great deal. In the past two weeks she'd visited tourist spots, stopped at points of interest, stayed in hotels. The camp was an impulse—he was sure of it—something she'd decided to do on the spur of the moment. But why? Just a visit? Or was she staying?

It didn't matter, he decided. If she stayed, he would too. He'd have to get rid of this car, though. Someone might recognize it. That was all right. He knew how to arrange accidents.

Then he'd buy another old junker. He had enough holiday pay, enough overtime to track her for—for as long as it took. When his cash ran out, he'd get another job.

One thumb poked the thin metal of the can, and a little hiss of bubbles broke the silence. He smiled. It was like the sound of a snake, sneaking up on its prey.

She was so big on that Bible stuff—what about "an eye for an eye"?

CHAPTER THREE

An hour after the dining hall had cleared and the last clean dish was stored away, Kent found Georgia MacGregor exactly where he knew she'd be, sitting outside the fence by the pool. There was something about the water that drew her. He knew it as clearly as he knew his own name, had seen the same preoccupation many times before in Christa.

As he walked toward her, he reviewed the information he'd been given. The woman from the church office knew her to be honest, trustworthy, and committed to her faith. The lawyer verified Georgia's words about her parents' restaurant, claimed he'd been her partner in the birthday party business. He'd known her most of her life and insisted Kent could trust her. Her former employers asserted that they'd found her to be honest and aboveboard in her work.

But all anyone would say about her personal life was that she'd suffered a great loss and was dealing with it in her own way.

Kent stopped two feet behind her, waited for her to notice him. When she didn't, he cleared his throat. "Miss MacGregor?"

Her body shuddered; she twisted to look at him. "It's Georgia," she said, lips curved in a faint smile. "Yes?"

The glazed look on her face told him he'd interrupted something private, that her thoughts had been a long way off. A faint shimmer of tears glossed the beauty of her eyes.

"If you want the job of head cook, it's yours."

He was given no time to probe. In a flash her vulnerability disappeared, and her manner became brisk, efficient. She nodded. "I can only promise you two weeks. Beyond that, I don't know. If you can manage breakfast, I could start with lunch tomorrow. I have to get back to town tonight, collect my things from the hotel."

Two weeks of homemade apple pie? He grinned. This was a no-brainer, even for someone who made as many mistakes as he did. "Lunch tomorrow is great. Two weeks is great. If you can stay longer, I'll be ecstatic. If not, I'll have to trust that God has something else in mind."

Kent was pretty sure he knew how David must have felt when he danced before the Lord. What an answer to prayer! The woman was gorgeous to look at, she made the best lasagna he'd tasted in years, and she baked apple pie he'd only dreamed about. Even better, tonight the operations staff hadn't said one word about too many pots and pans to wash, remarks they'd made loudly in his presence for the past week.

But surpassing even that, Christa had actually eaten something. That alone was cause for celebration. Kent sighed. He had a head cook and, maybe, a nurse. What else could he want?

Maybe a reason for the sadness clouding her eyes?

"So staying on is all right with you?" He found himself holding his breath, hoping she'd say yes.

"I'd like to stay. But . . . there's a condition." She held his gaze.

"A condition?"

Nothing about her quiet competence had prepared him for the gleam of gritty determination shining in those deep brown eyes. His hopes sank. The salary was a pittance. He knew that. She probably made five times that much nursing at even the smallest hospital. But finances were tight, especially for the past two years, after their . . . problem. He daren't offer more.

"Actually there are two. Conditions, I mean."

"Ah." He tried to remove the grimness from his voice, forced a smile to his lips in spite of the misgivings fluttering inside. She wasn't an answer to prayer after all. Well, that would teach him to stop assuming God's plans coincided with his.

"Do you want to hear them?"

He didn't, not at all. He wanted to hire her, forget about menus, and do what he had to do to prove to head office that he was worth a promotion out of the desolation that Camp Hope had become.

In your dreams, Anderson. You haven't begun to pay reparation for the damage you've caused.

No, he wouldn't go there. Not now.

"The wages for our cook are paltry." He offered the ridiculously low sum with meager apology. "I'm sorry but that's the best we can do."

"I see." She waited calmly.

She was going to turn him down. He tried to steel himself for it. *Keep praying about it,* he reminded himself. *But, Lord, I really want her to stay.* "Of course, you do get your room and board with that."

"Uh-huh."

As an enticement, it didn't seem to be working. Why didn't she say what she wanted? Kent shuffled from one leg to the other, head bent, eyes on the ground. Georgia MacGregor, he noticed, stayed exactly where she was, waiting.

After a minute or two, he got a brain wave. "Of course, if you wanted to take on the position of camp nurse as well, we could probably do a little better." Nobody at the head office would quibble about that. Nurses were hard to come by. "You'd have to hand out meds, bandage scrapes, that kind of thing. It's not a tough job, but we can't open without one."

Her eyes widened. "So that's what Ralna meant about needing a nurse."

He nodded, embarrassed by his ineptitude at finding either a nurse or a cook, even basic staff to keep the place going. Once it had seemed so much fun to run this place. But all that had changed last year with one bad decision. If there were problems, it was his fault.

"You do need help." She smiled. "The wages are fine."

"They are?" He stared, his whole body going still. Was she for real? He lifted his hand to shake hers, then dropped it back to his side as he realized she still hadn't agreed. "Does this mean you'll do it?" he asked, a hint of suspicion surfacing in his voice in spite of his attempts to hide it. "You'll take on the position of head cook? and nurse?"

"Yes." Georgia MacGregor seemed frozen in place, her face a mask. "With provisos."

"Oh yeah. Provisos." He slumped in defeat, shoulders drooping as he waited for the axe to fall. "Your conditions. Of course."

She leaned forward, as if she almost hadn't caught the last few words. He saw the confusion on her face, knew she didn't understand what he meant. Every time he spoke to her, Kent expected the worst. He didn't know why. She hadn't done a thing to create a bad impression. Perhaps it was just part and parcel of the legacy of guilt from his past.

One he'd do well to get over, he told himself sternly.

"Well, what is it?" His impatience bubbled over onto her, and he immediately felt ashamed.

She blinked, refocused on his face. Suddenly he felt tired, old. The mirror this morning had shown him the weary lines around his eyes and the tired slope of his shoulders under the faithful old shirt he'd chosen for church.

Why is everything about this place so hard, Lord?

"It's the pool," she blurted out.

"The pool." He twisted to stare at the shimmering aqua water, searching for problems, wondering what she'd heard. "What's wrong with it?"

"Nothing. Absolutely nothing. In fact, it's perfect."

"Perfect." *What does that mean?* "Well, I'm glad to hear you think so." Confusion lent a tinge of sourness to his voice. "So now that we've got that out of the way, you said you could start tomorrow?"

Georgia shook her head. "Not so fast. If I'm going to be head cook and resident nurse, I want your assurance that I can use the pool whenever I get a free moment and it's not already occupied."

"We don't allow anyone to swim alone." His mouth tightened to a forbidding line, remembering. "Those are the rules from head office. I couldn't change them even if I wanted to. Not that I do want to, you understand."

She nodded. "I understand."

"I certainly won't have the time to watch you." Though it would be no hardship, he admitted. She was beautiful.

"I wouldn't ask you to watch me. I'm perfectly capable of looking after myself. For your information, I have all my lifesaving courses. I took them years ago. I even taught lessons one summer."

"I see." He didn't actually. He had no idea what was going on in her brain to make her eyes go all big and shadowy. He only knew it had something to do with her past.

Kent kept watching her, caught the glint of anger that flashed across her face, observed how quickly it was doused when she stared into the water. Georgia MacGregor seemed mesmerized by that water. In a way, he understood her fascination. He'd derived plenty of pleasure himself from diving into the pool in the early morning hours when the sun just slipped free of the horizon or after a long, hard day when the night sky let him forget.

Christa had relished the pool. Heaven knew she'd built her entire future around it.

"I'll make sure someone responsible is with me when I go."

"But—"

"It's my first condition. I don't care about the money. I don't care about the hours. I don't even care if you ask me to cook hot dogs every day." She stood tall, determined. "But I do care about using that pool."

"I'm beginning to realize that." He'd meant it as a joke, but she didn't smile. "Just for your information, Miss MacGregor, we are *not* eating hot dogs every day, no matter how tight our budget gets." The joke fell flat. He regarded her unsmiling face. "Is swimming some kind of an obsession with you?"

"No."

Kent knew better. Even he could see she was inordinately drawn to the pool. Why was that? Add another to the stack of questions piling up in his brain, all of them to do with Georgia MacGregor.

Still, dense as he was, Kent understood that she'd found some kind of solace here. Hadn't he seen the same gleam in Christa's eyes once, a lifetime ago?

"If you have a thing for water, you probably already know that our water here isn't the greatest."

"I'm sure you have chemicals to correct any water problems that might show up in this swimming pool."

His comment had fallen flat. He hadn't meant the pool water, but she'd sidestepped his curiosity. Again. Kent shoved one hand into his pocket, his mind sifting, sorting, listing. Her friends were right—she was hurting. But it was equally clear she wasn't asking for sympathy.

Kent studied her, hoping for some clue to her past. But her emotions were a closed book. He clicked off his observations one by one. There were lines of fatigue around her eyes, and her glossy blonde hair was mussed. Her face retained a pink flush that was probably due to the heat in the kitchen. She wore a sundress that hadn't come from Sears, and her nails were perfect ovals—smooth, unvarnished—certainly not the hands of a workingwoman. She was a qualified nurse, well qualified if her mention of college meant anything, and yet she was willing to bury herself in these backwoods, not practicing her profession but spending hours over a hot stove.

What was Georgia MacGregor running away from?

"Maybe you'd better explain that other condition now." He tilted back on his heels and waited for the words that would make her impossible to hire.

"I don't want to answer any questions." She bit her lower lip. Eyes downcast. "Personal questions, I mean."

She hurried the words out, as if afraid he'd interrupt before she'd said everything. But Kent had no intention of interrupting. He stood where he was and let her continue, while inside, the web of curiosity in his gut spun a more intricate design.

"I'm speaking beyond the scope of the job of course." She looked him straight in the eye. "When it comes to work, I'm an open book, but I don't want to talk about my past or share personal histories. With anyone. I'm here to do the job, if you want me." She straightened her shoulders. "Beyond that, my life is private."

He knew she was trying to forget her past. But why here? Why choose *his* camp?

Kent jerked back to reality. She was a cook *and* a nurse—the very things he'd been praying for. She could rescue him from wasting precious hours out of every day that should be spent on camp duties. And he was questioning her reasons for helping him? How stupid was that!

"The job is all I'm interested in, Mr. Anderson."

It was a challenge thrust out with bravado but also with a touch of spunk. In effect, she'd dared him to turn her down. He admired that boldness.

"My name's Kent." Where did he go with this? "Well, beyond certain personal questions to do with your relationship to God, Camp Hope isn't really interested in your past, Miss MacGregor. Unless you're a convicted felon."

He'd always covered by teasing, but Georgia apparently knew his intent. Eyes blazing, she took up his dare, her hands smacking onto her hips. Look out!

"Oh, come on. I'm quite sure you mean, am I a Christian?" Her hands fisted at her sides. "Yes, Mr. Anderson, I believe in God." She pulled a cell phone out of her pocket, brandished it in front of him. "According to my conversation with that pastor in town, you and I share many of the same beliefs."

The briefest skeleton of a wistful smile touched her lips, then dissipated. "Though I wouldn't say God and I see exactly eye to eye on some things," she muttered through tight lips.

Now what did that mean? Kent frowned, his attention snagged on the painful tinge that colored her soft words. She was hurting about something. A man? His eyes slid down, took in her bare ring finger. Bare now, maybe, but she *had* been wearing a ring. There was a faint tan line still visible on the slim finger. Was she running away from a man?

His brain itched for every bit of information he could glean about this unusual woman. The question spilled out of its own accord. "You're not in trouble, are you?"

She smiled, a true smile, brimming with mischief. It made her eyes dance, her skin radiate. "No, I'm not in trouble. At least, not in the way you mean."

"No legal difficulties that would affect the camp adversely?"

Her grin grew until her sun-kissed skin glowed with the same mirth that sparkled in her Belgian-chocolate eyes. "Didn't everyone on my list give me a good report?" She obviously saw the flush that bubbled up from his neck and laughed. "No, sir. I'm not a bank robber or an escaped convict. Just a nurse who's willing to cook for a couple of weeks."

"But you are running from something."

Bingo! Kent could see he'd hit the nail on the head with that statement. Georgia MacGregor blanched, all pleasure drained away until she stood limp and exhausted, like a wildflower plucked from the hills. Shadows crept into her eyes, clouded their sheen.

"More like *to* something." She squeezed her eyes closed, took a deep breath, then looked into his eyes. "I'm sorry. I shouldn't have come here. It was a mistake. Good-bye."

She turned and moved toward her car, her strides automatic, as if she forced herself to put one foot in front of the other.

It was hard to watch, harder still to know he'd done the one thing she'd asked him not to—probed where he had no business. She'd proven she could cook, and she'd answered the questions that mattered to head office. Why had he pushed?

"Wait! Please." The words slipped out of their own volition. Kent strode across the grassy patch that should have been mowed last week, his breath whooshing out in relief as she faltered to a stop.

At first, Georgia MacGregor didn't turn to face him. She craned at the squawk of a crow. Her eyes found the bird, and she followed its flight across the field. Only when it disappeared from view did she glance at him. "Yes?"

"I'm sorry." He apologized quietly, guilt gnawing at him. He'd caused that suffering in her eyes. "I shouldn't have said that. Your private life is your own business."

"It's all right." She shrugged listlessly. "Maybe I'm too sensitive. It's just that—no, never mind."

Kent stood silent, eyes watching, assessing. Now what? Did he offer her the job, knowing that she was probably going to leave at the drop of a hat? He almost laughed at his own stupidity. Like there was some other alternative here? *Lord, You better stop me if this is wrong.*

"Welcome to our staff, Georgia MacGregor. If you want the job, you can start Tuesday morning. That will give you a full day to arrange matters." He'd do one more check through head office on Monday, but Kent already knew that Georgia MacGregor would be staying. He thrust out a hand. "We're like one big family here at Camp Hope. Glad to have you join us."

Several moments elapsed before she finally reached out far enough to slide her palm against his. Her skin feather-touched his, left the impression of coolness, a dewy soft encounter that sent a shock wave up his arm before she drew her hand away. Though he mocked himself, Kent sensed that connection was somehow very important to their future relationship.

"Camp Hope." A glimmer flickered through her mysterious eyes, distant now with thoughts he couldn't share. She pivoted, surveying the grounds from every angle. "Maybe," she whispered. "Just maybe it is."

———⟨◆⟩———

He stepped back into the shadows of the trees, choosing his retreat with the same thoughtful precision he always employed. From the protection of the overgrown ferns, he kept a silent vigil, watching, waiting, until the long spring evening finally ended, until the sun disappeared, until the moon climbed high in the sky and nothing but furry night creatures moved through the brush around him. Only then did he retrace his steps, three miles down the road back to his car hidden in the trees.

The woman was probably back in town by now, safely asleep at her quaint hotel. She'd be back and he'd be ready for her. The man— now that was a problem he hadn't counted on. But then, he'd dealt with problems before. He could do it again.

As he settled himself in his lonely campsite for the night, he studied the moon through his back window.

It's time to make the first move. The sentence cannot be commuted. You will pay.

The words were silent, inaudible.

Like all his plans.

CHAPTER FOUR

Georgia forced herself to store the last roaster on the shelf in its familiar upside-down position, even though her body screamed with protest.

"Mercy sakes, child, it's hotter than an inferno in here, with enough humidity to sink a ship! Why don't you take a break?" Ralna fanned herself with a magazine, her plump face bright red.

"What I'd like to do is dive into that pool." Georgia plucked two lumps from her precious store of ice cubes, dropped them into her tumbler of water, then held the glass against her cheek. "I'm bushed."

"I should think so! This place is far too warm for you to be working so hard." Ralna frowned. "I wish there was a way we could afford an air conditioner. You shouldn't be cooking in this heat. But with funds so tight, the best I can offer is a suggestion to change Kent's menu. Cold cuts and salads tonight."

"No can do." Georgia smiled at the older woman. "Already have the pizza buns made up. I'll get them into the oven later. For now I guess I'll go for a swim. Does that work for you?"

"Sure. It's too hot in the office anyway. The air conditioner there can't possibly keep up with this heat." Ralna grinned. "I'm almost tempted to jump in that water with you."

"Well, why don't you?" Georgia crunched on what was left of the melting ice cubes, relishing the icy slide of frigid chips down her throat.

"Me? In a bathing suit?" Ralna hooted with laughter. "I'd give everyone a heart attack, including me." She patted her chest, then eased to her feet, her body drooping with fatigue. "Not in this lifetime, girlfriend. Give me fifteen minutes, okay? The kids will be off to their skills classes by then, and you'll have the pool to yourself."

Georgia nodded, then left the kitchen to walk across the grass to her little cabin. Though it was shaded by huge trees and had two windows to allow a cross breeze, the cabin was hot. Everything was hot. At this rate, if the heat wave continued, the staff would be worn-out before the regular camping season even began. As it was, the school groups found it onerous to sit inside the stifling building and eat their meals, so Kent often requested impromptu picnics outside. Given the surge in the blackfly population, that wasn't much better. Tempers flared constantly.

Georgia lay on the bed in her cabin, her mind replaying the past with particular clarity.

"Promise me, Georgia."

"I can't promise that, Evan."

"Sure you can. If I die before you, I want you to make some gesture in my memory and then get on with your life."

"What kind of a gesture?"

"You'll think of something."

She'd forgotten that conversation. A week after their wedding, Evan had insisted they make out their wills. He'd been impressed with her parents' bequest to a children's group home.

"I like the idea that their legacy will live on because they've laid up treasure where it counts. Do that for me, Georgia. Promise?"

But she hadn't kept her promise. The money still sat in an

account in Calgary, waiting. Evan had loved kids. She could imagine the quirky smile that would have lifted the corners of his lips if he'd seen the campers' antics in the pool last night.

"*Promise me, Georgia.*"

She'd been so wrapped up in herself she hadn't done the one thing Evan had asked of her. That would have to change, and now, thanks to Camp Hope, she suddenly knew exactly what Evan would have wanted.

Georgia lurched upright on the bed, snatched up her cell phone, and made a long-distance call to the only person who could handle this for her.

"Sure, I'll do it. I'll ask for several quotes right away. Once we choose the installer, we can get going." A long pause. "Are you all right, Georgia?"

"I'm fine, Doug. Really. I'm going to stay here for a while. Help out a little." She made a face at the phone. "Isn't it funny? When we were sixteen I never thought I'd want to see the inside of a kitchen again, but I'm actually enjoying this."

"Good for you. But don't expect me to visit and peel potatoes," he teased. "There's no way I'm going back to scrubbing pots or hosting birthday parties. Your dad cured me of the first one, and you cured me of the second. I like my life the way it is now. Though I'll confess that sometimes I wonder if your father would think practicing law was an improvement over scrubbing pots." He chuckled.

Georgia couldn't suppress a smile either, remembering their antics when Doug had worked for her parents during high school and college. He was the brother she'd never had. "Those were good times, Doug. I miss them."

His sigh rebounded across the line. "I know you do. But good times will come again, Georgia. Just hang on, keep the faith, and don't lose hope."

Hope? That word again. "I'll try. Is there anything that's come up?"

Silence. An odd silence.

"Just one thing."

She waited, curious about the note of concern she detected in his low rumbling voice. "Well? Go ahead."

"Man, I wish I didn't have to say this." He huffed out a breath. "The fire, Georgia. It's about the fire."

The pleasure she'd found in their conversation vanished. Pain webbed around her shoulders and neck, knife hot as it stabbed between her shoulder blades straight to her heart. "I can't talk about that, Doug. Not now. Not ever."

"I know, sweetie. I know. And you hate it that I've stuck my nose in your business when you were so careful to keep all the details from me. Believe me, I know."

"You couldn't have done anything. I didn't even know you were in town until after the funer—" She couldn't say it. Instead she focused on a fly speck on the wall, distancing herself from the hurt the memories brought. "I managed."

"You did a great job. But, Georgia, there's something I have to tell you."

She swallowed, tried to prepare herself for the inevitable questions. Evan's insurance had left her a wealthy widow, even if she hated the thought of that money. Doug was only trying to protect her interests. Wasn't that why she'd hired his law firm in the first place?

"Georgia?"

"I'm here."

"Someone has been checking up on you."

"I know. I told Kent to phone you. I needed a reference. Was it a problem?"

"No. That was fine. I think I managed to ease your boss's mind on your trustworthiness. Our firm is well-known for its commitment to ethical practices. I'm not talking about that."

"Then what?"

"I mean really checking up."

There was something in his voice, a particular quality that caused her to sit up straight. She frowned. "Really checking up how? Why?"

"I sublet your apartment as you asked, left my number with the super, just in case something came up." Doug cleared his throat. "I've had several calls, Georgia. Someone's trying to find you. They've contacted your former employer too."

"I told Kent he could phone Sharon. She was my supervisor before—" She gulped the words down, wished she could forget.

"No, not Sharon."

He was scaring her. Georgia shivered despite the oppressive heat. "Then who did they phone? The hospital?" His silence told her all she needed to know. Georgia shook her head. "Why? What would anyone want with them? We hadn't lived in Calgary that long before—" She would not cry. "I haven't exactly been a social butterfly, Doug. What could they want?"

"Maybe a reporter rehashing an old story? I don't know. I don't think it's anything bad," he emphasized. "It's just . . . strange."

"No kidding. My life is about as boring as it gets." Georgia shrugged, glancing around the small room. "Well, whoever it is will never track me here. Even *I* didn't know I was going to stay at Camp Hope. Not until I arrived, anyway."

"So you like it." His voice lifted, resumed its teasing timbre. "I had a feeling you would. What's the best part?"

She sidestepped the question, reminding him instead of the camp they'd attended in their youth. "This place is a lot like that. Remote. Rustic. Beautiful." She took a deep breath. "And then there's the pool."

"Ah, a pool." He whistled his admiration. "Then how could you not stay? You always were a water baby, Georgia. It's like your natural habitat. It's good you decided to check out the place. Now you can relax and regroup."

"Relax? While cooking for a hundred starving teenagers?" she hooted in derision. "In your dreams, buddy. I'm so tired at the end of the day I can barely stagger to the bed."

"But I'll bet you sleep," he said so softly she almost didn't hear.

"Some nights I drop off the second my head hits the pillow. But something always wakes me up." She stopped, pushed away the words that would articulate her grief. Doug was the only friend she had left. She wasn't going to grind him down with her misery. "Anyway, I'm sure it would help if the kitchen and dining hall had air-conditioning."

"A little oasis in the middle of the oasis?" he said.

But Georgia caught the thread of sadness lacing its way through his words. Dear Doug. He always knew. "Kind of. It's a change. But I think I need that."

"You do. And I'm glad for you, honey. Really glad." He sounded relieved. "Your boss sounds okay. A little huffy maybe, but then he'd have to be to keep all those kids in line."

Georgia shied away from discussing Kent Anderson with Doug. "So you'll get someone out here to install whatever has to be done? The sooner the better, please," she told him. "I'm roasting."

"I'm on it. You take care of yourself."

"I will."

A pause.

"Georgia, you never did give me the number of your new cell phone, and I'll need it to give to the police. You know they said you should stay in touch." He hurried past that. "I wouldn't mind having a backup number either. Just in case your cell doesn't work. I thought I had the camp number, but I can't find—" Shuffling papers crackled across the line.

"My cell phone always works." Georgia suddenly remembered the gravel road and the "no service" message she'd gotten once before. "Actually, having the number for the camp might not be a bad idea, Doug. There's a gravel road out to the main highway, and the relay towers don't seem to cover that area. You have to remember to drive slowly on that gravel because you can lose traction in a second."

"I wasn't planning to visit you!" He sounded shocked.

Georgia giggled. "I know. That would get the Vette all dirty.

Especially if it rained. You've had that old death trap for fifteen years. Why don't you trade up?"

"Never. Don't even think it."

No, he wouldn't get rid of the car. His memories were tied up in it. Georgia nodded, then remembered he couldn't see her. "Well, I don't recall the camp phone number offhand. I'll have to go to the office for it. You know I have no mind for numbers. Besides, I've been working like a beaver."

"I can imagine. Never mind. I found your Kent's number. He can pass on any messages from me. And I'll have someone contact him about the AC. Don't overdo, okay, Georgia?" His concern wrapped around her like a long-distance hug. "And don't feel you have to stay there. If it gets too much for you, my condo has lots of room. You could relax here."

"You're very sweet." Georgia swung her feet off the bed, her eyes on her watch. "But, Doug, I do need to work. Working here is the one thing I absolutely *have* to do. Don't ask me why. It just feels good to focus on someone else for a while."

"Okay, honey. You know best."

She knew he was smiling.

"Promise you'll take it easy, all right? I don't want to lose my best bud to a bunch of rowdy kids."

"You won't, Doug. Not ever. And if you need a friend, I'm here. Anytime."

"You're the one I'm worried about, Georgia."

"Don't worry about me. I'm getting better. I think."

By the time she ended the call, Georgia's spirits had lifted immeasurably. Maybe having air-conditioning installed would accomplish something that would lend meaning to the past two painful years. She might be here at the camp for only a few weeks, but whoever followed her would find blessed relief in that kitchen and the kids would have a cool spot to eat in.

"I'm trying, Evan," she whispered, glancing at the photo on her nightstand. "I am trying." She trailed one finger over his smiling face, then moved her hand to touch the other picture.

It wasn't there.

"What—?" She reached out, her hand grazing the brush, the comb, the bottle of water. The picture was gone.

Georgia glanced around, her heart throbbing wildly in her chest. It was her only picture. Well, technically she had more that had been rescued after the fire, but they were in storage in Calgary. This one she carried with her all the time.

"It was here this morning," she muttered, checking behind the stand. "So what happened to it?"

"Is anything wrong?" Kent stood in the doorway, an air mattress in one hand, a screwdriver in the other. "I thought I heard you call out."

When she didn't answer, he crossed the threshold, his eyes on her face. "What's wrong, Georgia?" he asked, quiet concern threading his voice.

"N-nothing," she said, her fingers lifting, probing, searching.

"Something definitely is wrong." He laid his materials down, stepped over them to grasp her arm. "Tell me. Perhaps I can help."

She couldn't ignore the offer so freely given. "I-I . . ." She closed her eyes, concentrated on remembering. But nothing would come. Aside from a generic round face with dark eyes, she could recall nothing. "I have to remember. I have to!"

"Remember what?" Kent squeezed her shoulder, turned her around until she faced him. "You're scaring me. Please tell me what's the matter. Please?"

The concern in his eyes coupled with the strength in his hands were her undoing. He was capable, competent. And she needed to tell someone. She drew in a deep breath and explained. "I had a picture," she whispered, tears clogging her throat, "a very important picture. I can't find it."

"What was it of? Maybe I can help." Without waiting, Kent

looked around the room. A second later he stalked over to the
battered dresser that sat near the door. "You've spilled your soda," he
told her, mopping up the mess with his handkerchief.

Georgia saw him pick something up, pinch it between two fingertips. He waved it back and forth to release some of the moisture. "Is
this what you're missing?"

The familiar face, now stained and discolored, grinned toothlessly
at her. Georgia snatched it from his hands and carefully wiped the
precious image with a tissue.

Kent scrutinized her actions in total silence, though she knew he
had questions. Well, they could wait. She scanned the face in the
photo and felt the rush of emotion as details returned.

After several moments Kent's voice broke into her reverie.
"I don't think it's a complete loss. Just a little orange around the
edges."

"Orange?" She frowned at the picture, then at him. "What do you
mean orange?"

"Your soda." He pointed to the can, motioned to the pool of
orange liquid on the floor. "I think most of it should wipe off, but it'll
be hard to get rid of the color."

Georgia froze.

"Are you all right? You look . . . white."

She shook herself free of the daze and met his curious scrutiny.
"I'm fine. Thank you. I wonder if it would be possible to get a lock on
this door."

"A lock?" He stared at her. "We never lock anything but the pool
at this camp. We've never had a problem with theft."

"Well, you've got one now."

Kent looked around, his eyes brooding. "What did they steal,
Georgia?" He saw her purse stuck in a corner and picked it up. "Are
you missing any money?"

She slipped the damp photo into her pocket, then checked her
wallet. "No," she admitted reluctantly.

"Then what? Clothes? Blankets? Jewelry?" He waited as she checked, then denied them all. "Then what's missing?"

"It's not that. It's just—" She stared at him helplessly. "I know someone was in here," she insisted. "Someone spilled that soda on my picture."

He spoke gently, as if to reassure a child. "Someone like you? Maybe you reached for something and knocked over the can, a can you'd forgotten you opened. Isn't that what happened?"

"No." She shook her head stubbornly. "Someone was in here."

"How can you be so sure, Georgia?" He sounded frustrated. "Isn't it possible you're blaming someone for something you did?"

"Not this time," she said, bitterness eating at her. She picked up the can gingerly, held it out to him. "This isn't mine."

"You're sure?"

"Positive." She smiled at his frown of disbelief. "Once, years ago, I reacted to some orange food coloring my mother put in the icing for my birthday cake. This particular soda has that same chemical. I learned a long time ago to avoid it and all orange food additives if I didn't want to sport big red hives for a week. That's why I get Ralna or someone else to mix up the orangeade. I get bumps if even a few drops land on my skin."

Kent glanced at the can, then at her, his forehead furrowed as he puzzled out her meaning. "Then what you're telling me is . . ."

Georgia nodded. "Yes. Someone has been in this cabin without my permission." She held her picture so he could see it. "I keep this on my nightstand. Always. They moved it from there to the dresser, then spilled that drink all over it."

"I'm sorry."

She saw him staring at the photo, saw the way his eyes opened wide. "This picture—it's important to you?"

She nodded again, unable to speak past the lump lodged in her throat.

"This is . . ." He stopped, waited for her to finish the sentence.

"This is—was—my son," she blurted out. "He died."

Then she raced from the room as if she could flee the constant sting of that horrible loss and the pain that wouldn't go away. But she couldn't. She would never forget.

Her two most beloved possessions had been stolen that night. But why had it happened? *Dear God, why?*

What had she done that God would punish her like this?

CHAPTER FIVE

If anyone had asked what he did for the rest of that day, Kent knew he wouldn't be able to cite a single thing. Whatever he accomplished was done by rote.

The only thing he saw, heard, and relived was the tortured ache in Georgia MacGregor's voice as she showed him the photo of her baby son.

Had he actually thought a beautiful woman like her would be free of relationships, that she would willingly bury herself out here without some strong internal motivation?

The thing was, he had. He'd been so relieved to finally be free of the kitchen responsibility that he'd willingly accepted her no-questions-asked policy. Avoiding her was easier than acknowledging his own unusual response to her presence. He'd left her under Ralna's care, hoping she could fend for herself while he concentrated on his own job, because it was easier than admitting that Georgia MacGregor got to him.

Guilt itched at Kent. He owed her more than a pat on the

shoulder, a few meaningless words. Clearly the woman was in pain. And he'd let her run and hide to nurse her wounds, done nothing to help her, offered no words of hope to ease the burden she bore. Wasn't that what Camp Hope was all about? But what was he to do?

"Kent?" The soft purr of Christa's wheelchair announced her even before she spoke.

Knowing how much she hated it when he hovered, Kent stayed where he was, seated on his own chair, staring out through the screened porch. "I'm here."

"What's wrong?" his sister demanded when she'd made it to her favorite spot on the porch. "What's the matter?"

"Nothing."

"There is something. You never sit out here when camps are on."

Kent sighed. "Camp hasn't officially started yet, Christa. It's only been the schoolkids, and they're not here tonight."

"Which makes me wonder why you're sitting here staring into space. You have ten thousand things to do. What's wrong?"

Though she'd lost the use of her legs, Christa's mind was as sharp as a knife. Nothing escaped her piercing regard. Kent didn't even try. "It's the woman I hired as cook. Georgia MacGregor." He told her about the events of the afternoon. "I couldn't think of anything to say. I just stood there like an idiot. Guess I don't have your way with people."

"Sometimes there aren't any words you *can* say," Christa said thoughtfully. "Sometimes it's enough to have someone there to listen. It's so terribly sad. What do you suppose went wrong?"

It was the first topic Christa had taken an interest in for months. Kent was only too glad to discuss the situation with her if it kept her mind off herself.

He told her what he knew about their new cook, including how beautiful she was. "I know it's not much, but the only way she would take the job was if I refused to ask questions. Not that her past matters much to the camp. She cooks like a dream. Did you taste those lemon bars?"

"You tasted enough for both of us." Christa uttered a hollow laugh, avoided his searching look.

Kent remembered Christa's almost-full plate of food he'd fed the dog. "You should have at least tasted something, Chris."

"I wasn't hungry." She shrugged. "Did you tell her that lemon anything is your favorite?"

"Christa, I barely see the woman! I'm up before dawn, I've got tons of chores, and the campers will start flooding in the day after tomorrow. How could I possibly find time to talk to her about lemons?" He couldn't help remembering the old days when Christa had shared some of his hopes.

"You obviously found enough time to notice her looks."

"You can't help but notice her. She looks like a model. Except for her eyes. There's something in her eyes, Chris. I can't explain it. Clouds." He shook his head, unable to verbalize what he'd only glimpsed. "It's as if she's hiding."

"Hiding? Hiding from what?" Christa rolled her chair down the ramp. She tilted her head back over one shoulder. "Are you swimming tonight or not?"

"I'm coming." He shifted to his feet, tiredness dragging at every muscle.

"We don't have to go, you know. You could take one night off."

"I'm fine." Once he was doing laps, he'd revive. Besides, no matter how bone weary he was, Kent didn't dare take a night off. It was the only time Christa budged from the house. She needed the outing even more than he did. Maybe this time he could coax her into the water.

He grabbed two towels and loped down the stairs. "It's a beautiful night. You could join me, Chris."

"No."

Kent sighed. Experience had taught him not to push.

They moved together through the darkness. The camp was silent now, the last of the school groups gone for the day, the exhausted staff long since asleep. This was their special time, his and Christa's. With no one to see her wheelchair, no one to stare at her leg braces, she used the cover of darkness to venture away from the house and the fenced-in yard with its perimeter of protective trees.

Tonight she even stopped long enough to bend over and admire the bedding plants that now flowered profusely along the south wall of the dining hall.

"You wouldn't believe how hot it was in there today. I felt sorry for Georgia cooking in that heat. It's a wonder anyone ate anything. But those kids never seem to lose their appetites." He kept up the chatter, allowing his sister an interlude to savor the sweet fragrance of lilacs almost past their blooming season.

As usual, the late evening brought a refreshing coolness with it, rejuvenating him as he breathed the pine-scented air. He stared down the trail toward the pool, remembering. "She's a swimmer too. A good one. She's in here every day after lunch."

"By herself?" Christa's head spun around to stare at him.

"Ralna watches her." He tried to pretend the tension wasn't there, building a wall between them. "She's fast."

"Really?" Christa's interest sparked. She didn't flinch as she usually did when he helped guide her chair up over the bump that let them through the back gate he'd fashioned when he still believed she'd use the pool.

"How fast?" she demanded.

"Very. Her turns are like lightning. And she stays under forever." When there was no response, Kent turned from latching the gate to look at his sister. "What?"

"For a man who's so terribly busy, you seem to have noticed quite a lot about this new employee." Christa squinted at him through the darkness, her lips tipped up in a saucy smile.

"I always notice swimmers. That's your fault. Nothing wrong with it, is there?"

"Nothing at all." A hint of his sister's former zest sparkled in her eyes. "In fact, I'd say it was about time."

"Forget it, Christa. She's still grieving." He shook his head at her teasing wink. "Besides, what woman would willingly spend the rest of her life out here?"

"The right one." Christa made a face. "It's me, the clinging vine, she'd have a problem with. And she might find your incessant determination to get promoted to head office a bit wearing. You are not a pencil pusher, Kent. You belong here."

"I belong where I can do the most good. I think a lot of people would agree I'm not doing much good here. Maybe if I was out of here, people would forget." He clamped his lips shut on the frustration. "You need anything?"

"I need you to wedge me farther back, out of the light."

"Everyone's in bed, Chris. No one can see you." He stifled the rest of it. It wouldn't do any good to keep harping.

"You don't know that. I hate it when they stare at me." She pressed the button, and the motor hummed with the effort of moving her chair forward and backward several times until she was hidden in the shadows of the shower building, dark blue towels draped over her legs. "I'm not some kind of spectacle to be ogled."

"No one would do that, honey."

"Someone did it today," she burst out, her cheeks bright red. "A man was poking around the house this afternoon."

Kent frowned. "What man?"

"I don't know who he was," Christa said. "I sent the dog out and he disappeared. More of those transients, I suppose. I wonder why they pick here. We're not exactly on any major routes."

"Maybe that's why. Or it could be that campsite down the road. I know it hasn't got any services, but some people like rustic. More private, fewer questions." Kent wanted to question her further, probe her certainty that someone had actually been here, but he was afraid he would frighten her. Because of her disability, Christa had already shut herself away from life. Adding to that insecurity would be foolish.

Tomorrow, before she woke, he'd check the yard, though he was pretty sure it had simply been one of those schoolkids messing around or looking for the frog their biology teacher had requested.

"If you sent Maggie to check, I'm sure whoever it was won't be back," he reassured her. "That dog would protect you with her life."

When Christa didn't respond, Kent sighed, removed the jogging pants that covered his bathing suit, and slipped into the water. Immediately the tension oozed away as he began the rhythmic strokes that had finally become almost second nature, though at first—no!

He stopped counting after fifty laps, content to let his muscles do the work, while he allowed the cool slip of water against his skin to obliterate his worries over his sister. For now.

The moon slipped under a cloud. Long shadows hid the cabins from view. He'd purposely left only the dining-hall yard light on tonight. No point in wasting power when there were no campers on the grounds.

"I see you don't follow your own rules."

Kent flailed, lost his rhythm. He searched the darkness for the owner of that sarcastic voice as his feet sought purchase on the pool bottom.

Georgia MacGregor stood at the far end of the pool, just outside the gate. She looked like a wraith in her white shorts and T-shirt. Or an avenging angel, he amended, noting her hands planted on her hips.

"I beg your pardon?" Kent ducked his head under once, so the water slicked his hair out of his eyes. He blinked at her, dislodging the moisture that clung to his lashes. "What do you mean? I always follow the rules."

"I assume then that your . . . er . . . partner . . . is changing?" She pinned him with a steely glare.

"No, she's—" He cut himself off, not daring to glance at Christa huddled against the wall, totally concealed by the shadows. "I did have someone here," he said, but even he couldn't hear any conviction in his words.

"Of course you did. How foolish of me not to have seen that for myself." She glared at him another ten seconds, then whirled around and stalked away, her white-clothed figure clearly visible in the night.

"That was your new cook—the one who likes to swim." Christa sighed, the words almost mournful in their regret. "I'm sorry, Kent. Now she'll think you're deliberately trying to keep her out of the pool, and it's all my fault."

"She already goes in the pool. A lot." He swam to the edge, hoisted himself out, and accepted the towel she held out. "Anyway, I'm sure she has no desire to swim if I'm here."

"Still, it doesn't look good—one rule for her, a different one for you." Christa flipped the brake on her chair and pressed a button to activate the motor. "I'm not doing anyone any good here, Kent. Why don't you let me enroll in that group home? That's where someone like me—a cripple—belongs." She whirred through the gate.

"No, it isn't. Christa, wait! I'll help you." He searched frantically for his pants and shoes in between quick glances to be sure she was all right.

"I don't want you to help me." She kept moving. "I can manage perfectly fine, Kent. See? You don't have to baby-sit me. I'm a cripple, not an invalid."

She disappeared into the gloom, her navy clothes a perfect camouflage in the darkness.

Stung by the pain in her voice, Kent sank down on the end of the diving board and clasped his head in his hands. "Please, God, help me help her. Make her whole." He knew as he said it that it was a foolish request. Paraplegics didn't suddenly rise to their feet and walk.

Christa would be in that chair for the rest of her life, and it was his fault. He'd accepted that. But there had to be something he could do, some words he could speak that would help her see she still had so much to give.

"I guess I should apologize."

"What?" He looked up, surprised that Georgia MacGregor had managed to sneak up on him. She'd found the back gate. "Apologize?" He frowned. "Why?"

"I heard your companion speaking a few minutes ago." She peered at him. "Christina, wasn't it? I wasn't trying to eavesdrop."

He said nothing. What could he say? His sister would never forgive him if he told her story to this stranger. She barely tolerated Ralna and Fred knowing.

"I'm sorry I intimated you were a liar."

"Is that what you intimated?" He sighed, shook his head. "Thanks for apologizing, but it really doesn't matter, Georgia. For the record, her name is Christa."

Kent gathered up his belongings and slid his feet into his shoes. He wrapped the towel around his shoulders, picked up his keys, and walked toward the gate.

After a moment, Georgia followed.

"I'm surprised you're not asleep. You've had a couple of busy days." Kent snapped the padlock closed, checked it, then began walking toward his office. "We've never had two hundred kids in one week before. I appreciate all you've done to help us handle these school groups. It's a new thing for us but a welcome source of much needed revenue."

"I was asleep. Something woke me up." She stopped when he did, waited while he locked the pool key inside the office. "You know, it's odd. The camp seems very poorly off, yet you have an expensive swimming pool that costs a lot to maintain. Why is that?"

He gulped and turned away to pretend he was checking the door as his brain searched for something he could say to explain what couldn't be explained. Not to a stranger. Not to anyone.

"We had some expenses a while ago that really set us back. Then the number of campers dropped. It's taken time to rebuild our base. The pool is our strongest feature, and we use it all we can. Pools around here are in short supply, so we spend a lot of time and effort to keep ours in top shape." He deliberately walked them toward her cabin. "I'm sorry you were awakened. What was it?"

"I don't know. Some noise. I think I've heard it before."

"Heard what before?" He wondered if Christa had been right. Did they have another transient on the property? He almost groaned at the thought of resuming those late-night vigils by the pool, hoping to catch their uninvited guests. "Can you describe this sound?"

"Yes. A kind of whirring noise. Like a motor, maybe?" She stared up at him, obviously thinking it through.

"A motor?" Kent closed his eyes, took a deep breath. Christa's wheelchair. They'd have to go around Georgia's cabin next time.

"Yes. But that was once I was awake. After the drea—" She stopped.

"After the dream?" he asked quietly. He smiled at her surprised look. "My sister has them too." It was his turn to fall silent. Desperately Kent searched for a new topic. "What was yours about?"

"Fire." She bit out the word as if it offended her to say it.

"Fire?" He frowned. "Like a campfire?"

She shook her head. Her voice dropped to a whisper. "No. It was a house. A house fire."

"Whose house?" He hesitated to ask more, unsure of her meaning.

"It was hot, so hot. I could feel the flames singe my skin." She stood, her body frozen in place.

Kent wanted to say something to draw her attention back to the present, but something stopped him. Instead, he waited and listened as she relived it.

"They were snapping at me. Crackling—" She glanced up at him, her eyes huge with shock and fear. "Crackling," she repeated. "It was the crackling of paper that woke me."

He couldn't just leave her here. He had to do something. "Paper?"

Kent led her toward a small bench under some trees, a few paces in front of her cabin, helped her sit. She was far too overwrought to go to sleep yet. Perhaps talking would help. "I'm sorry you've had such a bad dream. Sometimes it's hard to drag yourself back to reality after those."

She was shaking. He moved automatically, gathered her cold hands inside his, trying to infuse some warmth into them.

"Yes. Yes, it is." She sat quietly, her shoulder against his, her hands still as they nestled inside the cocoon of warmth his fingers provided.

It felt right to sit here, to listen. Kent brushed his thumb over her delicate skin, noting the blue veins that showed translucent. Her hands seemed frail, as if not used to the challenges of everyday life. But then so did her face. Drawn, blue circles ringed her beautiful brown eyes. Georgia MacGregor needed a good night's rest.

"Would you like to pray about it?" He felt her immediately shudder in response.

"Pray?" She whispered the word as if unfamiliar with its connotation. "To God?"

He smiled. "Yes, of course. He's our heavenly Father; He wants us to lean on Him."

"He doesn't hear me." The admission was so soft, so forlorn he almost didn't catch the words.

"He always hears, Georgia. Always."

"Then why doesn't He answer?" she asked.

The brokenness in her voice stabbed his heart. She, too, was hurting, no matter what outward facade she presented to the world. A band tightened around his chest. Kent found himself wanting to ease her pain, to get to the bottom of her suffering, to bear it for her. He squeezed her fingers in empathy.

Suddenly she shifted, straightened her back, and tossed her head. In a flash her hands were free of his. "Answer me! You said He heard." The words exploded, brimming with anger and frustration.

"So why doesn't He answer? Is He mute? Does He enjoy hanging people out to dry and leaving them there? Is that the kind of God you pray to?"

"No, Georgia. That's not my God. My God is love."

The fight drained out of her like sand from an hourglass. "That's what everyone says," she said. "A God of love." A smile devoid of mirth lifted the corners of her lips. "I'm having a little trouble with that picture."

"That's okay. He can handle your questions. He's God, after all." Kent hoped that was the right thing to say. He was out of touch, more used to counseling kids than a broken young woman.

"And that gives Him the right to do whatever He wants with people?" She stood. "So who am I to argue with God, right?"

But the questions were still there. Kent knew it. He could see it in her dulled eyes, her drooping body. He stood, too, wishing he knew how to help. "God isn't offended when we ask why, Georgia. He knows we're human, that we can't understand all of His ways."

She stared at him for a long time, her face in shadow so he couldn't read her expression. After several moments, she backed away. "I'm sorry I bothered you on your night off. You've got enough on your plate running the camp. I shouldn't have annoyed you with my problems." She surveyed the grounds once more, a curious speculating look on her face. "It seems different here tonight, doesn't it? Empty." She shrugged. "Good night."

He let her walk a few steps. "Georgia?" He deliberately called her by name, enjoying the familiarity of it. It felt good to be on a first-name basis with this unusual woman.

She turned, looked at him.

"We have two days until regular camp begins. Take tomorrow and Sunday off. I don't want you back at work in the kitchen until Sunday evening. Get some rest. Drive into town if you'd like. Whatever. You deserve a break. You've earned it."

She stood there, watching him, her eyes blank. At last she

nodded. "I don't need any time off. I like being busy. But I might drive around the countryside, investigate the hills."

He frowned. He hadn't expected that. He'd thought she might relax by the pool. Kent shook his head to clear it. "All right. If you prefer. But please, let someone know where and when you're going, will you? People have gotten lost in those hills."

She grinned the cheeky smile she'd used so often in the past week to hide her own emotions. "Afraid we'll run out of apple pie, huh?" She laughed at his flush of embarrassment. "Don't worry, boss. I'll be back. I'm starting to like this place."

And he was starting to like having her here. Too much? "Does that mean you'll be staying with us the entire summer?" he asked, hope surging inside.

But Georgia shook her head. "I don't know that yet. I'm just taking it one day at a time." She pulled open the door to her cabin. "Good night."

"Good night." Kent waited till a lamp flicked on inside her cabin. When he turned toward home, a flash of white on the ground underneath her window caught his attention. He bent down and shifted a stone to free it.

The white turned out to be a corner torn from an old newspaper. He couldn't read the faint words in the dim light, so he carried the bit of paper with him, stopping under his own porch light. "Nurse Georgia MacGregor implicated in hospital." The caption was written under the picture of a smiling woman. Georgia.

Uneasiness rippled down Kent's spine. Implicated? What, after all, did he know about this woman to whom he'd entrusted the welfare of the campers? And who had left this incriminating paper outside her cabin? It hadn't just fallen there; he was sure of that. The stone had been placed deliberately on top of the paper to keep it from blowing away. Someone had wanted this paper found. What had she said—crackling. She'd been awakened by crackling.

Georgia was right—the camp did seem different tonight. Lonely.

Not even the rustle of birds twittering in the trees disturbed the stillness. Almost too quiet.

"Lord?" he whispered helplessly.

An eerie silence was his only answer as a hush descended on the woods surrounding the camp.

It was not the answer he sought.

CHAPTER SIX

"Georgia?"

The following morning, Ralna scurried toward Georgia's car, her breath coming in short gasps. She clapped one hand to her chest and leaned against the front fender. "I'm glad I caught you. Kent wants to talk to you before you leave. He's in the craft shack pretending to organize next week's projects."

"Thanks." Georgia frowned at her friend. "Sit down and catch your breath. You know you shouldn't be rushing around in this heat."

"I'm fine. Some exercise is supposed to be good for me." Ralna plopped down on a huge boulder. "I hope you enjoy the break enough to get some color into those pale cheeks."

"I'm always pale. It's part of my natural beauty," Georgia teased. But as she walked through the trees following the little arrows to the craft cabin, she knew Ralna's comment was bang on. She *was* pale. In the past she'd always been healthy; her complexion, far from the wan color it was now, usually bloomed.

And it would again. It was just a matter of getting back on her feet, of regaining a feeling of security. That odd perception of being safe, almost protected, grew stronger with every day she spent here at Camp Hope.

"Anyone home?" she called, pushing open the plank door. It stopped with a thunk, followed by a grunt of pain. "Oh, sorry. I didn't see you there. What are you doing?"

Kent glanced up from the mess he'd created on the floor, rubbed one elbow. "Organizing, of course. There are too many bits and pieces thrown in here. They take up all the room. One of these days it's going to rain and the kids will have to work inside. They'll need the table free."

"I think maybe the rain thing may be wishful thinking, and I'm not sure what you've done here could be classified as organizing, but whatever works." She leaned one hip against the log wall. "Ralna said you wanted to speak to me before I left."

"Yes, I did. Let's sit outside. It's too stuffy in here."

Three picnic tables sat just beyond the door, and he dropped onto the end of one. Immediately the plank he was sitting on protested with a wrench. It flew upward and he landed on the ground. Georgia barely managed to smother her giggle.

"Go ahead and laugh," he grumbled, dusting off his worn jeans. "I would too if I weren't so tired. Another repair. I'll add it to the thousand and one I already have."

"Too bad you couldn't find a volunteer who'd handle these little projects," she mused, testing her own seat before sinking down. "An extra pair of hands would go a long way, and the work isn't that complicated, is it? I'm sure you have other things to do."

He raked a hand through his hair, rolled his eyes. "One or two other things," he admitted. His hand dropped to his knee as he stared at her.

The silence lengthened between them.

"So what did you want to tell me?" She waited, her nerves kicking up a flutter when he didn't immediately speak. "Is something wrong?"

"Not exactly." He sighed, then shrugged. "Look, there's no way around this. I know you specifically asked me not to discuss your past. And I'm willing to abide by that. I just wanted you to see what I found outside your cabin last night. I don't think it blew there by accident."

Georgia stared at the grainy photo of herself and the newspaper caption beneath it. Her heart sank. "It's not what you think," she whispered. "I didn't do anything wrong."

"I believe you, Georgia."

She scrutinized his face, searched for some hint that he wasn't completely sure. But nothing in that open, honest gaze gave her cause for doubt. She heaved a sigh of relief. "Thank you."

"You're welcome." He offered her a crooked grin, crinkles appearing at the corners of his eyes. "But it bothers me that someone would leave this for others to find. I can't imagine who would do it or why. I thought you might know."

Was that the truth, or did he expect her to explain? She shuddered at the thought of rehashing it again, then remembered he'd already contacted the hospital. He would have said something if they hadn't cleared her. "It's an old story," she murmured. "Look at the date."

"I did."

"A patient died. There was an investigation. I was cleared." She had the sense that he hoped she'd say more, but Georgia shied away from that. The past was dead and gone. For once, she could almost feel the future beckoning. "Maybe it just blew there."

"It's not really that weathered." He fingered the edges of the paper. "Doesn't feel like it's been rained on or sat under a drift of snow."

"Well, I can't explain it. Though I did haul out a bunch of newspapers from the basement yesterday. Maybe that was in them."

"This particular piece?" His face told her how improbable her explanation sounded.

"I really don't know how it got there, Kent," she told him. "But however it did, it doesn't matter. Does it? I have nothing to hide. You checked my references. Did anyone—?"

"No one has said a word against you, Georgia. It just seems . . . odd."

It did. More than odd. For the past two days Georgia had concentrated on this new surrounding, but now the questions were back. "There are a lot of odd things in the world." She gazed past him. "Unless you have some other explanation, I guess that's one of them."

A sound broke the crackling tension between them.

"What on earth—?" Kent twisted to look.

They both gaped as a big gold button moved across the floor inside the gloomy craft shack.

"What, exactly, is that?" she asked.

"Good question." He stood. "We sometimes get animals inside the cabins. I'd better check it out."

"Now you tell me. Animals. Like mice?" She shivered at his nod. "Thanks. I won't get any sleep tonight." She stayed exactly where she was and watched Kent move toward the cabin.

"They're harmless. Usually." He turned back to grin at her, then stepped inside the shack.

"Yes, well, it's that *usually* that bothers me," she called out.

He was gone for several minutes, but Georgia decided he was old enough and big enough to look after himself no matter what was inside. She remained seated. A few moments later she heard a rustling sound, then the pad of tiny feet running away.

Kent appeared in the doorway, a big grin splitting his face.

"I know there are no snakes here, and besides, they can't run. So what was that?" she demanded.

He held up the button. "A pack rat. Must have come in while I went for lunch. Doesn't happen often, but they do wander into camp once in a while."

"A rat?" She stood, edged away. "I think I have to go. Now."

"Nothing like a little rodent to speed you on your way. Enjoy your day off." He chuckled at her scrunched-up face. "Where exactly are you going?"

"There." She pointed. "Years ago I took a trip to Scotland. Those hills remind me of it. I think I'll drive in a little way, have a picnic, and look around. Maybe take some pictures. I should be back tonight before dark. Tomorrow I'll go into town. I need to pick up a few things."

"Shopping." The disgust he forced into that word told her his thoughts on the subject.

"Yes, shopping. I need some shorts and T-shirts if this heat is going to continue." She felt his stare move to her bare legs. "I've washed these shorts so many times this week, I don't know how much longer they'll last."

Kent said nothing, but his eyes continued their scrutiny.

"I'd also like to get a pair of sneakers." She babbled, trying to change the subject, hoping to get his focus off her. "I can't find my old ones. I thought they were in the trunk of my car, but—" She scanned the ground, frowned.

"Don't worry," he told her with a solemn nod. "Pack rats don't steal shoes."

"Ha-ha." She felt a blush burn her cheeks. "Anyway, I need to get some. Sandals aren't the best thing for working in a kitchen."

"I don't imagine they are," he mumbled, his eyes on her feet. "But they sure look good."

"Oh. Thanks."

As if suddenly aware that he'd been staring, Kent raised his eyes. "Have fun, Georgia. Just be careful not to go too far off the main road. There are bears out and about back there, and they're hungry after snoozing all winter. Wouldn't want you to get lost and turn into their lunch."

"Very funny." She turned away, stopped when he called her name. "Yes?"

"If you do get lost or confused about how to get back, look for markers. They look like this." He sketched in the sand, explaining the system some locals had identified for hikers. "Follow the directions on the markers and you'll be fine."

"I don't get lost easily. I was a Girl Scout."

"A Girl Scout? That settles it then. I'm sure you'll be fine. See you tonight." He smiled, but his eyes didn't dance the way they usually did when he found something funny.

"Bye." Georgia scurried off, as anxious to get away from his scrutiny and the questions he hadn't asked as she was to see those hills.

⎯⎯⧫⎯⎯

Three hours later Georgia pushed away all thoughts of Kent. She found a small stream hidden in the V of two tree-covered hills clothed in variegated shades of fresh green. It was an ideal place for a picnic and since her stomach had been rumbling its complaint for the past twenty minutes, she drove her car beside a grove of willows and parked.

Over one arm she draped the old quilt Ralna had given her to sit on. In her other hand she grasped the small blue cooler she'd packed earlier and ambled down the gentle incline in search of the perfect spot. In the midst of a puddle of dappled sunshine, a big granite boulder sat waiting, quartz chips winking in the light as if to welcome her. Georgia reached out a hand, felt the warmth of the stone, and smiled. Perfect. And not a bear to be seen.

She spread the quilt so she could lean back against the granite yet stretch her legs out. It was an unbeatable vantage point. To her left the brook bubbled over small rounded pebbles. In front of her stood the valley of the forest with its gently wavering ferns. To her right the land rose above her, hiding her in the lee of its protective embrace.

Had a plain cheese sandwich ever tasted so good? She couldn't remember. The apple juice she sipped was like nectar—cool, sweet, refreshing. All around her, birds twittered and sang as they darted among the trees, searching for food for their babies.

A mantle of peace rested on Georgia. In her mind's eye she could hear her father's voice: *"The heavens are telling the glory of God; they are a marvelous display of His craftsmanship. Day and night they keep on telling about God. Without a sound or word, silent in the skies, their message reaches out to all the world."*

She'd memorized that psalm with him when she was ten. Funny how the words still stuck in her brain.

Georgia spent a long time in the glade. Her soul absorbed its peace and beauty. For once she asked herself no questions about the past. Instead her heart eased in the silent reverence of the forest, content simply to be. She thought about the camp a little and about Kent a lot.

He was an unusual man in many ways. He had patience, a lot of it. The kids could ask him anything about the camp, and he always took the time to explain. He was strong but also protective. She'd seen him send Ralna to rest, then watched him quietly finish her tasks when the older woman seemed to sag in the heat.

He carried his own problems. She knew his self-reliance cost him from watching his shoulders slump when he was alone and thought no one could see. Several times this past week, very early in the morning, she'd spotted him sitting beside the stream that ran through the camp. He'd been speaking intently, the concern reaching her, though the words didn't. She'd watched, mesmerized, as the pain on his face transformed to a glow enhanced by the first sun rays of the day. Only later had Georgia realized he had been lost in prayer.

That communion, that absolute faith in God—he'd shown it often. It was something she envied but knew she'd never have. To Kent, God was love, and that was enough. But Georgia couldn't understand a love that had allowed such terrible things to happen to her family. Until she did, her faith would never be like Kent's, no matter how much she wished it.

Eventually the shadows lengthened, and the sun no longer warmed her rock. She packed up the little cooler, folded her quilt, and climbed up the hill, muscles protesting at the effort.

Her little car was like an oven inside, so she rolled down the windows to let in some of the freshening breeze while she speculated on her next stop. Funny that once she'd turned off the main road, she hadn't seen any of those markers Kent had mentioned. She'd go back to that road, look for one. The rest of the afternoon waited to be filled, and given the long summer evenings of the prairies, she had plenty of time to return to Camp Hope.

But the road she found looked different. There were no markers to give direction. In fact, she could find no indication that any one of the graveled roads was more traveled than the other. To her they all looked the same.

Surely Camp Hope lay to the west? Yes, that was right. She remembered driving east into the sun, then south.

A wiggle of worry nagged at her, but Georgia refused to give it credence. She was fine. There was plenty of daylight left. Sooner or later she'd find a farmhouse. Or something.

With each valley she told herself to be patient, to wait, to have faith. With each climb she anticipated another vehicle, someone who would show her the way out. Once or twice she thought she saw the glint of metal up ahead. But as she crested each hill her hopes died all over again. Except for a few deer, some rabbits, and a glimpse of brown fur, which could have been a bear, the area seemed virtually deserted. There was nothing. No one.

By now the road had become little more than a dirt track, barely discernible in the growing dusk. It should be gravel. Had she taken a wrong turn? Georgia drove slowly, scanning the sides of the road for a marker. One sign. Just one. That's all she needed.

Her stomach rumbled again, its complaint less easy to ignore. After she drove another half an hour without spotting even one marker, Georgia stopped the car and pulled out the apple she'd been saving. If she ate it, she'd have nothing left but a bottle of water. But that was all right, wasn't it? Surely she wouldn't be here much longer. She bit through the vivid red skin, savoring its crunchy moist texture against her dry tongue.

Twice in the past hour she'd thought she spotted dust whirls in her rearview mirror. But whenever she slowed down to wait, they disappeared. Whirlwinds, no doubt. When that didn't work, she told herself they were dust eddies, common to the prairies.

Someone would come, she thought. She imagined Kent arriving to find her sitting here. He'd rant and rave about her getting lost so easily, but he'd make sure she was all right and then he'd lead her home. Why she was so certain of that, Georgia wasn't sure. Maybe because she wanted to believe it.

She'd finished the apple and was about to toss the core out her window when she saw it. A bit of metal lying in the ditch, its dull gleam caught a shaft of the setting sun.

Georgia shoved the car door open, got out, and walked toward it. A marker. The post it had stood upon was broken, jagged spears pointing toward the sky, as if someone had run into it. The sign itself lay on the ground. She hunched down, peered at the words: *Granby 2. Camp Hope 4*.

So she was only a short distance from town and twice that far from the camp. Relief flooded her. She had plenty of gas to make it there and at least an hour before it grew totally dark.

Not long now and I'll be home.

Home. It felt odd but strangely comforting to think of Camp Hope as home.

Back in the car, she started the engine and shifted into gear, eager to get going. But the car did not move smoothly forward.

What's the matter? She climbed out and walked around the car. The engine was purring properly, so the problem wasn't there.

Then she saw it. The front right tire was completely flat.

"How did that happen?" She hurried to turn off the motor to

conserve what fuel she had left. It wouldn't be easy to change a tire in this dim light, but she could do it. She had to. It didn't look like any Sir Galahad was about to appear to do it for her.

In a second Georgia had the trunk open and was lifting the thin matting that covered her spare tire.

Only there was nothing there. A gaping hole in the floor was all she saw.

That wasn't right. She'd had the spare checked before she left Calgary. Had they forgotten to put it back? No, she distinctly remembered the serviceman talking about what he called the doughnut tire, telling her that if she had to use it, not to drive above fifty because the car wouldn't handle the same. It *had* been here.

So where had it gone? Though she'd packed and unpacked many times since leaving Calgary, she'd never removed the spare.

But someone had.

Though the heat shimmered over the landscape, she shivered, scanned the hills once more. The sun's last rays streaked across the sky in a ribbon of flamingo red. Seconds later even that light was gone, and a murky darkness slowly descended over the hills, creating heather shadows that wavered in the dimness.

Still clinging to some faint ray of hope, Georgia peered down at the tire once more. Still flat. What should she do now?

When no obvious alternative came to her, she returned to her seat behind the wheel. She leaned her head back and tried to relax a little as a cross breeze brought fresh, if not cool, air through the open windows.

"Perhaps I could walk out," she mused aloud, as if speaking could build her courage.

But Kent's reminder about hungry bears and a memory of brown fur soon halted that thought. She'd seen one. There could be others. The truth was, she could do nothing but wait and hope someone would pass. Someone with a spare tire would be nice, but a ride back to the camp would do just as well. She scrabbled in her bag for her cell phone, but when she turned it on, the "no service" sign flashed prominently. There was no dial tone, no way to contact anyone.

As the world grew darker around her, Georgia suddenly realized the precariousness of her situation. She was alone in a thickly forested countryside, where finding a lost vehicle would not be easy, even if someone was looking for it. After all, she'd told Kent she could look after herself. He had no reason to doubt her.

The air cooled rapidly. She rolled up the windows, leaving hers open about two inches. She wanted to hear if a motor sounded in the distance. What else? It cooled off at night, and she was already chilly. Georgia retrieved the quilt from the trunk. As she drew out the worn and tattered fabric, a sound behind her, from the thicket of shrubs that shrouded a homestead from long ago, drew her attention. She squinted, trying to see what had made the noise. All at once a small flock of birds lifted out of the trees, fluttering overhead.

Someone or something was out there.

"Hello?" she called, listening as her own voice reverberated back to her. "Is anyone there?"

But the world around her remained silent.

Georgia slammed the trunk closed, then took her seat inside the car, locking each door before draping the quilt over herself. She sat behind the wheel, gazing into the night sky, bright now with evening stars. The Big Dipper—where was it? Wasn't there something about the brightest star being the North Star?

Evan would know. Evan who'd loved to traipse over mountain paths with his compass firmly in hand.

Why did he have to die, God?

The question rose from her heart, but as usual there was no answer. The emptiness that yawned inside her hadn't changed. It only waited for an appropriate moment, then washed over her in a new wave. Georgia stared in front of her and willed away the pain by filling her mind with other thoughts.

The moon, a huge yellow-orange disk, slipped over the treetops. South. That must be south. She glanced at her watch. Ten-thirty. Surely if anyone had gone looking for her, he would have given up by now.

A flare in the northeastern sky snagged her attention. Wavering ribbons of silver-washed blue shot across the sky in ever-increasing arcs that moved and danced, directed by unseen hands. No sooner did one flare waver and fade than another appeared, expanding in a band of vibrating color that grew more beautiful until finally it waned, withered, and faded away.

The northern lights.

She hadn't seen them often in Calgary. The city was too brightly lit to allow a good view. But here, alone in this vast space, there were no glowing streetlights to obstruct.

She watched them for a long time until gradually they merged with the stars and she fell asleep.

Sometime later a thump against the car woke her. A chill of fear grabbed the muscles in her shoulders and wrenched them tight. She searched through the side windows, trying desperately to see who or what was out there. The window was still open a scant two inches, and she put her mouth near the glass.

"Hello?" she whispered, voice shaky. "Is someone there?"

Nothing.

"It could have been an animal. A skunk, perhaps." She scrunched up her nose. "There's no way I'm getting out of this car to look at a skunk." Talking out loud bolstered her courage. "You'll have to wait till morning, skunk."

Somehow that wasn't an encouraging thought. Maybe if she flashed the headlights, it would scare away whatever animal was out there. She pulled the switch, watched as the road in front of her lit up. She couldn't leave the lights on too long or the battery would die, but just for a few moments she needed the courage those beams could impart.

Determined to fight the fatigue that swamped her, she took a sip of her precious water and stared out the window. What was out there?

Later she noticed the time. Surprised by the swift passage of twenty minutes, Georgia sucked in a breath of courage and clicked off the lights. The world plunged into inky darkness. She blinked to adapt her eyes.

There, to the left, was that a shadow in the trees? She squinted, but then it was gone. Georgia couldn't decide whether she'd dreamed it, or whether there really was someone out there. So why wouldn't they help her?

An eerie rush feathered over her skin. She grabbed the knob and pulled the headlights on once more, desperate to drive away whatever skulked in the darkness.

"Don't be silly," she scolded herself. "If someone really wanted to frighten you, they've had plenty of opportunity. It's just an animal, a deer or something."

Half an hour later she was able to turn out the lights once again. Sleep was not an option. She began to recite whatever affirmations she could remember while staring at the distant ridges. "'I look up to the mountains—does my help come from there?'"

Where had that verse come from? Georgia couldn't remember the reference, but the words were clear and certain, flooding her mind with promise.

"My help comes from the Lord, who made the heavens and the earth! He will not let you stumble and fall; the one who watches over you will not sleep."

"God is always love, Georgia. Always. Always." Her mother's voice echoed from some far-off memory. "He's just waiting for us to ask Him to help."

Was that all there was to it? A plea for help? Not for escape from life's pains, perhaps, but help—now?

It was too hard to believe. God had taken her family, stolen them. How could He love her, want to help her? How? Why?

The arguments whirled round and round inside her head until Georgia couldn't think straight. She leaned her head against the cool window.

"'An eye for an eye,' the Bible says. Justice will be done." The voice breathed through her open window, brushed against her ear in an intense whisper filled with . . . hate?

Georgia jumped to see who was there, caught only the faintest glimpse of a shadowy figure in her side mirror. But the thud against the car's rear bumper was unmistakable. What was happening?

Fear clawed at her as she scrambled for the knob to wind the window all the way closed. She was alone at night without any protection. Was her mother right? Did she dare trust God to be here with her?

What other choice did she have?

"Please, God, help me," she whispered, her fingers clutching at the lock to be sure it was still in place. "Please. Help."

Honk the horn.

"What?" There was no one in the car with her yet the voice was as clear as if someone had spoken aloud.

Honk the horn.

She didn't stop to argue or reason but reached out and pressed the silver button as hard as she could, then released it. The blast echoed across the countryside.

Again.

She nodded, pressed again, then turned on the lights for good measure.

In her rearview mirror Georgia thought she saw a shadow slip into the woods, but she couldn't be sure. Maybe she was hallucinating. The whole evening seemed utterly surreal, like a movie that was happening to someone else.

Honk again.

She didn't understand why she obeyed. Perhaps it was the reassurance that voice offered, the flutter of peace that rippled inside after she'd done as asked. All she knew was that she had no other options. She obeyed.

Kent's voice from last night made her sit up straight. *"He always hears, Georgia. Always."*

Was . . . was God speaking . . . to her? The very idea of it awed her. She hadn't asked God for anything since . . . and yet—

In the distance, Georgia caught the flash of lights through the trees. It had to be a vehicle, bouncing over the rutted road in front of her. Someone was coming. She turned on her own lights, then hit the horn once more.

Moments later a van burst over the crest of the hill. It halted in front of her, gravel spewing all over.

Kent Anderson jumped out. "Georgia?" He ran over and rapped on her window, peering through the glass at her. "Are you all right?"

"I am now." She unlocked the door, then tried to climb out. But her wobbly legs got tangled in the quilt. Grateful for his support, she leaned against the car while he freed her legs. Georgia savored her freedom, trying to control the rush of emotions that threatened to swamp her.

Kent's fingers brushed her cheek, then dropped to her shoulder. "Georgia, what happened? Why didn't you come home?"

Home. She felt a flicker of joy at that. "I have a flat tire."

"And you don't know how to change it?" He frowned, fingers tangling in her loosened hair.

"Not exactly." Grateful for the human touch, she pondered how much of this crazy night she should share. "My spare is missing."

"Missing?" One eyebrow flicked up in surprise. "What does that mean?"

"It means it was in my trunk when I left Calgary, and I haven't used it since. It's missing." She shivered as a breeze rustled over her skin.

"You're cold. Here." He wrapped her in his jacket.

"I can't take your jacket. You'll freeze. Your arms—" She

clenched her teeth together to stop them from chattering, the limey tang of his jacket a welcome shield.

"My arms are tough enough to withstand a little summer breeze." He smiled, squeezed her shoulders. "I'll be fine, Georgia. And I'll get your car fixed tomorrow. Right now you need to get back to camp. I don't imagine it was very nice sitting out here by yourself, but I'm very glad you didn't try to walk. It would have made locating you much more difficult."

"H-how did you find me?" she asked, accepting his hand as she climbed up into the van.

"Your horn. Which is rather strange. These hills have a terrific echo. I heard the horn and thought I knew where it came from, so I was turning around to go the other way." He shrugged. "But then I saw a flash of lights. It seemed best to come this way. Then, just as I was wondering about my choice, you hit the horn again. It was much louder so I knew I was going the right way. I don't know how you knew when to honk that horn, but it sure helped."

Who or what had directed her to honk at exactly the right time? God? Georgia swallowed, shuddered.

His eyes darkened with concern. "You're still shaking."

"I'll b-be fine. Really."

"If you say so. I'll lock up your car." Kent apparently took her silence as agreement, for he closed the van's passenger door, pulled a flashlight out of his pocket, and walked back to her car. She saw him looking at her tires, noted the way he stared at the front right tire. Then he kneeled down beside it, and he was hidden from her view.

Georgia fidgeted in her seat, scanning the area as she waited. What was he doing? Why was it taking so long? What if that person came back? Georgia rolled down the window. "Kent? Could we go? Please?"

"Yeah, right away." He stood, switched off her lights, and locked the car, then returned to the van, his face marred by a faint frown as he climbed inside.

"What took so long?"

"I just wanted a look at the tire—you know, to tell the garage what they'd need."

"What they need is some kind of air-pressure thing. It's flat."

"Yeah, it is." He put his hand on the gearshift and stared at her. She met his stare, frowned. "What?"

"Nothing." He put the van in reverse, then paused. "You're awfully pale. And your hands are trembling. I didn't realize it would shake you up so much to be out here alone."

"It's not that." She bit her lip.

"But you are upset. Why? Is something else bothering you, Georgia?"

How much should she tell him?

The truth.

Shocked by the quiet insistence of that inner voice, she gulped. "You'll think I'm crazy."

"No, I won't," he promised. He reached out, pushed a tendril of hair from her face, and tucked it behind her ear. "I just want to help. Tell me."

"Someone was watching me. I know it sounds crazy, unbelievable. But I also know what I heard."

"What you heard?" he asked.

"I had the car window open a little to let some air in. He whispered something." She clutched the jacket tighter as she remembered the feathery brush of his breath against the curve of her ear. Prickles rose on her neck.

"I'm guessing you didn't know this person?"

She shook her head. "I didn't see who it was."

"What did he say?" His mouth clamped tight; little white lines etched themselves around his eyes. "Tell me the rest, Georgia."

"He said the Bible said 'an eye for an eye' and that justice must be done." She blinked away the tears. "What does it mean? What am I going to do?"

Kent grabbed her hands and cradled them in his. Georgia didn't ask herself any questions. She simply threaded her icy fingers through his warm ones and hung on, allowing the strength of his hands to soothe her.

"You're going to relax while I drive us back to camp and get you something to eat," he told her. "You're safe now, Georgia. You're safe with me. I'll get you home. I promise."

"Okay," she whispered, relief washing through her as the warmth of his hands chased away the chill.

"I need my hands to drive," he teased when several minutes had passed and she still clung to him.

"Oh. Sorry." She pulled back, blushed.

"Don't be." He winked. "I enjoyed holding hands with you."

She heard him but decided to ignore it. Her mind honed in on something else. God. Had that been Him speaking to her? She'd prayed for help. Had He really answered her prayer?

As they rumbled toward Camp Hope, Georgia clasped the wonder of it to her heart. God had heard her prayer. And He'd answered by sending Kent.

At least now she was no longer alone.

CHAPTER SEVEN

Rick Mercer is on the phone, Kent."

Ralna's summons blared from the radio clipped to his belt, cutting across the garrulous chatter of kids at their first day of camp. Kent forced his face to remain blank, pulled the radio up, and spoke into it. "I'll call him back as soon as I finish dinner."

Then he continued his appreciation of the delicately browned pizza buns Georgia had prepared for the campers' first meal of the week.

Fred, Ralna's husband, paused, his food halfway to his mouth. "The RCMP are calling here? On a Sunday evening? What now?" he asked, his voice low enough that none of the kids surrounding them or the wranglers and other staff seated farther down their table could overhear.

"Nothing to worry about. I asked them to check something out."

"Something about last night?" Fred scanned Kent's face and nodded. "I thought it was funny when you brought her back last night, then disappeared after she'd gone to bed."

"Nobody else noticed, did they?" Kent had no intention of broad-casting this newest worry to anyone.

"Don't think so. Most of the other staffers were pretty tuckered out from their trip to the city yesterday. They make the most of those jaunts, I'll say that for them." He took a bite, chewed it thoughtfully. "So what's the problem?"

"Her." Kent inclined his head toward the slight woman behind the serving bar who was laughing and chatting with her kitchen helper as if nothing untoward had occurred in the past twenty-four hours.

"Doesn't look like much of a problem there. The woman is as pretty as a princess and cooks like a dream."

Kent couldn't disagree. Georgia MacGregor was very pretty. When he looked at her now, it was easy to see something had changed since last night. This woman looked entirely different from the quivering mass of nerves he'd brooded over. He'd spent the wee hours of the morning wondering if she was all right, and she showed up this morning laughing with Ralna—something about a skunk. Her eyes sparkled with fun, and she seemed excited about something. But as far as he knew, she'd told no one about her adventure. He was fairly certain something else had happened, some private event she'd tucked away inside. That was okay. Kent wanted the answer to one question though: Had she made up the story about the voice?

Immediately he tossed that idea away. She'd been terrified. That's another reason why he'd installed a lock on her cabin this afternoon. He didn't have to close his eyes to see those big round eyes brimming with panic. She always looked fragile, but last night when he'd found her, he'd struggled with himself not to gather her into his arms and soothe her fears, block out the dread and evil that had tormented her.

Even now, that rush of emotion he felt toward her shocked him with its intensity. He'd been a loner for years, except for Christa, only daring to hope in his heart that he might one day meet someone who'd share his dreams. But since his sister's accident he'd shut down his foolish plan to make the camp a raging success, not just financially but spiritually.

Every action Kent now performed had one goal in mind—to get the office job at head office, to earn a bigger paycheck, so he could afford to get Christa into the environment she needed—a place that would challenge and encourage her to rebuild her life.

Fred placed his knife and fork in the center of his clean plate. "You listening to me?" He waited for Kent's nod. "Ralna says Georgia's a nurse as well as a cook. Seems to me your troubles are solved. What's wrong with that?"

Kent stole another peek at Georgia, noted her rosy cheeks, bright with color from the heat of the kitchen. Her giggle was a warm joyful sound he hadn't heard before. It danced across the room, infusing light into shadow. Would he ever understand how the female mind worked? Last night she'd clung to his hands, yet today she barely looked at him. Georgia MacGregor had him stumped. He knew something in her life wasn't right, knew it was his job to watch out for her, to protect her, to help if he could. But she wouldn't let him in on her secrets.

He sighed. "Have you got a minute, Fred? I need to talk to you."

"Sure." In one gulp Fred swallowed the scalding coffee he always drank black and picked up his dishes. "Be right with you," he said, then grabbed his cap and strode across the room.

Kent watched him sort his dishes into the appropriate bus pans. As usual, the older man stopped to compliment Georgia on what he'd just eaten. She beamed at his praise. But her smile faded when it slid to Kent. He wasn't sure why.

"Go ahead, Kent. I'll get rid of the dishes for you." Mina Forrester, a local woman who volunteered as a kitchen helper from time to time, swept his empty plate and cup away. "I know how busy you men are. Get on with you now." She smiled at him, her lips poised to say a whole lot more.

"Thanks, Mina. I appreciate it." Kent hurried away before she could draw him into conversation. She had a good heart, but the young widow Forrester needed a new husband, and she kept looking to him. That made him nervous.

Fred waited by the door, a grin spreading across his face. "I figured Mina'd be in hot pursuit." He waited until Kent had walked through the door, then followed him down the steps.

"You want to go to the office to talk?"

Kent shook his head. "No offense, Fred, but Ralna is there, and she's lousy at keeping secrets. For now this stays between us." He motioned ahead of him. "I've got to check out a pellet gun. Let's go out to the range."

One thing Kent had always appreciated about Fred was that he could bide his time without nagging for answers. Now Fred worked quietly alongside him, checking each gun for problems, waiting for Kent to find the right words.

Only there were no right words. Not to explain this. Better to dive in and get it over with. "You know Georgia had a flat last night."

Fred nodded. "I heard."

"Well, I don't think it went flat. In fact, I'm pretty sure someone cut that tire." Kent saw he had a rapt audience. "It looked funny when I found her, but it was dark and I didn't want to say anything. She was pretty shook up. Even claimed someone had been watching her, whispering stuff."

"Nerves, maybe?"

"Maybe. But I doubt it." He was fairly certain a nurse with Georgia's credentials didn't get jangled nerves from a few shadows. She'd heard something. Kent set the pellet guns back into place, locked the cabinets, then checked their stock of pellets.

"She's too strong for a case of the vapors. I agree." Fred inspected the stock of bull's-eye sheets.

Target practice, particularly marksmanship, was one way they tried to visually demonstrate the importance of training yourself to focus on a goal and the rewards of working to reach it. Patience and persistence weren't easy for anybody, but the results were worth it.

In this case, Kent had figured patience wasn't necessarily a good thing.

"But why slash her tires?" Kent surprised himself by saying it aloud. "Who would do that?"

"So you asked Mercer to check it out." Fred quirked one bushy eyebrow. "You think it's those transients again?"

"I don't know." The truth was, Kent had gone over possible scenarios a thousand times last night, and none of them seemed plausible.

Not unless Georgia had made an enemy who had followed her all the way out here. Which was ridiculous. Georgia MacGregor wouldn't hurt a flea. He'd just watched her slip an extra dish of peach slices to a young, half-starved waif who'd come to camp on a scholarship. He'd noticed how careful she was to ensure that each child had enough on his or her plate, that the meals were tasty as well as nutritious. At Camp Hope, everyone loved Georgia.

"Some of 'em like to play tricks." Fred scratched his sunburned nose as he thought about it. "That dead tree—the transients put that across the road after we said they couldn't build a fire by the barn, remember?"

"Yeah." Kent nodded. As if he'd soon forget hacking that eighty-foot pine into firewood.

"And remember the night those teenagers got into the pool? They must have dumped every toy we own in the pool after we kicked them out. Though you didn't seem to find retrieving them any hardship." Fred winked. "Want me to remind you of some other shenanigans?"

"No, thanks. I remember all their tricks. Especially the last one. Haven't needed soap for months." He grinned, knowing Fred wouldn't easily forget the soap bubbles they'd had to hose out of the shower complex. "But none of the things they did were malicious, Fred. Just pranks."

"And the tire was?"

"Oh, that was deliberate. Rendered useless. Cut six ways through

Sunday." He flopped down on the grass outside the door to the pellet shed. "I don't know what to think."

"You considered maybe it's us they're aiming at?" Fred hunkered down beside him in the peculiar fashion he had of never quite sitting but still balancing on his heels so he was at eye level. "Lots of people around here haven't forgotten that a girl almost died in that pool. Some of 'em wanted the camp shut down, thought it would be a good idea to end this ministry. Not enough time has passed to forget that."

"Yeah, I've considered that." And blamed himself for it every night. "But the question is, what do we do about it? Hire security?"

Fred snuffled his laugh. "Who's gonna come way out here to run a check every few hours? And how would we pay 'em? We're barely functioning now. If we don't get some more registrations, head office will—" he stopped, swallowed—"sorry."

"Don't be." Kent patted his shoulder. "You and Ralna have been rocks through all of this, and I appreciate it." Sheer frustration nipped at him, and he raked his fingers through his hair. "So what am I supposed to do? We can't take any more negative publicity. If anything else happens—"

"Head office will close us down, and that promotion you're aiming at will evaporate like that." Fred snapped his fingers.

"Yes." Kent sighed. "I've got to get this place back on the map. It's my only ticket out of here, the only way I can see that Christa gets what she needs."

"No change there?"

"None. If only—" Kent jumped to his feet, fed up thinking about it. "Come on. We're only going round and round. We might as well get on with what we can manage. Only, if you don't mind, keep your eyes peeled, will you? I don't want to spread any rumors so I asked the garage to keep quiet about it. I'd appreciate it if you didn't tell anyone what I suspect."

"Of course not." Fred locked the pellet shed. "You're pushing yourself pretty hard, Kent. I admire your desire to do right by your sister, but ultimately she's going to have to face reality and deal with her problems. You can't keep shielding her."

The gentle remonstrance offered sympathy and understanding and as such, it was impossible to take offense.

"I know you're right." He walked beside Fred through the over-long grass. "And I keep hoping and praying. But until something changes—" he shook his head—"we slog on. Look at this place! There's so much to do, it's wearing us out. How much more can we handle?"

"We can handle exactly what God gives us. No more than that. He will not suffer a bruised reed to be broken." Fred pulled his work gloves out of his back pocket, slapped them on his thigh to release the dust. "The Lord put this camp here and placed us in it for a reason. We have to keep it available for when He decides to use it."

"Uh-huh. I just wish He'd send along someone with some money to help get things moving." Immediately he felt guilty for saying it. Hadn't God sent Georgia to shoulder a huge part of his load?

"Along that line, I might have some good news. Pastor Ben phoned this afternoon. He said some guy spoke to him after church today about wanting to volunteer at a camp his niece had attended." He grinned. "A camp called Camp Hope. Apparently this girl had some dramatic turnaround after being here and is now doing so well, her family is delighted. This fellow has the summer off and wants to help out for a few weeks."

Kent blinked. "You're kidding? Well, bring him on. Another set of hands is exactly what we need."

"Pastor doesn't know when he'll show up, but he said the guy's eager and willing to pitch in." He laughed at Kent's whoop of excitement. "See, the Lord's busy working for our side, son. You just have to keep the faith and push ahead as best you can."

The truth of Fred's words pinged his conscience. How often would he need to hear them before they sunk in? Kent grabbed Fred's hand and shook it as appreciation flooded his heart. "God gave this camp a precious miracle when He sent you and Ralna, Fred. Thanks for adjusting my focus."

"My pleasure. Now I suppose we'd better get that volleyball net fixed before it gets dark."

They smiled at each other, then turned and walked toward the camp office, toward the next problem that faced them.

It came sooner than either expected.

"Kent? I . . . maybe you better come to the office. Now. Right now." The radio crackled its summons. Ralna sounded breathless, surprised. She was never surprised.

Kent scowled at the van parked in front of the office, glanced at Fred. "Plumbers? After hours?"

Fred shrugged.

Kent pushed open the office door and walked inside. "Ralna, I thought we'd decided to hold off on calling out the plumbers."

"We did."

Then what are they doing here? "Okay." He frowned at the shock on her face. "But there is a van outside. What's the matter? Can't they calibrate the ovens? Are they too old or something?"

"Oh, we can calibrate those," a big man in denim overalls said. "No problem there. I'm just wondering if you can sign this work order. Tomorrow morning, bright and early, I want to get my men out here and get started. Can't do that without your John Henry." He held out a clipboard.

"Your *men*? For two ovens?" Kent took the board and looked at Ralna. "A work order? We never used a work order for fixing those ovens before, did we?"

"Oh, this isn't for the ovens. This is for the air-conditioning."

"The what?" Kent inspected the paper he was holding. *Install air-conditioning unit for dining hall and kitchen with appropriate ductwork and thermostats.* "I-I didn't order this," he stuttered.

"Don't know about that. Just know I need your signature before I can get started." The man shifted from one booted foot to the other.

"I was on a job in town on Saturday and stayed over to go fishing with my brother. I figured I'd stop by here on the way back and get an idea of the supplies I need. It's kind of a big job," he hinted, holding out the pen. "Might be a good idea to get things started right after breakfast tomorrow."

"I'm sorry but—" Kent turned to Ralna. "Did someone authorize this?" he asked hopefully.

"Apparently. But I can't seem to find out who."

Kent faced the plumber again. "I'm truly sorry to hold you up, but I wonder if you might check with your office again. I think maybe you've got the wrong place."

"There's more than one Camp Hope?" The guy scratched his head, then picked up the phone and dialed. "Nobody in the office today, but lucky for you, my wife keeps it all in her head. Hey, Martha . . . you know this air conditioner I'm supposed to install tomorrow? . . . They said they didn't order it."

He hunched over the phone, turning his back to them. But his whispered voice was loud enough for everyone to hear. "I think maybe they can't afford to pay for it. . . ." He froze, straightened. "You don't say? . . . Well, then . . . no problem. See ya in a bit."

He hung up the phone and faced them. "Well, that settles it. Sir, if you'd sign that work order, I'll get measuring so I can do my job."

"But . . . but—"

He clapped a hand on Kent's shoulder, his grin wide. "This is your lucky day. Seems the whole thing's already been paid for. Top-of-the-line system, no holds barred. By tomorrow evening, those little tykes will be eating their dinner at a cool sixty-nine degrees." He pointed one beefy finger. "Put your John Hancock right on that line."

"It's all paid for?" Kent saw the nod, but he couldn't quite understand it. "We won't owe anything?"

"Not one thin dime. Okay?"

"Very okay. Best donation we've had in a long time." He winked at Fred. "Boy, sometimes that faith you were talking about sure works fast."

Kent scrawled his signature on the crumpled piece of paper, handed back the clipboard, and watched the man leave. After several minutes, he turned, only then realizing that Ralna was staring at him openmouthed. "Fred, I think you'd better explain your thoughts about faith to your wife. I'm going to talk to Christa, but I'll meet you on the court in twenty minutes. We should still be able to get that net up."

"Sure, boss."

His ATV was where he'd left it last night. Kent dug out his keys, started it, and headed for home, excitement coursing through his veins. It had been so long since anything good had happened. He could hardly wait to share this with his sister, watch her eyes sparkle with excitement.

A camp with air-conditioning! I intend to find out whoever you are and thank you personally. He gunned the engine and rolled down the path toward home.

What he saw there had him pulling up short to stare.

Christa in her wheelchair sat beside their cook. She took a bite out of the sandwich Georgia handed her and began chewing, her attention riveted on her guest.

Neither noticed his presence, so Kent quietly turned back the way he'd come, stunned that his reclusive sister was actually speaking to a stranger.

He moved inside the chapel and began organizing things for the evening service, feeling as if his ordinary world had been turned upside down. Everything was mixed up, out of order. Christa was actually talking to someone else!

Why was that?

The silence, the dimness—it was the perfect place for prayer. *I don't know what You're doing, God. But whatever it is, please keep it up. For Christa's sake.*

She didn't belong here.

Georgia scanned the sea of young faces and knew these kids had more faith than she'd ever had. They were halfway through their week and they'd begged her to come tonight, to sit in on their service, to listen to the speaker they termed *awesome*. So she'd given in, silently slipped into the chapel after the first few songs. She'd stay a minute or two, then leave.

But the singing got to her. It was lively, sometimes discordant, but so full of joy. It bubbled out, rose to the rafters, and bounced back down again. Some of the youth leaders didn't look a whole lot older than her physically, yet their devotion to God, their utter peace in His presence held her amazed as she listened to their prayers. Confident, secure, they petitioned God about the smallest request, utterly serious.

She could have tolerated that.

But this speaker—she didn't remember his name or where he came from. But the words he was speaking were unforgettable. They bit deep into her soul.

"Lots of people have the wrong idea about God." His eyes roved his congregation. "They think He's there to help us, to make us strong. And He is. But only if we're serving Him. You see, we're saved to be His servants. We serve God, not the other way around. Getting that relationship right can save you a lot of grief later on."

Something in what the speaker said didn't make sense. Surely God couldn't have wanted her to lose Evan and Ty? That would be— ungodlike. God was supposed to be love.

"You see, the trouble is, we don't know God. Not really. We think we do because we read some Scriptures about Him. We've gone to Sunday school and church for years and heard that God is love." He grinned. "It's a funny thing. Whenever someone wants to blame God, they quote 'God is love' as if that's all He is."

Georgia could see frowns on some of the kids' faces. She knew there was one on hers. She'd never heard anyone speak like this before. What was this about?

"But just loving us and giving us everything we ask for, that's Santa Claus, not God. God's way is bigger than that. Of course He promises that He'll always be there for us, but He expects something in return. He expects us to follow Him no matter what, not to waver in our faithfulness. He expects us to keep our promise."

Kent slipped into the seat beside her. He smiled, then turned his attention to the speaker. But Kent's close proximity made Georgia nervous. Could he tell that her faith was a sham, that inside she was empty?

The fresh tangy scent of his lime aftershave assaulted her senses. She thought of that night in the woods, of his gentle care, of his protection. She'd been terrified out there, yet what she remembered most today was the coaxing warmth of his hands, the way he'd hastened to give her his jacket, his careful probing questions. The next day he'd rushed over to install the door lock she'd asked for. She was an employee, a temporary one at that, but he acted as if she were a valued member of this camp. Why would he care?

"God offers us unconditional love. But once we accept it, we are His to do with as He wishes. We're just like this." The speaker held up a handful of sticky brown mud. Several kids giggled. "It's clay. Now say I want this clay to be a lovely big bowl. First I work it until it's pliable; then I press and bend until it has exactly the shape I want."

He pulled a big clay bowl out from behind the piano. A hush fell over the chapel. Georgia leaned forward, curious about his point.

"Now suppose I was working this clay and all of a sudden it said, 'I don't want to be a clay bowl. I want to be a flower.'"

A child in the front row burst out laughing.

"Why, Jonathan, what's so funny?"

"Clay doesn't talk," he sputtered. "It's clay. You decide what it's going to be and then make it into that. The clay doesn't decide."

"Exactly. And that's how it is with God. We're of no earthly good to Him if we won't get pressed and molded. Even this nice clay bowl isn't any good to me. Look what happens if I put water in it." He called up a girl, asked her to hold the bowl, then poured in a pail of water. "Now just stand there a minute, Desiree. We're going to sing another song and then I'll finish talking."

Of course, in the middle of the song, the bottom of the bowl dissolved and water spilled onto the floor. Georgia couldn't stop her own giggles as she watched the mess he'd created.

"Do you know why that happened? Because the clay hasn't been fired."

The speaker went on to explain the refining process that produced usable pots, but Georgia didn't want to hear the rest. The humor was gone. Was that supposed to comfort her? The knowledge that God had taken her husband and child to make her a better person?

No! She wouldn't accept that.

"Excuse me." She slipped past Kent and hurried outside, drawing deep drafts of fresh air into her lungs to slow her racing heart. She headed toward the pool, to the bench at the end where she'd spent many hours thinking.

<hr />

Kent didn't hesitate. He followed Georgia out of the chapel, stood watching as she scurried toward the pool. After a moment he went after her but at a distance, giving her time to sort through the shadows in her mind.

"Are you all right?" He kept his voice low, soft, hoping she wouldn't feel like he was intruding.

"I'm fine. I just like to come out here and think." She sat on the bench, drew her legs up onto the seat, and stared into the starlit sky.

"I don't blame you. It's quite a view." He sat beside her, not quite touching but close enough that she couldn't ignore him. Georgia

MacGregor needed to displace some of her stress. How could he help her?

"Sometimes when the camps aren't running and we're all alone, I sit out here and watch the night sky." He pointed. "See that flurry of stars that looks like someone tossed them into the sky like seeds? I'm pretty sure that's the Milky Way."

"Pretty sure?"

"I told you I was an amateur. There's Orion. The Big Dipper."

"They're beautiful." She tilted her head back and obediently scanned the inky sky in its star-studded majesty.

"Yes, they are beautiful. But they all seem dimmer once the moon rises. I wish you could be here in the fall, in the midst of harvest when the moon is low on the horizon, a massive orange ball. Or just before Christmas. Some nights the moon is so bright against the snow you'd think we had floodlights on."

"I'm sure each season has its own beauty."

He nodded, searching for the right words. "Looking at the sky— it helps put life in perspective sometimes. All my petty frustrations and worrying about the camp and its future, how we're going to pay for things—it all seems slightly foolish in the midst of this master plan."

He lowered his focus to her face, gazed at her skin gilded by the moonlight. "Who needs money," he whispered, "when you have all this?"

"You do," she whispered back, a slow smile curving her lips. "You need it to share all this—" she waved a hand—"with kids who need it."

He smiled at her perception. She understood that much about him anyway. "Did something upset you back there?" He hiked a thumb over his shoulder toward the chapel.

"No." She chewed her bottom lip.

Kent was fairly certain she was searching for a way to avoid his questions. He told himself not to push, to wait.

Finally she spoke. "I promised the kids I'd sit in on a session. They seem to really enjoy the speaker."

"Ron is a master storyteller when it comes to kids. Every year he takes his summer vacation out here and spends it teaching. The kids love him." Kent saw her cheek muscles tighten. "Did he say something that bothered you?"

"I don't want to talk about it. I just want to unwind a bit."

He'd have to respect her wishes. But if she could open up a little . . . "You should unwind. You work too hard. The kids didn't need fresh doughnuts this afternoon. Chips would have filled their stomachs just as well, though the doughnuts were excellent." He grinned at her. "I checked. Thank you."

"You're welcome." A flicker of fun danced through her eyes. "Though if you aren't careful, some of the counselors are going to complain that you got more than they."

"Let them," he told her airily. "I'm the boss. I get to make the big decisions around here."

"I see." She unclipped her hair from the silver barrette she always wore. Her fingers riffled through the golden mane. "That feels better. I'm not used to wearing it up all the time."

"I like it down," he said, watching as the shimmering strands resumed the curl she never quite managed to suppress. "You have beautiful hair."

She turned her head away, though not before he saw her frown. "Cooking in that kitchen is fun now with the air conditioner."

"Ah yes, the air conditioner." He hadn't yet managed to find out who'd lavished such a wonderful gift on them, but with temperatures still hovering far above seasonal norms, he enjoyed the cool refreshment the dining hall offered as often as he could. "You changed the subject."

"Yes." A smile quirked the corners of her lips. "The doughnuts were a special treat for a friend."

"The little guy with the big blue eyes?" He nodded, felt a wave of tenderness curl inside him for this woman who'd lost her own child yet found joy in another. "Toby. I know the feeling. He could ask me almost anything and I'd do it, just to wheedle a smile from him."

"He reminds me of—" She swallowed the words.

"Of your son." Kent finished her sentence, fought to control the wobble in his voice. She was finally opening up, just a little. *Don't push too hard.* "What was his name?"

She twisted to stare at him, her big brown eyes wide. "Ty," she whispered a moment later. "Tyler. He'd just learned to walk."

The smile transformed her already lovely face with a translucent kind of beauty that came from inside. "He was such a good baby. I know all mothers say that, but Ty had this funny little chuckle. He'd wake up in the morning and pull himself up in his crib. If he stood the right way, he could see into our room. He'd wait and wait until I finally looked at him, and then he'd give a little chortle as if he was wishing me good morning."

She hesitated. "I never told anyone that before."

"I'm glad you told me. It's a very precious memory."

It was the wrong thing to say. She drew herself up, shifted away from him. Immediately Kent felt the invisible wall return.

"Yes, that's all I have left. Memories." She turned her head. The wind tossed her hair across her face. She scraped it back with one hand, her eyes dark, secretive. "Please don't be offended, but I'd like to be alone now. Please."

"I'm not offended, Georgia. You can say anything you want to me, anything, and I'll understand. If you need a friend, I'm available. Remember that."

"Thanks."

Kent didn't want to go, didn't want to leave her sitting here alone with nothing but memories. The tiny vine of protectiveness that had rooted inside him the day Georgia MacGregor showed up at Camp Hope had begun to wrap its tendrils around his heart. Which was absolutely ridiculous. He had one goal, and it couldn't include Georgia, no matter how much he wished for it.

He had to stick to his plan, get the camp back in the black, and impress head office. A promotion out of here, that was the only way he could help Christa.

With that plan in mind, he forced himself to leave Georgia, to walk away. Sometimes doing what was right seemed all wrong.

CHAPTER EIGHT

When she heard the muffled cries, Georgia had no idea how much time had passed since Kent had left. The camp seemed unusually quiet until she remembered that squirt-camp kids were the youngest campers, so they usually went to bed the earliest.

"Help me!"

The breathless gasp shocked her into action. She whirled, saw wild splashes in the water, and knew immediately that someone was in trouble. But the front gate was still locked. Then she remembered the night she'd found Kent swimming alone.

Georgia raced around to the back, found the open gate. She ran through it, only then spotting a wheelchair hidden in the shadows. "Christa!" She scanned the pool.

"Help me, Georgia. I've been hanging on for ages, trying to get you to notice. My fingernails are about to give way. Please get me out of here. I-I can't swim anymore." Her face, so like Kent's, begged for help before she sank under the water.

Georgia kicked off her sandals and dived in. In a matter of seconds she found Christa and dragged her to the surface.

"What are you doing in here alone?" she demanded as she towed Christa over to the ladder beside the diving board. "You know the rules."

"I'm the reason for the rules." Christa sucked in several deep breaths, let go of the ladder with one hand to swipe it across her eyes. "I just wanted to see if it was like I remembered. Talking to you this afternoon made me think of it. It was so hot. I wanted to feel the old feelings, remember how it used to be."

She slapped the water with her free hand, the other clinging to the metal support. Her blue eyes blazed with temper. "I couldn't move my legs; do you know that? Not even a little. I sank like a stone!"

Georgia ignored the anger. "Of course you did. Your arms aren't strong enough to support you. But they could be. If you'd practice." Her sundress wound itself around her legs as she treaded water. "Practice *with* someone," she added.

"But—"

"Shh. Someone's coming. Oh no, it's Kent. He'll kill me." Georgia could imagine his irritation when he found her here with his sister.

"Quick! You have to hide me," Christa said. "He can't see me in here. Not like this. He'll worry and—oh, please, just hide me under the diving board."

Georgia wanted to argue, to point out the merits of gaining Kent's help. But Christa had taken a giant step today. There was no way Georgia wanted to say or do anything that would send Christa back to her self-imposed reclusivity. Anyway, there was no time to argue.

"All right, whoever you are. I want you out of that pool. Now."

"While you're hanging there, pray that he doesn't see your chair," Georgia whispered. She left Christa clinging to the metal supports and moved away from her to the side ladder, hoping it was dark enough that Kent wouldn't notice her dress. "Please don't come any closer."

"Georgia?" He stood in the center of the gate. "What are you doing?"

"Swimming. What else do you do in a pool?"

"Is Ralna around?" He glanced left and right.

Georgia held her breath, wondering if he'd see the chair.

But evidently Kent wasn't looking that hard. Actually, he was glaring at her. "She's not here." He shook his dark head in confusion.

"No." She couldn't get Ralna in trouble.

"Then why are you here? I told you that no one is allowed to come in here without a buddy. You even agreed to my rules."

"Technically I didn't—"

"Don't go there, Georgia!" He was furious. One hand smacked the cement wall of the showers. "We have these rules for a reason. Someone almost died swimming in here alone at night. If head office heard of this—" his voice hardened—"I could lose my job."

"I'm sorry." And she was. He'd been so kind to her. Now he'd probably have to fire her. But what else could she have done?

"Sorry doesn't cut it. I want you out of here. Now."

"I can't."

"Then I'll help you." He stepped forward.

"No!" Georgia paddled backward, hoping the moon would stay behind the cloud. "My swimsuit is . . . er . . . well—" She took a deep breath. "Couldn't you go away for a minute? I promise I'll get out right away. Just . . . uh . . . give me a few minutes to fix things. Five minutes. Please?"

At first she didn't think he'd budge, so she glanced at Christa, hoping she'd have an idea or announce her presence.

But finally Kent nodded, if you could call the jerk of his head a nod. "Five minutes. Not one second more. If you're not out, I'll haul you out myself. In this case modesty is outweighed by safety." The metal gate clanged closed. "I'll be back to lock up in four minutes, fifty-eight seconds."

"Yes, sir." She waited until he left, then swam to Christa. "Come on; let's get you out of here. Your skin is like ice. You'll be lucky if you don't catch pneumonia."

"S-serves me right."

Weakened and tired by her ordeal, Christa could offer little help as Georgia dragged her over the lip and onto the cement apron. She looped her arms around Georgia's neck as she was told, but she was deadweight. Georgia was gasping by the time she got Christa seated on the diving board, but she had no time to waste. Quickly she handed her a towel, then helped her pull on a fleecy black sweatshirt.

"Bringing this is about the only bright thing you did tonight," Georgia muttered, pushing the wheelchair close, then locking the brakes. "Now get in this thing and get out of here before your brother comes back."

"I don't know how to thank you. I could have drowned," Christa said through her tears.

"Yes, you could have. Which is kind of the point here, Christa. Next time you want to swim, you tell me." Georgia saw the denial rise to Christa's lips and forestalled it. "I mean it. You don't promise, I tell Kent about what really happened here. It's that simple."

"Okay, okay. I promise." Christa pressed the button that moved her chair across the deck, over the bump, and down the ramp.

"Just a minute. I want your key to the pool." Georgia held out her hand, waited until Christa removed the silver key ring from her chair and tossed it over. "Now get going. I'll see you tomorrow, and we'll talk about this."

"You look too small to be such a bully." Christa whirred away in her chair.

"Yes, I'm a real tough guy." Georgia wrung out her hair, made a face at her limp sundress, and groaned. "Also a mess."

She'd just finished snapping the lock shut when she saw the towel still lying on the diving board. Would Kent recognize it as his own and figure out what had happened? She had to get it out of there.

Hastily she unlocked the gate, trying to stay in the shadows as she crept across the deck. The towel was near the end of the diving board, and she had to stretch to reach it. As her fingers closed around the end, searing pain stabbed the back of her head.

And then she was falling.

⋙⋅◆⋅⋘

He'd waited long enough.

Kent headed back to the pool, grinding his heels into the dirt as he went. She knew better. So what had possessed Georgia to swim alone? Didn't she realize one little accident could cost him everything?

He moved through the trees, scanning the darkness. The gate was still open.

Lips pursed tight, he surged through, prepared to lecture her long and loud about the inherent dangers. But the words died in his throat when he saw her lying facedown in the water, her white sundress floating around her slim body.

Kent ignored all the questions and dived into the water. In minutes he'd eased her unconscious body out of the pool. Squatting beside her, he saw no sign that Georgia MacGregor was breathing. *Not again. Oh, God, not again.*

He tilted her head back, held her nose, and began the short breaths of air he prayed would coax life back into her. Her silken skin was cold. It was as if time stood still—as if nothing had changed. "Come on, Georgia. Breathe. Come on, honey."

In and out, in and out—he kept the rhythm going until finally she sputtered, coughed, and then spit out the pool water from her lungs.

"You're okay. Just lie still and take deep breaths."

He should never have left her in the pool alone. He'd risked her life to save what? Her pride? Her dignity? It was a poor trade-off.

He took careful inventory of her limbs. No broken bones. One thing to be grateful for. But how had she fallen into the pool? She was a strong swimmer; he'd seen that firsthand.

Kent could come up with only one conclusion. Georgia must have slipped on the cement and knocked herself out. That's why she had her dress on. But where was her suit?

"Ooh." The groan eased through her white lips.

Kent chafed her chilly fingers, noted her slow pulse. "Georgia? Are you okay? Anything hurt?"

"My head." The whisper came faint but heartfelt.

"Okay. Just lie still for a minute." He slipped his hands into her sopping hair and checked for bumps. Instead he encountered a sticky wetness behind her left ear.

"Oh, that hurts. Please! Don't touch it."

"All right." He drew his hand away, shocked by the blood on his fingers. "You've injured yourself." Fury rose, white-hot, mixed with a choking fear in the pit of his stomach. "I told you not to swim alone," he grated, his heart racing with fear. "You could have died. Did you slip?"

She opened her mouth to respond, then closed it.

"Nothing to say for yourself, I see." He saw her struggle to sit up and slipped his arm around her shoulders, offering support as she eased upright. "Sit on the diving board for a minute. Make sure everything's where it's supposed to be."

"I'm fine. I think. It's just . . . my head." She drew her fingers away from the injured spot, looked at them in apparent surprise. "I'm bleeding."

"I know." This angry churning in his gut was more than simple fear for her safety, but he couldn't waste time trying to figure it out. Not now. He'd failed to prevent this. It was his fault, but his anger spewed out over her.

"Do you realize that I could fire you for this? You deliberately disobeyed me, Georgia. How can I keep you on when you won't follow the rules? How did you get in anyway?"

"I wish you'd stop yelling at me."

The soft plaintive complaint made him feel about one foot tall. He grabbed the pool hook, snagged the towel from the water, and wrung it out, all the while ordering his emotions in check.

When his heart had finally slowed, he sat down on the board beside her. "I'm sorry I yelled, Georgia. I just can't understand why you'd do something like this. I thought you understood."

"I do understand. And I didn't break your precious rules." She sighed, wiggled closer. "You don't mind, do you? I'm freezing."

"Of course not. I should have realized." Guilt washed over him. He unzipped his windbreaker and wrapped it around her, then hugged her close against his side. "Are you ready to go back to your cabin?"

"Not yet. My legs are a little wobbly."

"I could carry you."

She started to shake her head, winced, then sighed. "No. I'd rather sit here for a minute. Just until things stop spinning."

He should be rushing her to the hospital, not sitting here in the dark fuming. The more he thought about it, the more something about her story didn't ring true. Georgia had been very careful to make sure Ralna was always with her when she swam. It didn't make sense that she'd sneak behind his back when she had only to ask.

"Why were you in here, Georgia? And I want the truth this time."

She studied him for a moment, chocolate eyes pensive. Her voice, when it emerged, was slightly above a whisper. "I was sitting on my bench thinking. I heard a noise, came around the back, and found the gate open. Your sister was in the water, barely able to hang on." She shivered. "She had this crazy idea—well, never mind that. I'd gotten as far as dragging her to the edge when we heard you coming. She begged me not to tell you what she'd done."

He couldn't believe what he was hearing. Christa had *wanted* to get in the water? Since when? Georgia shuddered again, and he rubbed her arms with his hands, trying to infuse warmth while he puzzled it out.

When she spoke again, Georgia's voice had changed, hardened. "I probably shouldn't have done it, but I agreed to let her hide under the diving board while you ranted and raved. As soon as you left, I got her out and back in her wheelchair." She peeked up at him through her lashes. "Are you more mad now?"

He was and he wasn't. She'd saved his sister. "But what was she doing here? Why would she even try to swim after all this time?"

"I can't answer that. It's something you'll have to discuss with Christa. All I can say is at that moment, she was worried about you, about your reaction."

He didn't get it, but he'd talk to Chris later. Right now he focused on her. "So what—you decided to go in for a dip while you were here? In your sundress? You had no right to go back in the water, Georgia."

She straightened, knocking his arm away from her shoulder. "I didn't *intend* to go back in the pool with my clothes on, Kent." Her voice sharpened, her eyes, huge with shock, bored into his. "Someone pushed me."

"What?" He wanted to laugh at her accusation, to deride the fear he saw on her face. But it made sense. Why else would she be floating, unconscious, fully clothed, in the pool?

"I felt the hand on my back and tried to turn, but my foot slipped." She touched the back of her head gingerly. "I must have overbalanced, hit my head on the diving board, and fallen in. I remember reaching for Christa's towel." She focused on the sodden mass lying in front of them. "Then pain. And nothing else." She stood slowly, tested her legs.

"Pushed you?" Kent couldn't believe this was happening. "Deliberately?"

She nodded. "That's what I'm saying." Her fingers touched her forehead. "I want to go back to my cabin now." Her full lips tilted in a lopsided grin. "Funny how my shoes stayed on, isn't it?"

Kent found nothing remotely amusing about any of this, but he clamped his lips together and said nothing, merely grasped her elbow and helped her across the deck.

"Where's the key?" he asked when they arrived at the gate.

"Must be on the bottom of the pool by now." Georgia shrugged. "I took it from Christa. I figured I'd take it back to the office in the morning and suggest Ralna hide it. I don't think it's a good idea for Christa to have access to it."

"You're intimating that she'd actually hurt herself. Deliberately?"

"This is awfully hard for you to hear, and the truth is, I don't know what she'd do, Kent. But I don't like her frame of mind. She's been sitting alone brooding for far too long. I wouldn't leave that key lying around."

She waited a moment, then laid her hand on his arm, her eyes brimming with sympathy. "I'm sorry. I don't want to hurt you. But I do know something about depression. I've only spoken to your sister briefly, certainly not long enough to judge her mental state. I'm just saying it wouldn't hurt to take some precautions."

At that moment, Kent saw Georgia MacGregor in a new light. She'd saved his sister's life and almost lost her own, her head still trickled a thin rivulet of blood down her neck and must ache terribly, yet her concern was for a woman she'd only just met. The little vine of tenderness sent out another shoot toward his heart and wrapped itself around it.

"Come on, Georgia," he said, his voice gruff in spite of himself. "You need a doctor."

"No doctor. Just to lie down." She pointed. "Lock the gate, Kent. You can find the key in the morning. It's either in the pool or lying on the deck somewhere." She turned and began to slowly tread the uneven path toward her cabin.

Kent snapped the lock shut, then hurried to catch up. "I don't want anything to happen to you. You should have a doctor check you out. Just to be sure. You could black out again." Were her pupils too large? Did her gorgeous oval face seem too pale?

"I'm fine. Truly. I know the signs of concussion. I just need to rest a bit." She unlocked her cabin door and smiled at him. "See you in the morning."

He put his foot in to stop the door from closing.

Georgia's eyebrows rose.

"Don't lock the door. I want to check on you. Just to be sure."

"I'm—"

He reached out, cupped her chin in his palm, and stared into her eyes. "You scared the daylights out of me tonight. I won't be able to sleep. I'll be around every so often to make sure you're all right." He shook his head when she opened her mouth. "Just accept it, okay? It'll make me feel better."

For a long time Georgia didn't move. Her skin against his fingers felt like satin with a hint of warmth. Her big round eyes peered into his, asking a thousand questions.

Finally she nodded. "Okay. Thank you, Kent."

For some reason her polite response made him smile. "You're welcome." Then before he convinced himself to give in to the temptation to lean forward and kiss her, he turned and walked toward home and Christa.

≡≈◆≈≡

By four in the morning the malevolent night shadows had disappeared. The dawning sky cast a sheen of rosy light over the camp. Kent walked over the familiar perimeter for the seventh time, checking and rechecking the area for anything amiss as his mind tumbled over the events of the night before.

Unresponsive was the best word to describe Christa's attitude. She'd refused to answer his questions, refused to apologize for her actions. Only when he'd told her of Georgia's accident had she shown any remorse, insisting that she would sit with the other woman for the rest of the night and watch for signs of problems from her injury.

His own reaction surprised him. He wanted to be there, to watch over Georgia, to make sure she was all right. But because he knew how inappropriate that would be, Kent contented himself with pacing the grounds, ensuring that nothing else happened to her or anyone else in his care.

Now he marched up the path to the pool gate, yanked on it hard. It stayed locked, as he knew it would. There was no one here, no one waiting in the shadows. It was so hard to know where to draw the line on his fears. And still he was left with the problem of that tire.

He turned to leave, taking the back route behind the pool. As he turned the corner, he tripped over something. Glancing down, Kent waved his flashlight across the trampled grass. A piece of wood. He picked it up. Firewood. How had it traveled from the woodpile to here?

Kent lifted his arm to toss it into the bush where no one else would fall over it. But as he did, a red blotch on the end caught his attention. He redirected his flashlight so the beam illuminated the mark.

It looked like . . . blood?

His entire body froze at the sight of the long, curling blonde hairs caught in the splinters.

Rage built, tore up his insides like a tornado. This was definitely no accident. Someone had deliberately hit Georgia MacGregor over the head with this piece of wood and left her to die in the pool.

Enough. It was time to make this an official police investigation. Kent held the stick between two fingers and marched back to the house.

It would not happen at Camp Hope again.

It would not!

He followed the tall, angry man back to the main house, sneaking through the trees, hiding in the shadows of buildings so no one would see.

The man was becoming a nuisance. If not for him, *she* would be dead. His job would be finished, the pretense over.

But he wasn't giving up now. Justice would be done.

Soon.

CHAPTER NINE

Georgia knew exactly how she'd begin. "Christa, I'm here because I care. You can't keep doing this to yourself—hiding away, pretending." Ironic that she was chiding Christa for something she herself had done.

"Believe me, I know what I'm talking about," she'd say. "You have to face the reality of your world and get on with living."

To Ralna's shocked surprise, Georgia had forgone her daily swim. What she didn't know was that Georgia intended to speak to Kent's sister. Christa had refused to talk last night, but she wouldn't get the chance to avoid it today.

For her part, Ralna seemed more than grateful to remain in her air-conditioned office, though the window conditioner seemed barely able to keep up with the soaring temperatures.

"You go ahead, dear. I've got plenty to do here. It happens every time someone surfs the Net. Kent's installed every protection he can think of, but the viruses are more cagey, I guess. Today my files are all scrambled. Again. I keep a backup, naturally, and I'll wipe the thing clean and reinstall if I have to. But still, it's frustrating to work with

117

this tired old machine. It's so slow." Ralna had swiped a hand across her perspiring forehead and groaned as she rebooted. "I hate machines. Mostly I hate computers."

Georgia had left the older woman glaring at the gray screen, wishing a computer was the sum total of her worries. Of course, Ralna didn't know about last night. No one did. Kent, his face white with strain, had waited till dawn to remind Christa and Georgia to go on as though nothing unusual had happened, but his attitude told her that he was clearly worried.

There was something he wasn't saying, something that lurked in the shadows of his eyes when he thought she wasn't looking. What was it? And why wouldn't he tell her?

She found Christa sitting in the shade and delivered her carefully prepared speech.

"You obviously don't understand." Christa's voice only sounded sad, not belligerent. "I want to do that, to face what the rest of my life is going to be like. I've told Kent a hundred times to ship me off to a nursing home for cripples." Now her eyes flashed with temper. "But he won't. He needs me here."

"Why do you say that?" Georgia had to understand this. There was something no one was saying. Ralna had hinted at it, told her it was Kent's story. Christa, whom she'd known barely one day, had alluded to it. "Tell me the truth," she ordered. "I have to know."

Christa grimaced. "You can't understand, Georgia. I doubt if anyone can. It's kind of an atonement thing with Kent, because he feels guilty."

"Why should he feel guilty?"

Christa shrugged. "You'll have to ask him. It's not really my story to tell."

There it was again, the hint that Kent was to blame for Christa's problems. Why? What had he done that was so terrible?

"All right, I will ask him." She sat down opposite Christa. "But that doesn't excuse you. Going in that pool last night was nuts. You haven't been doing any physio. I don't imagine you've even been in the water since your accident, have you?"

Christa's downcast head gave the answer.

"I believe you can swim and enjoy the water again." Georgia held up a hand to silence the protest. "It's not going to be the same; we both know that. But you could learn to maneuver yourself in the water. Believe me, I've seen it before. You already understand the buoyancy of water. So use it. Learn how to harness it and enjoy what you've been denying yourself. I'll help you."

"Why?" Christa frowned. "Why would you do it? You're working yourself to death in the kitchen. You sit up at night watching sick kids. I've heard how you challenged the crafts counselors to devise new projects. Why would you want to take on more?"

"You make me sound like some kind of a martyr! I'm not, believe me. My job is to cook and care for sick kids. But I've always enjoyed crafts. Why shouldn't I do them? You could help with that, you know."

"Help with crafts?" Horror washed across Christa's face. "No! They'd stare at me, at the chair. They'd want to ask questions."

"So? No one would be unkind. Kids are just curious. Give them a chance and you'd be surprised. Besides, you'd have the perfect opportunity to talk about water safety."

If only she could get through to this hurting woman. Georgia leaned forward, placed her hand over Christa's. "Your brother is running himself ragged. He was up all last night because of us. Today he's out there roofing in this heat. And when he finishes that, he's got more jobs to do."

"I know I'm a burden to him."

"That's not what I meant and you know it." Georgia waffled between sympathy and an earnest desire to help Christa see beyond herself. She decided to offer a dose of reality. "You sit here all day feeling sorry for yourself, when the truth is, you have a lot to give if you'd just dig yourself out of your self-pity and look around." She winced, tried to soften her words. "Your brother is carrying a huge load of guilt that no one will talk about, and it's eating at him. He could use your support, your help. Instead he's bending over backward to shield and shelter you. But he can't do it forever, Christa. Sooner or later something will have to give. Then what?"

"Nothing's going to give." Kent stood in the doorway, his cheeks blazing red. "I will be there for my sister whenever she needs me. I'd appreciate it if you didn't interfere when you don't know what's going on."

"I was trying—"

"To help. Yes, I know. Thank you." His rigid face gave no hint to his feelings. "The best way you could possibly help us is to stay out of trouble."

Indignation vied with frustration as Georgia glared at him. He was trying to protect his sister not hurt her; she knew that deep inside her heart. But why couldn't he see that it wasn't helping Christa; it was only prolonging her push back into the world? Why take out his anger and blame her? It had to be because he was concerned about last night, that she'd cause more trouble for them.

"Do you want me to leave Camp Hope, Kent?" she asked, her voice low. Deep in her stomach a fist clenched. To leave—now when she'd begun to feel a measure of peace? "If you think I'm adding to your problems here, then perhaps it's better if I go immediately. I don't want to cause anyone more trouble."

Something akin to regret flashed across his face, but there was no sign of it in the cool timbre of his voice. "Perhaps that might be for the best—"

"Be quiet, Kent, before you say something even more stupid." Christa positioned her wheelchair between them. "He doesn't want you to go. And neither do I. We appreciate everything you've done for the camp, for us. For me." She glowered up at her brother. "Don't we?"

He waited a long time before answering. "Yes, we do," he said at last, raking a hand through his hair. "I'm sorry, Georgia. I know you don't understand. How could you? You weren't here."

"So tell me." Georgia rose, impatient with the stalling. "Let me in on the big secret of Camp Hope. Maybe I can help. Maybe not. But at least I won't intentionally do anything to make matters worse."

Kent slanted a sideways glance at Christa, pursed his lips. "It's not that easy," he mumbled. "Some things—"

"Some things have been bottled up for too long." Christa moved away from them. "This is stupid, Kent. You can't protect me anymore. Anyway, I don't need protecting. I've been trying to tell you that I'd be perfectly fine in the city."

"No." His jaw tightened. "Christa, this is private."

"Private?" A harsh laugh distorted her face. "Georgia could go to town, and anyone there could tell her some version of what happened. Why not tell her the truth first?"

"I'm not sure our truths are the same, Christa." Kent shook his head, turned away, weariness evident in the slope of his wide shoulders.

"Then maybe that's the problem. Sit down, Georgia. This could take a while."

Georgia sat, eager to listen. Perhaps at last she'd understand what kept these two apart.

"I was a member of the Olympic swim team," Christa began, closing her eyes. Her voice dropped. "My times were off, and I was supposed to be working on them."

"What she's not saying is that I pushed her." Kent whirled around, eyes flashing with pain as he met Georgia's quiet stare. "I admit it. I nagged and pushed and prodded her."

"I'm telling this story. You only did what any big brother would have done." Christa smiled at Kent. "Anyway, swimming had always been my thing, the Olympics my dream. I'd worked hard to get on the team, and I was good. I had a chance at a medal, my coach said. But my turns needed work. Our parents had been dead for about four years back then, and I was living with Kent."

Her face whitened, and little lines of strain appeared at the corners of her eyes, but she pushed on. "Then he got the job here and insisted I come with him. I thought it was supposed to be a temporary assignment. Kent thought it would be perfect for me. I could swim for two hours in the morning before anyone was up, teach lessons to earn some money, spend another hour practicing in the afternoon before the kids' free swim, and go back for another hour or so in the evening. I had the ideal pool schedule, and it cost us nothing. All I had to do was practice."

The landscape shimmered with heat, but nothing interrupted to destroy Christa's recollections. In the distance, children's happy voices wavered on the hot afternoon breeze. A fly buzzed against the screen. The water from her precious fountain offered a soothing swish. Georgia waited for the rest.

"But there was this boy, a counselor here at camp. I . . . cared about him, and it was more fun to be with him than to spend hours practicing. Kent didn't like Phil, and he liked it even less that I was neglecting my workouts. Kent was trying to help, to get me back on track. I'd been skipping out, neglecting my pool time to be with Phil, who was neglecting his campers. They'd been getting into trouble, and the other counselors were tired of covering for him just because he was playing with the boss's sister."

"Tell *all* the truth, Christa." Kent faced Georgia. "I was afraid she'd lose her position on the team so I pushed her. I nagged her nonstop. Every morning I clocked her times, and if she was off by a second, I read her the riot act. I also let Phil know I didn't appreciate the job he was doing. In fact, I pushed them both so hard Phil finally quit." The pain in his voice could not be hidden by his harsh laugh. "Not that I minded that."

"He should have quit a month earlier. He wasn't here to work, and he did a lousy job." Christa's sad smile tugged at the corners of her mouth. "But I wasn't thinking like that at the time. I was furious and I blamed Kent for breaking us up. I decided I'd show him. I'd get so fast, I'd take gold. And then I would be able to find enough sponsors to leave him, to go out on my own." She fell silent, remembering.

Georgia's heart ached at the misery each still carried.

Kent took up the story. "We had a bad string of lightning strikes. For three days in a row I ordered everyone to stay out of the pool. It was terribly hot, dusty. Thunderclouds were always present, which meant it never cooled down in the evening. Everyone was overtired. A swim would have meant the world to them, but I was afraid to risk it."

"I thought Kent was just trying to boss me again, and that made me furious. I'd worked hard to build up my speed, and now I was losing any gains I'd made because I couldn't get my pool time in. Once Phil walked away, that goal—the Olympics—had become all important to me, a way out. I wasn't going to risk losing my chance to get away from my big brother and this camp he seemed to adore."

Kent's head jerked up.

Christa smiled. "You thought I liked it here, didn't you?" She shook her head. "It was an act."

"But why? What did I do?" He seemed dazed by her confession.

"It wasn't you; it was me. I was seventeen, Kent. I felt hemmed in, restricted, frustrated. I wanted to be with the rest of the team in the city. I wanted—" she made a face, hunched her shoulders—"what every teenage girl wants. For a while Phil seemed like the answer, but then he left and I was alone again. I was biding my time."

"Until you could leave me." The words oozed sorrow.

"Yes." Christa took a deep breath and looked directly at Georgia. "I waited until I thought everyone had gone to bed. 'He wants a medal; I'll get him one,' I told myself. I knew it was wrong, and I knew it was stupid. But I needed to do something to show the world that I was capable of more than making crafts at Camp Hope."

"Oh, Chris." Kent's eyes glistened with sadness. "If only—"

"There aren't any *if onlys*," she told him softly. "You never let me talk about it, never let me explain. I need to say this, Kent. I need to tell you so you'll understand." She gulped. "I'm the one."

Her voice died away, her memories cutting a canyon of silence between them as tears rolled down her white cheeks.

"It's okay. It doesn't matter now." He stood where he was, staring at his sister's broken body. "It's the past, Chris. Forget it."

"I can't! Because this—" she pointed at her legs—"affects the future. My future. And yours as well." Christa's sobs were loud, painful.

There should be something she could do, but Georgia didn't know what it was, so she sat silent, wishing she'd never opened this can of worms, yet knowing the catharsis would do brother and sister good.

"Kent? Can you come to the office immediately? Rick Mercer is here to see you. It's important." Ralna's urgent tones burst from the radio clipped to his belt, cutting off any further explanations. "And if you see Georgia, can you bring her along? We've got a problem."

Kent grabbed his radio. "We're on the way. Hang tight." He motioned to his ATV. "You'd better get on. Ralna sounds upset."

Georgia only nodded, frustrated by the interruption. She wanted to know the whole story, to understand what drove brother and sister apart, but she'd have to wait.

Kent walked over to Christa, leaned down, and murmured something only she could hear.

She nodded, turned her back on them.

"I'll come back as soon as I can."

"It doesn't matter." She adjusted the footrest on her chair. "I'm not going anywhere."

The hopelessness in Christa's voice was hard to hear.

"I'm sorry you were interrupted, Christa. But we will talk. I'll see you later." Georgia climbed on behind Kent, her fingers gripping his waist as he accelerated, and they bounced over the rutted back trail toward the office.

An RCMP cruiser was parked in front of the office building, its navy crest gleaming against the white paint. A man sat in the back-seat, head down, eyes closed, apparently oblivious to their presence.

"What now?" Georgia heard Kent mutter before he climbed off the bike, helped her off, then waited as she preceded him inside the building.

"Rick," he greeted the lean man who was leaning against a file cabinet, his tall figure authoritative in his blue gray shirt and yellow-striped navy trousers, shoulder crest glinting in a shaft of sunlight through the uncovered window. "What's up with you today?"

Georgia was puzzled at the look that passed between them.

"Hey, Kent. I was hoping you could do me a favor." The Mountie surveyed Georgia for a moment but didn't speak again.

Assuming he wanted privacy, Georgia approached the desk. "Did you need me, Ralna?"

Ralna shook her head, her eyes on the two men. "Not me. Him."

"Georgia MacGregor?"

"Yes?" She turned toward the policeman, wondering what it was all about.

"Rick Mercer. I'm a corporal at the local detachment. I under-stand you are a registered nurse."

"Yes, that's correct."

"We had a situation last night. I'm not sure how much you heard." He glanced from Georgia to Kent.

"I'm afraid we had our own little crisis last night. That's why I phoned you earlier, but you were out." Kent paused. "We can talk about that later. In the meantime, what do you need?" He motioned toward his office, then led Rick and Georgia inside. Once there, he offered them coffee and with no takers was forced to sit. "Go ahead, Rick. We're listening."

"You noticed the fellow in my car?" He waited for Kent's nod.

"Who is he?"

"That's just it. We have no idea."

"I don't get it," Kent said. "What is this about?"

"Yesterday a member of the force found this man in a ditch. He carries no identification, and he can't seem to remember who he is or where he's from. He's been checked over by the hospital staff. The doctors could find nothing wrong with him, specifically no head injuries to account for his lapsed memory." Rick tipped back on his chair, his gaze moving from one to the other. "As far as we know, he's done nothing wrong. His fingerprints are not on file."

"He's given you no indication of memory, something faint that flickers back and forth through his mind, a picture of some sort?" Georgia leaned forward. She'd treated only one person with amnesia, but even that hadn't been total.

Rick shook his head. "We sent him to the city, just to be sure. They did the scans. Nothing. The doctors tried different stimuli to elicit something, but he's a blank."

"And you need us because . . . ?" Kent frowned, obviously concerned.

"Because if you look on the underside of his forearm, you will see two words printed there: *Camp Hope*." Rick's voice dropped a notch. "I think he was coming here or he'd been here, but I suppose you can't confirm my hunch."

Kent walked to the window. "What is he doing?"

Rick moved beside him as they both watched the man he'd brought to Camp Hope climb out of the car and walk over to the camp van. One hand reached up to trace the lettering on the side. After several moments, the man returned to his seat in the car.

Kent shook his head. "I can't say if he was on his way here, but he certainly hasn't been here before."

"I didn't think so. Well, you have a trained nurse on staff who can watch Mr. Riddle—that's what we call him, John Riddle. We thought maybe your nurse could keep an eye on him, see when and if his condition alters." Rick sat up straight. "I know it's an imposition, Kent, and at the beginning of your season as well, but we literally have nowhere to put this guy. You know how small our hospital is and there are no empty beds, thanks to an accident last night. So they won't keep him. I'm not allowed to lock him up indefinitely without a reason, and no one seems willing to cover the cost of his staying in a hotel. I was hoping he might be able to bunk down out here, maybe help you around the camp."

"You think he's fit enough to do that?" Kent's skepticism was evident. "What if he does something to one of the kids?"

"He's not dangerous. He's perfectly reasonable and logical. He just can't seem to remember anything about himself." Rick sighed. "I know it's asking a lot. But I thought since Mrs.—Miss MacGregor is here, and she has all the qualifications . . ." He shrugged. "I hoped she could act as kind of a medical monitor."

"Did the doctors specifically name his condition as amnesia?" Georgia wondered aloud, her curiosity about their visitor growing by the minute.

"No. They said his condition could have been caused by some incident that caused him to wipe all memory of it from his mind, along with his identity—as a means of protecting himself, I guess."

"PTSD," Georgia said. "That makes sense." She caught Kent's frown and explained. "Post-traumatic stress disorder. His brain couldn't deal with what he was seeing so it shut down that part. Sort of. It's complicated." She looked at the Mountie. "Can I speak to him?"

"Sure." He stood, strode out of the office and the building, beckoned them to follow. After opening the car door, he said, "John, some folks would like to talk to you. Would that be all right?"

"Certainly." The man slid across the seat and stepped from the vehicle. He wore baggy jeans a few sizes too large and a plain white T-shirt that also didn't fit. When he moved, one of the filthy sneakers he wore fell off his foot.

He was tall, perhaps six feet three, with the well-honed physique of a man, perhaps in his late twenties, who had spent plenty of time working out. His sandy hair drooped in a curious wave, almost shielding his dark blue eyes. He reached up and raked it back with his hand.

Georgia began sorting details. He was paler than she'd expected from someone so fit, though it was obvious he had not spent the winter in the ice and snow, or if he had, he'd visited a sunlamp. She spotted a faint untanned band around his wrist and assumed he usually wore a watch. If she had to judge, she'd guess he was an executive of some kind. His hands were clean and uncalloused, his nails groomed.

"I apologize for my appearance," John said, standing before them calmly.

She could easily visualize him in a custom suit, with a white shirt and a red tie. He'd wear wing tips, Georgia decided, buffed to a glossy sheen. The picture took little imagination, even given his current state, but she had no idea why she thought this.

"My name is Georgia MacGregor," she said, holding out her hand. "I'm the staff nurse and chief cook here at Camp Hope. This is Kent Anderson. He's responsible for running the place."

John Riddle shook both their hands, his eyes scouring the camp in a quick assessment. "Beautiful location. Perfect for company retreats, that sort of thing. Needs a cash infusion, though." His eyes honed in on a little girl playing on a nearby swing. "Sally," he called, stepping forward.

The little girl turned around and he froze.

"John? Is something wrong?" Georgia shook her head when the Mountie moved toward him. She had a hunch that something important had just happened, but what, she didn't know? "Do you know that child?"

He stared at the girl, then glanced at Georgia, his head slowly moving from side to side, while a frown wrinkled his forehead. "I don't think so. Do I?"

Whatever his brain had seen, it had shut down now. The blue eyes were cloudy, vacant.

"It doesn't matter. Are you all right?" she asked, grasping one arm as she checked his pulse. Slowing to normal.

"Do you have a computer?" he asked suddenly.

"Yes, we do. Would you like to see it?"

He seemed puzzled by her question. "No. I don't think so. Thank you." He stood silent, gazing into the distance.

"John?" Rick shook his arm, smiled when the man looked at him in startled surprise. "Sorry. I wondered if you'd like to sit over there on that bench and have a drink. I have some business to do here, and I might be a while."

"That would be very nice, Officer. Thank you." John waited until Rick returned from inside the office with a can of soda, accepted it, then walked to the bench beside the chapel. But his fingers never popped the tab.

"Eerie, isn't it? He has the manners and bearing of a statesman, but he looks like a hobo." Kent shook his head.

"Oh, the clothes aren't his. They're just what we could dig up for him. He was found wearing tattered rags that I'm fairly certain weren't his either. Too small. Also, the labels had been removed."

"So with no labels to check, you have no way to trace a buyer. Unless these are very specific rags," Georgia mused.

Rick grinned. "Garden variety."

"It's odd. Almost as if he didn't want anyone to know who he is."

"Or someone else didn't want him found." Rick held up a hand when Kent opened his mouth. "I don't know that for sure. I'm only speculating. We have no idea how long he's been wandering around. At any rate, you can see why I don't think he'll be a problem." He inclined his head toward their guest, who sat perfectly still, holding the unopened can.

"I'm not sure about this, Rick. I'd like to help; you know that. But I have to think of the kids," Kent admitted.

"I'll only be as far away as a phone call," Rick promised. "Besides, it's a long weekend, and there simply isn't anywhere else but a cell until we can free up someone to take him back to the city. Technically, as far as we know, he hasn't done anything wrong. I hate to lock him up just because he can't remember anything."

"He does seem quite gentle." Georgia glanced at Kent, who shrugged. "What if we try it for a little while? If it doesn't work, we'll call and they can find somewhere else."

"I suppose a couple of days won't hurt. But you'll have to explain it to him, Georgia. See if he agrees." Kent looked at Rick. "I don't want any more incidents. If head office found out . . ." He let the rest dangle, shook his head. His voice dropped. "I've got to be careful, for Christa's sake. We've already had trouble. If this guy acts up, gets violent, I could lose my last chance."

"He won't get violent." How Georgia knew that was a mystery, but a sweet sense of confidence gave her the courage to say it. "He's confused and trying to make sense of everything. But he's not violent. He needs a place to relax and let the memories return. He mentioned a computer. Maybe we can get him busy on something there. I have an idea."

She walked over to John. He stood as soon as he saw her, calmly waiting for her to speak first.

"John, I wondered if you'd help us with something. We have a problem with our computer files. Would you mind taking a look?"

"Certainly not." He set the can on the bench, then followed her into the office. "What seems to be the problem?"

"We think a virus has affected our files. This is Ralna. She's finding it difficult to unravel things." She inclined her head toward the older woman. "Ralna, this is John Riddle. He's going to look at the computer for you."

"Oh. How nice." Slightly confused, Ralna nevertheless rose, moved out of the way so the big man could sit at her desk.

They both gawked as John's fingers flew over the keyboard at lightning speed. As he worked, the images on the screen flashed for mere seconds, then disappeared, to be replaced by baffling configurations. Georgia couldn't follow what he was doing, and she was certain Ralna was just as mystified.

"It's an old machine, and your virus protection isn't great," John stated. "You should update it every few days, especially if you've more than one user."

"Yes." Ralna blinked as her list of files suddenly reappeared on the screen. "How did you do that?"

"It's quite simple." He launched into an explanation that made Georgia's head spin. This wasn't basic knowledge. This was something advanced far beyond a normal person's scope. Which only emphasized her belief that he had something to do with offices, business.

"You must do a lot of work on the computer," she said. "Are you any good at Web pages?" It was a guess, a stab in the dark.

Bull's-eye.

At first he stared at her as if he hadn't understood. Then his hand moved to the mouse. Without speaking, he clicked on the dial-up icon and waited for a connection. As soon as the screen appeared, he began typing faster than Georgia had seen anyone keyboard.

"No," he whispered, blanching. "Don't." Without hesitation he cut the connection, clasped his head between his hands.

"John, what's wrong?" Georgia scrutinized his face for some answers to the many questions rolling through her mind.

He twisted to look at her. His face mirrored her confusion. "I don't know," he replied, shaking his head. "It's just . . . numbers."

She crouched beside him, rested her hand on his arm. "What do you mean, numbers? What are you talking about? Tell me what you're thinking about right now."

Panic wavered in his eyes. "I'm not thinking anything!" he insisted. "Numbers keep rolling around inside my head. A bunch of numbers."

"Leave it for now," she coaxed, urging him away from the desk. "Thanks to you, Ralna has her records back. That's more than enough for one day."

"Simple data recovery," he mumbled.

"Easy for you to say." Ralna watched him walk toward the door, waited till he was outside. She shrugged when Georgia glanced at her. "A true techie. He must be. There was nothing simple about what he did. I've been working on this thing all morning. Nada."

Georgia stepped outside, saw Kent and Rick deep in conversation, and guessed Kent was relating the incident from last night.

"Well, gentlemen, John has fixed our computer glitch. Now I've got to get back to the kitchen or no one will be eating tonight. Kent—" she focused her attention on him—"perhaps John could sleep in that camper-van you have at the back of the property. It's clean and has a heater, though I doubt he'll need it."

Kent nodded. "I'd forgotten about that thing. We were given the use of it for the summer. Good thing, too, because our cabins are full."

She'd talk to him later about moving it away from the kids' cabins.

"Do you have something John could help with for the rest of the afternoon?"

Kent blinked as if she'd asked for a snake, then grinned. "How are you at painting, John?"

She watched while their visitor turned the idea over in his mind. It was obvious from his bewildered look that he found no visible clue.

"We've been wanting to get a fresh coat on the office building. Can you handle that?" Kent's query was filled with hope.

"I think so. Yes, I'm sure I know how to paint a building." As his confidence increased, John seemed to grow taller.

"Well, since everything here seems under control, I'll get back to work. Officer, I'll talk to you soon." Georgia hoped he understood that she couldn't be in charge of John's medical condition. She'd watch him, certainly. But ultimately, the man wasn't her responsibility.

"I'll look forward to it. Thanks for your help." Rick said something sotto voce to Kent, then got in his patrol car and drove out of the camp.

"Okay, you need paint. We'll have to go to the supply shed." Kent motioned to his ATV. John climbed on the back without hesitation.

Before Kent could start the motor, Ralna appeared in the doorway. "You'd better read this," she said, shoving a white sheet of paper in his direction. "It was just faxed."

Kent read it, glanced at his secretary, then read it again.

"What's wrong?" Georgia asked. Uneasiness feathered over her skin at the tightening of Kent's lips. "What is it?"

"Head office is coming for an inspection of the camp. This is not their usually scheduled time. In fact they've been through twice this year already. I think we can safely assume they're looking for problems."

"And you think the camp will reflect negatively on you? But we're taking more campers every week." Georgia frowned. "I don't get it."

"There has been some talk of closing the camp down unless we can manage to carry ourselves," Ralna said. "We were hoping that this year we'd be able to really make an impression, that they'd see how much we've accomplished."

"Because if we don't . . ." Kent's face was grim. "If I can't somehow manage to show them progress, I can kiss that job at head office good-bye. And Christa will never get out of here."

He handed the paper back to Ralna, climbed on the ATV, and headed toward the supply house with John seated behind him.

"We've got to pray, Georgia. Harder than ever. He's driving himself too hard. He needs help."

"Excuse me?" a quiet voice interrupted.

Surprised, Georgia and Ralna spun around and stared at the man standing not five feet away.

"I'm sorry," Ralna apologized. "I didn't hear you drive up."

The man nodded. "Perfectly understandable. You were deep in discussion." He took off the dusty red cap he wore and held it against his chest. "Not long ago I spoke to a man who said you wouldn't mind if I volunteered some time out here. I thought it would be an appropriate way to thank the camp for all the help they were to my niece last summer. The girl's made a real turnaround."

"I'm glad to hear it." Ralna studied him. "You found us through your niece?"

"Well, I also spoke with a Pastor Ben in town. I was asking how I could best help the camp, and he suggested you needed another pair of hands." The stranger didn't look at Georgia but kept his focus on Ralna. "I'm on holiday for six weeks with nothing to do. I've done some carpentry, maintenance, that kind of thing, so I have a little experience if you can use it."

"Camp Hope can always use help." Ralna motioned to Georgia. "This is our camp cook and resident nurse, Georgia MacGregor."

"Hello." He barely acknowledged her, his attention still on Ralna. "To whom would I speak?"

"I'll introduce you to Kent Anderson, the director. He'll have some questions to ask you, and he'll need to check your references before you begin," Ralna explained.

Georgia frowned. It was almost as if he was deliberately ignoring her, which was ludicrous because she was positive they'd never met before. Perhaps he was just anxious to make a good impression. "I think I'd better get to work, Ralna. I'll leave you. It was nice to meet you, Mr. . . . . I'm sorry, but I didn't catch your name."

"Herb. Herb Armstrong."

"Welcome to Camp Hope, Mr. Armstrong." When he simply nodded, Georgia had no other recourse but to turn and walk to the kitchen, where she buried herself in preparing pizzas for dinner.

As she worked, she mulled over the fax Kent had received. She'd been here long enough to know he was worried far more than he'd let on. If only she could do something to help. An idea began to simmer. Maybe she could help. Hadn't Christa worked on crafts before her accident? Maybe she would again—given the right incentive.

While her helpers prepared toppings for ice-cream sundaes, Georgia went to talk with Ralna. She found Herb repairing the rotted fascia boards on the office. An idea swirled through her brain.

"You know how to run power tools. That's good, Herb. That's very good." She watched him miter the corners of two boards. Her idea blossomed with possibilities.

"It is?" He tilted his head to stare at her. "Why?"

"Because I have a project for you. As soon as you're done with this job, you and I are going to lend Kent a hand getting this place back on the map. We're going to do it by preparing a new and very different craft project for those teens that are coming next week. But we aren't going to tell Kent my idea. Not yet. I want it to be a surprise."

"Secrets?" he asked, his forehead furrowed in disapproval.

"Only the very best kind," she told him. "He'll like it." *I hope.*

———◄►◆◄►———

He stood in the shadows behind the office and watched her interact with the children as they gulped down ice cream. Fury rose inside. To allow her to be around kids after what she'd done . . . with deliberate control he quashed the terrible memories, forced his fists to unclench.

This was a part, a role he had to play. There could be no cracks in his presentation, nothing to cause suspicion. No one suspected him— yet. No one would.

Not until it was too late.

CHAPTER TEN

You're not going to back out now, Christa." Kent pushed his sister's chair over the familiar bump and onto the pool deck. "You promised Georgia, and she's been looking forward to getting you in that pool all day. You might remember she's missed her swims for the past few days because of you."

The words had no sooner tumbled out than Kent regretted them. Being dog tired was no excuse. Everyone was tired. They'd been rushing full out for days now, trying to get the camp shipshape while maintaining camper activities as usual. It hadn't been easy, but it had been worth it. The latest group had left after lunch, leaving Camp Hope rather silent without all their newly created wind chimes tinkling in the breeze. Georgia's idea.

From the corner of his eye he saw his sister brush her hand over her face. Remorse swamped him. "I'm sorry," he said. "I shouldn't bark at you."

"Sure you should. I'm being a wimp." Christa wheeled her chair into the darkest spot. "It's time. I know that, Georgia knows that, and so do you. Tonight's the night. But I am curious. Wasn't it you who was talking about her leaving not too long ago?"

He couldn't stop the red tide of embarrassment that burned his cheeks.

"You mind telling me what's changed?"

Everything. "Nothing," he muttered, unwilling to discuss his reactions to Georgia MacGregor. "I spoke to Rick about the problems she's been having. He intimated that she might be safer here with us watching than roaming around on her own."

"Why?"

He shook his head. "I don't know. I get the feeling there is something she isn't saying about her past, but I get nowhere asking questions."

"And suddenly we've got two more to watch out for." She raised an eyebrow at his frown. "That John person and the handyman."

"How do you know about John?" A frisson of fear crawled up his spine. "Did something happen, Christa?"

She had the grace to face him. "I fell out of my chair."

"What?"

"I was trying something and it upset. I yelled and he came. He was very kind." She stared into the night, her forehead pleated. "There's something . . . odd about him, Kent."

"What do you mean, odd?" *Oh, God, haven't I got enough to deal with? Not another problem.* "Weird, you mean?" he asked, heart sinking at the thought.

"No. Just that—" She paused, obviously organizing what she wanted to say. "Most people who haven't been trained or don't understand about my injury just grab me and assume it doesn't hurt. John knew exactly how to lift my legs, to support my back. At the very least, he's been around paraplegics before."

Kent mentally ticked off what he'd learned about the man so far: a computer whiz who thought Camp Hope should branch out to the corporate world and knew how to deal with Christa's condition. Who was this guy?

And another thing—why hadn't John's sudden appearance, his

obvious knowledge of her condition, upset his sister when before she'd always refused to let anyone see her?

So many questions. Where were the answers?

"Don't you want to wait for Georgia?" he asked a moment later, surprised to see her shedding the towel that always covered her legs.

"Why?" She grinned up at him, eyes snapping in a fashion he barely remembered. "Afraid I'll drown?"

He choked.

"You're not going to drown, Christa. I promise." Georgia stepped through the gate, her hair streaming behind. She tugged on the arm of the man beside her. "Christa, this is John. You remember I told you about him? He's been slaving all day, and I hoped it would be okay if he joined us. I tried to find Herb, too, but he's left for the day. Probably worn-out after cutting all those boards for the toolboxes we're going to make. Isn't that right, John?"

"The boys will enjoy making them. Hello. Are you all right?"

Kent's attention immediately swerved to his sister. Her gaze was riveted on the tall man in front of her. His eyes seemed slightly glazed as he stared back at Christa. Kent held his breath. Christa hated anyone staring.

"We've already—"

"Sally," he said, his voice barely audible.

"—discussed that," she finished. "And my name is Christa." She glared at him for a moment. "It's rude to stare. I told you that before."

Kent was at a loss, so he looked to Georgia.

"That's twice he's said that name," she remarked for his ears alone. "I wonder who Sally is or was."

Kent opened his mouth to answer, but Georgia shook her head. Her attention moved back to their unusual visitor. "Watch," she whispered.

"Is anyone going to help me out?" Christa's plaintive voice broke John's trancelike state.

"You don't really need help," John replied. "Look, if you put your chair here and lock the brakes, you can grab onto the handrail and lever yourself in." He smiled at her. "Go ahead. Try it."

Christa didn't move for a long time. Eventually she shrugged, wheeled her chair to the edge, and did as he instructed, John's gentle voice guiding her until at last she was in the water.

"If I hadn't just seen that for myself . . ." Kent tilted his head down, his voice soft. "What do you make of it?"

"He knows what he's doing. Either he has experience working with paraplegics or he's studied the subject. Maybe if we leave them together, some of his memory will come back."

"I'm not sure I want a total stranger with my sister—"

"Look."

Kent tore his gaze away from Georgia to watch the couple in the water. John picked up the water wings Georgia had brought along and lowered himself in the pool. Once he'd fitted the bands on Christa's thin white arms, he began to show her how to maneuver herself through the water.

"He's very good," Georgia said. "But then he seems to be good at most things. I wonder how he got those marks on his back."

Kent didn't want to waste time staring at John when Georgia was nearby. He motioned for her to precede him into the pool. Georgia remained where she was, her eyes on John and Christa.

Why did this guy have to look like some kind of male model, he wondered miserably, and why should it bother him? It wasn't as if he wanted Georgia's attention on *himself*.

"I saw the prototype he made for your tool-kit project this afternoon. It's impressive."

"I know." She grinned at him. "And it's all out of our own wood. I mentioned to Herb that we needed a serious craft for the older boys, something not too easy that they'd want to keep when they left here. John overheard and just started cutting."

"That came out of his head?" Kent could hardly believe it. "Do you think he was some kind of craftsman?"

Georgia shrugged. "I don't know. But he knows computers, and he knows wood." She glanced at him, a question in the depths of her gorgeous brown eyes. "How's Herb doing?"

"Equally surprising. His references are glowing. He certainly knows what he's doing. Took us half the time I'd planned to replace those shower stalls, and the caulking looks like it was done by a professional. I wonder why he's wasting his time here."

"Wasting his time?" She glared at him. "You got a gift from heaven with these two, Kent. They've done more to get this place knocked into shape than we could do all summer. You should be thanking God He sent them here." She tossed her cover-up on the diving board, then took a header into the water.

Ashamed of his ungratefulness, Kent followed, catching up with her in the shallow end. "I'm sorry, Georgia. I didn't mean I wasn't thankful for their help. I am. Almost as delighted as I was when you showed up."

She swiped the water from her eyes, averting her face, but a crooked grin lifted the corner of her mouth. "Before you killed yourself from food poisoning." She chuckled.

"Or worse." He matched her stroke for stroke until they came near the deep end. Before he could speak again, Georgia flipped down and around. She was three-quarters of the way to the other end before he'd pushed away from the wall.

"How do you do that?" he demanded when she finally surfaced.

"Do what?" She glanced at him, shrugged, then did it again, beating him back by several meters.

"Do that. I've seen you do it a hundred times, and I still can't figure out how you can go so far on one breath."

"Neither can I." Christa bobbed closer, one hand on John's shoulder. "Where did you learn a turn like that?"

"I never really learned it," she mused, trying to remember. "I just started doing it. If you pull down with your hands and scull your way across the bottom, you can make really good time."

"Show me," Christa ordered.

Georgia obliged by swimming to the end and partway back before she surfaced.

Kent watched, noticing she wasn't particularly winded. "You said you used to swim," he said, trying to remember what else she'd told him. Maybe this was a chance to learn more about their mysterious cook. "What kind of swimming?"

"Uh-uh. Diving."

Then he remembered. She'd said it the first day she arrived, when he'd found her admiring the pool. *I used to dive.*

"Professionally?" he asked, praying she'd answer just one of the many questions about her that plagued him.

"No." She shook her head, her smile quizzical. "I tried out for the Olympics, that's all. Never got as far as Christa."

"Georgia Cook," Christa whispered, eyes huge as she stared at her. "I remember you. High dive, back flip. You kept everyone guessing where you'd surface. There was never a ripple when you went in; then you'd just appear. Everyone was sure you'd take gold. But you never competed. What happened?"

"My mom got sick. I had to help my dad with the restaurant."

Kent watched her hands fluttering through the water as she bobbed beside him.

"You quit?" Christa demanded. "Just like that?"

Georgia frowned as if she couldn't understand the question. "I had to. My family needed me."

"Family always comes first." John's quiet voice broke the taut silence.

Kent's attention swung from Georgia to John. Suddenly he had a thousand doubts about this man and his presence here in the camp. Had John really forgotten everything about his past? Or was that simply some kind of pretense, an excuse that allowed him to get closer to Georgia? Was he her nemesis?

A fierce wave of protectiveness swamped him. She would not be harmed again, not while he was around. *Please, Lord.* And just to make sure, he'd stick as close as she'd let him.

"Well, Miss Georgia Cook MacGregor, Olympic wannabe, why don't you show us how to do that turn?" Kent asked, hoping to lighten the atmosphere that had suddenly become almost introspective.

She gave him a long look, then nodded, flashing a smile. "Follow me, boss."

In many ways, the evening was a roaring success. In the pool, Christa shed her inhibitions and became a new person. Freed of the hated wheelchair, she giggled wildly with each new discovery of freedom in the water. Solemn as always, John refused to relinquish his position as her guardian, though Kent offered to relieve him several times. Did anyone else see how closely the enigmatic man scrutinized his sister when Christa laughed at her own ineptitude?

But no matter how closely he watched, Kent found nothing threatening or worrisome about John's attitude toward his sister. But then, why would he? Georgia was the one who'd been threatened.

Weary beyond measure, he pulled himself up to sit on the side, watching as Georgia cleaved through the water in a clean, even stroke that never faltered. Time after time she flipped through the water, disappeared, then bobbed up when he'd begun to worry.

The questions mounted: When had she learned how to swim? Who had taught her? Did she have brothers? a sister? None of those things were the least bit important in solving the reason behind those curious incidents, and yet he wanted to know every detail.

"You're glaring. I suppose that means I've been in here long enough." Georgia hauled herself out of the water, pulled on her cover-up, then sat down next to him. "I notice you gave up on the turns."

He nodded.

"It's not easy to master. You have to keep your focus on the wall and know exactly the right moment to start the roll."

"Sounds a lot like life."

She seemed to think about that for a few minutes. "I suppose it does," she agreed quietly. "Seems quiet without the kids, doesn't it?"

His gaze feasted on the pure oval radiance of her face, illuminated by the overhead lights. "Who's Doug to you?"

The question shocked him as much as it surprised her. She raised one eyebrow, lips pursed. "Doug is a friend."

He hadn't meant to ask, though he'd mentally wondered every time he'd overheard her talking to the man who could make her eyes dance and her laughter tumble out like silver sleigh bells echoing through the crisp purity of a Christmas Eve.

"A very good friend," he added, not needing the nod of her head to confirm what he already knew.

Her eyes sparkled with pleasure. "Very good. We grew up together. What I didn't think up, he did. Once I met Doug, it didn't matter that I hadn't any brothers or sisters. He filled the void."

One question answered.

Georgia turned away from him to reach for something. Only then did he notice the picnic basket she'd pushed underneath the diving board. "I made coffee. Want some?"

He nodded. There was nothing like Georgia MacGregor's coffee. Rich, full-bodied, with just a hint of . . . something. She'd even added the cream he preferred. He checked, saw that Christa and John were chatting as they sat on the steps in the shallow end. Just for a minute, he'd relax. He closed his eyes, letting his senses inhale the coffee's richly satisfying flavor.

"Doug and I started kindergarten together. Whenever I needed him, he was there." Georgia had curled her legs underneath her body. Both hands snuggled her cup against her chest as she stared into the night.

"His dad was a doctor. Kids lined up to get a chance to play at his house. But for some reason, he'd always invite me. In grade three I asked him why and he said, 'Friends are special, Georgie. Good friends aren't like other friends. Good friends are always there—no matter what.' And he was." She blinked, her smile tremulous. "I never realized how much until these past two years."

Kent took a risk. "That was after . . ."

She frowned at him, but eventually she answered. "After my . . . family died. Yes."

Kent remembered the picture he'd seen in her cabin. *Family*, she'd said. Not *child*. Had her husband died then too?

"Doug never pushed, never asked me questions, never demanded I do all the things grieving people are supposed to do." One finger wiped across her eyes leaving a shiny wet trail. "He was just there, for whatever I needed."

"Sounds like you really care about him." The gruffness of his words didn't faze her. She simply smiled, nodded, her eyes fixed on something Kent knew he couldn't see.

"That's what families do. They care about each other. And Doug is the only family I have left."

That had to mean she didn't think about him romantically, didn't it? More like a brother?

A mocking voice inside his head asked why he cared where Georgia MacGregor's romantic feelings lay. Kent ignored it. From the first day, when he'd accepted his appointment here, he'd prayed for God to send him a helpmate, someone who saw, as he did, the potential in Camp Hope. For a while he'd believed that person might be Christa. Now he realized that he'd only seen what he wanted. Christa had stayed because he'd insisted, but working to build up Camp Hope wasn't her heart's desire. Apparently it never had been. How could he have been so wrong?

"Kent?" Christa was sitting in her wheelchair with John at her side. "I'm tired. I want to go back. John said he'd walk me."

Given the little they knew about the man, Kent wondered if that was a good idea. But the look in Christa's eyes silenced his protest. She'd swum with him, laughed with him, even agreed to allow him to take her home. For the first time in almost a year, Christa had left her self-imposed exile.

He'd smothered her once before with disastrous results. This time he'd leave his sister's protection up to God.

He nodded, watched them leave, John carefully steering the heavy chair over the rough ground.

"That was hard for you, wasn't it?"

He turned, found Georgia watching him. "You noticed." Embarrassment forced his gaze to lower. "Apparently I'm overprotective. I'm trying to get over it."

"Don't beat yourself up. Overdoing it is a lot better than not caring at all."

He felt better immediately, until her next words. "But you can't keep this up, Kent."

"I don't know what you mean."

She shook her head, and he knew she'd read him like a book. "Sure you do. You're a perfectionist. You want everything to be at its peak, everyone to be on their best behavior. You're trying to expect the unexpected and prepare for every scenario."

"I'm not—"

"It's a noble attempt. But Camp Hope is what it is. You can't make it into an upscale glossy spread for some magazine just so your head honchos will give you their approval. Neither can you foresee every possible eventuality. You're not God."

This was new. She was trying to preach to him?

Apparently Georgia read his facial expression. She flushed a rich, dark color, then shrugged. "I might have my problems with Him," she muttered defensively, "but at least I recognize that I'm just a cog in the whole operation. You're trying to take over His job."

Her words forced him to think. "I know I'm pushing it pretty hard," he admitted at last. "But I've got to get that promotion. Ensuring a good inspection will help with that."

"Why?"

The quiet question surprised him. "Why what?"

"Why do you need that promotion?" She tapped her forefinger against her mug, forehead furrowed. "Your focus is clearly here with the camp, Kent. Part of your problem is that because this place is your baby, you can see the possibilities here, and it frustrates you that you can't make them materialize."

She didn't understand. Kent sighed, handed her back his cup. "I'm doing this for Christa."

"Again—why?"

Frustration lent an edge to his response. "Because she's my sister. Because I'm trying to help her. Because she needs me—" He stopped, surprised by the angry shake of her head. "You must understand what I'm doing, Georgia. Isn't that exactly what you said your Doug did when your husband and child died?" He knew it was a risk to bring up the past. She'd asked him not to question her, and Kent hadn't meant to go back on that.

But in her desire to explain herself to him, Georgia barely seemed to hear his words. "They died in a fire," she told him, her voice wavering. "There was nothing I could do for them. But this is different." She leaned forward, her eyes scant inches from his, imploring him to understand. She laid a hand on his arm, her fingers warm against his skin.

"I know you love her, Kent. And that you feel somehow responsible for what happened to her." She ignored his sputtered interjection, her fingers tightening on his arm. "I have to say this to you because I care about you both. Christa doesn't want you to take that job for her sake, she doesn't want to move with you, and she doesn't want you to try and fix what's wrong in her life."

It was too hard to hear. Pain shafted a spear through his heart, and the only thing that kept him focused on her words was the soft, comforting touch of her hand against him and remembering that she'd said she cared about them. The little vine expanded its grasp.

"You can't fix this, Kent. You have to let her find her own way.

She needs to do that. For her own peace of mind, Christa has to know that she can handle whatever comes her way. Otherwise the future—"

He couldn't think about that. In one fluid motion he rose, paced across the deck. What did she know? How could she understand the responsibility he had to his sister? He'd been left to care for her. His parents had *trusted* him. And he'd blown it.

"Kent?" She stood there, waiting for him to answer.

But what could he say? "You don't understand."

"Of course I do. You love her; that's obvious. But you are not your sister's keeper."

"Take care of Christa, Kent. Be there for her." His father's voice echoed the order from long ago.

He wheeled around, anger kindling at the words she spoke so easily. "It's very interesting to me that you're so knowledgeable on this subject," he growled, refusing to heed the warning inside his head.

"I-I don't know what you mean." She backed up a few steps, her eyes wary but focused intently on him. "What's wrong? What did I say?"

"It might be easier to let Christa manage on her own. It would certainly be simpler for me to back off and let her do as she wants, whatever that is." He picked up the basket, motioned for her to precede him through the gate.

Georgia moved slowly, sliding on her sandals, folding her towel. When she walked in front of him, Kent reached out, prevented her from going farther. Her skin was heated silk under his rough fingertips. The yard light magnified her eyes, huge orbs glowing with a thousand questions. Conflicting emotions raced through him—he wanted to hold her, to make her understand. He wanted to push her away so she'd leave and thus end the rush of feelings she made him so aware of—emptiness, loss, incompletion.

"I'm not like you, Georgia. I can't run away from my life, no matter how bad it gets." He saw the hurt cloud her eyes and winced.

Hurting her wouldn't help. It was like wounding something within himself, and he regretted the hasty words.

She would have slipped away then, but he held her by the simple gesture of reaching up to brush the strands of hair back from her face, then cupped the soft curve of her cheek in his hand.

"Christa *is* my responsibility. I have to do what I think is best, no matter what." He brushed his thumb over the dimple at the corner of her mouth. "Can you understand that?"

Georgia said nothing for a long time. Her words, when they finally came, were more powerful for their gentle remonstrance. "It's true I was running, Kent. But I thought I was running *to* something— peace, a new life, answers." She mirrored his gesture, lifted her hand until her fingers grazed his chin. "You're running away, but you're using Christa as the excuse."

"I'm not."

She smiled. "You're a wonderful brother, Kent, a man any sister would be proud to have. You genuinely care about the kids who come here, and you'd willingly give up your own agenda if it meant helping them. You're a man of many talents, but you're trying to give your own explanations for life's problems. I don't have any answers. Only questions."

She was fragile, a waif in the moonlight. And yet her courage was mighty; her words challenged him to look at his own motives. At least she was still asking questions. She hadn't shut God out. That took a lot of inner strength.

He'd hurt her with his anger and recriminations, yet she returned the favor with gentleness. Standing there, staring into her molten eyes, his throat clogged at the absurdity of it. Georgia MacGregor had lost her family, but she was trying to fix his. How could you not admire a woman like that?

He bent his head, touched his mouth to hers in a caress that didn't come close to saying the things that filled his heart.

But just for a moment, she responded, her ardor matching his.

Then she turned and was gone, gliding through the gate into the darkened compound beyond, her whispered good night barely reaching his ears.

Bemused by what had just happened, Kent closed and locked the pool gate. He followed the path toward home, spied the wavering blackness of a shadow that moved to stand at the corner of Georgia's cabin. He saw a flicker, heard the sibilant hiss of a match quickly doused.

"Who's there?" he called, racing toward the spot. There was nothing, no one there. *What is going on here, Lord?* He knocked on Georgia's door.

No response.

"Is something wrong?"

Kent wheeled around, searched the darkness. John stood under a puddle of nearby light, a white Styrofoam cup in his hand.

Kent ignored the question.

"If you're looking for Georgia, she's gone to the shower house."

"What are you doing here, John?"

"Just taking a walk. I found this." He held out the cup, partially filled with a clear liquid. A single match floated on top.

Kent's brain raced to absorb the information. Was John the one who'd been terrorizing Georgia? He knocked the cup away and grabbed his shoulders. "Who are you?" he demanded.

But though his mouth worked, John gave no answer.

Was that because he couldn't . . . or wouldn't?

CHAPTER ELEVEN

We need a break." A week later, Christa pushed her chair into the circle of light that illuminated the diving board and stared at the faces bobbing in the water. "Today I have cut out more fabric than I've ever worn in my entire life. The kits to make kites are ready, the camp is spotless, and the kids don't come until Monday morning. I have an idea."

"Oh no. Not an idea." Georgia groaned as she stepped down the ladder and stroked across the pool, not daring to look at Kent for fear she'd remember that kiss. "The last time Christa had an idea—"

A unanimous moan went up from all three.

"I don't know what you're complaining about. Fishhooks would have made a great craft." Christa eased herself into the water, accepting John's help as if it were completely natural. "Georgia did ask for help with the crafts, you know."

"And I've repented of that. Many times." Georgia giggled, paddling in circles around the younger woman.

"Very funny." Christa ducked under, emerged spluttering. "I wonder if I'll ever get the hang of that."

"I've tried to tell you that it takes—"

"Never mind, John. Christa is one of those who has to learn for herself. You tried." Kent smiled. "Now, what's your grand idea, Sis?"

"Tomorrow's my birthday. I think we should have a picnic in the meadow after church." She announced it triumphantly, then waited for their response.

"You're going to church?"

Georgia wished she'd been quick enough to poke Kent in the ribs and forestall that comment. Sometimes he couldn't see the forest for the trees.

"I think a picnic's a wonderful idea. I'll make you a cake." Georgia tried to cover the yawning gap of tension between brother and sister, edging closer to Kent. "What would you like for your birthday, Christa? A few fishhooks?"

"I don't want anything except to get out of here for a while." Christa ignored Kent, paddled toward John. "A picnic would be fun. Ralna and Fred would be here if anything came up."

"I don't . . ."

Georgia didn't hear the rest because she ducked beneath the water and grabbed Kent's heels, dragging him to the bottom of the pool. Then she darted through the water, scooping handfuls as quickly as she could to get away. It didn't work. He pulled her to the surface, his fingers tight around her forearm.

"Penalty," he gasped, his face streaming with water. "Unfair advantage, no warning. Time for retribution."

In a side-swept dive, Georgia slipped away from him, pushed herself to the bottom of the pool, and sculled her way to the other end, holding her breath so he wouldn't see her bubbles. Then she swam back to the other end, her lungs burning. But Kent was too smart to be fooled so easily. A second after she touched the cement wall, he was there beside her, his underwater grin ghoulishly wide and threatening. With his hand clamped over her shoulder, she had no choice but to float to the surface.

"There is no escape," he said, his fingers flickering in front of her face. "Prepare to accept your fate."

For the next several minutes, she used every tactical maneuver she could remember to avoid Kent. They both ended up clinging to the edge, gasping for breath.

"If you two can stop chasing each other long enough to listen, John and I are leaving." Christa sat in her chair, her face sober. "Is the picnic tomorrow on or off? And no, I'm not going to church with you, Kent."

"It's on, of course." Georgia flushed with embarrassment as she realized how their antics must have appeared to the other two. "Are you all right, Christa?"

"Does it matter?" A second after the words left her lips, Christa's attention was on John. "Yes, I'm fine. I'm sorry," she said. "I guess I'm just a little tired."

"Probably tried to do too much at once." John grabbed the handles of her chair and turned it toward the gate. "That's the way it always is."

"Always? How does he know that?"

At least Kent had waited until the couple was out of earshot before speaking. He hauled himself out of the water, then sat on the plastic bench against the fence.

"You have to admit—John does seem to possess some knowledge about people in Christa's condition." Georgia wasn't ready to leave the water's silky embrace yet. "She probably has overdone it. Those muscles haven't been used so much in a long time."

"She's not the only one who's tired. I feel like I've run a marathon." He stretched his arms overhead, working the kinks from his shoulders. "But I will say one thing: the place looks good. There's nothing the least bit neglected-looking about it now. I was concerned about the cabins looking shabby, but Herb managed to get another coat of stain on three of them—the worst three."

"Speaking of Herb—how come he never joins us for a swim?" Georgia floated on her back, eyes closed, and let the peace of the evening fill her senses. She kept her head aloft just enough to hear Kent. Georgia continued, "I only see him at meals or after dinner when he's trying to finish a job. Then he's gone. Think he'll come for the picnic tomorrow?"

"I doubt it. He's never shown up on a Sunday before. Besides, he told me he likes to be alone. He seems to really enjoy just meditating on his own. I don't think he's had a particularly happy life. Or maybe it's his job he doesn't like. It's hard to find out much about him; he's pretty tight."

Like other people I know. Georgia heard the words, even if he didn't say them aloud.

"I guess I can understand that." She pressed her toes against the wall, pushing herself back into the center of the pool. "But he's so quiet. He never even speaks to me except to say thank you. It's almost as if I've done something to offend him."

"You're being silly. He's shy; that's all. I asked him about his niece the other day, told him I'd like to call her and tell her what a good job he was doing. He almost dropped his hammer." Kent chuckled. "He's really very modest. Told me he doesn't want his niece to know he's here. That this is between him and God. I kind of liked that."

"Hmm." It sounded plausible, didn't it?

"It's something like your situation, isn't it?"

The question stunned her by its simplicity.

"I mean, you came here because of some personal issues between you and God."

"Yes." She did *not* want to talk about that.

"You were hurting. I think Herb is too, though he's never said anything."

"Then why do you think that?" Georgia stood up in the water, eager to hear what Kent had to say. He was the kind of man who, most of the time, had very good intuition about people. One that she trusted.

"I'm not sure. Sometimes when he's working, he'll pause, get this faraway look on his face, and almost smile. It's as if he's remembering something." Kent's voice changed. "It's the same look you get some-times."

"Me?" What had he seen?

He nodded, his stare intent. "Last week you were watching that couple who brought their twin daughters to camp. The woman had a baby on her hip. You took one look and time warped to somewhere in the past. I'm guessing the baby reminded you of your own child. Tyler."

"Yes, he did." Georgia waited for the stab of pain, blinked when she realized it had become more of a tug of sadness.

"And the man?"

"He reminded me of Evan. The hair—that flaxen stick-straight mop that wouldn't behave—that's what his was like. Not that he'd ever let it get that long. Evan hated untidiness."

She remembered their first argument. She'd wanted to try a new paint technique in the dining room, but halfway through the hospital had called. Evan hadn't said much when she came home and tumbled into bed, but the next morning she noticed that the wall was back to plain white. Such a silly memory.

"Georgia?" Kent perched on the diving board, peering down at her. "I'm sorry. I didn't mean to upset you."

"But you want to know, don't you?" She treaded water, watching him. He wanted to help; she knew that. But he couldn't. No one could. "I don't want to talk about my past, Kent. I told you that a long time ago."

"Because it hurts. I understood that. But surely, after all this time, you've begun to heal, to for—"

"To forget?" She shook her head, spraying water droplets from the ends of her hair. "I don't think it's possible to forget a husband and son. There are just too many memories."

"They don't sound like very good memories."

"Some are. Some aren't." She shrugged. "It was my life. Now it's gone. I have to learn to deal with that." She swam to the ladder, climbed out of the water, and pulled on her wrap.

"But you might be able to deal with it more effectively if you talked about it."

She glared at him, angry that he kept pushing when she'd made it clear she didn't want to answer any questions.

"Sometimes it helps to share your memories, Georgia."

"I've heard that before, but in my case, it doesn't apply." She slid her feet into her sandals, bent to fasten them. "I have to make sense of this my own way."

"But—"

She held up a hand, tamped down her frustration, and tried to explain. "Listen to me. I had a husband and a child I loved, work I adored, a life that was full and happy and blessed. Then suddenly it was all stripped away. Why? That's what I don't understand. What did I do wrong? How could I have been so bad that God would take away the two things I loved most?"

She smiled at Kent to show there were no hard feelings. "You see— more questions. That's my problem, Kent. And talking to you or anybody about my past won't solve the problem of my faith. I feel like God has punished me, and I don't even know why. I'm not sure I want to."

She gulped, grabbed her courage, and told him the truth. "Because the God I believed in would never have done this."

The loss of a faith that had once sustained her brought tears to her eyes and she wheeled away, anxious that he not see her weakness. "Good night," she whispered, then hurried into the night, toward her cabin.

"Good night, Georgia."

<hr/>

Long after Georgia's lights had been switched out, while the moon rose higher in the sky, until the first flickers of flamingo daylight chased away the shadows, Kent prayed. For what, he wasn't sure.

Only God knew.

If he had to describe this afternoon, Kent decided *halcyon* was the word he would use. Seamless blue sky, just enough wind to moderate the heat, and very few bugs. Even Christa's favorite meadow looked calmly serene, especially since he'd made certain the bull standing in the pasture next door couldn't get through the sturdy wire fence.

"Do you think heaven is like this?" Christa's eyes were invisible behind the dark lenses of her sunglasses.

Kent felt Georgia's stare, met it, shook his head. "Good question. I never really thought about it. Must be pretty close, I'd reckon. That cake seemed like manna to me." He'd always used a joke to lighten things up, but suddenly he felt uncomfortable, as if he were deliberately avoiding deeper issues.

And perhaps he was.

"It was a delicious birthday cake, Georgia. I guess you figured out lemon is my brother's favorite. Maybe you didn't know it's mine too. Thanks for making it for me."

"You're welcome."

Kent watched his sister turn her head toward the remaining cake, now covered by a plastic dome. He'd eaten two pieces, but Christa had barely touched hers.

"It's a good thing there's some left over. Ralna and Fred will want a piece."

"And John," Christa added. "I hope he's feeling better. These headaches—do you think they're a bad sign, Georgia?"

"It's very hard to judge. If they continue, I think we should suggest that Constable Mercer take him back in for tests." She leaped to her feet. "Come on, you two. This is a birthday party! You look like you're both ready to nod off."

"I was just thinking about that. I hope you won't mind. Sitting out here makes me sleepy. And now that I have these—" Christa held up the two books Georgia had given her—"I want to look through them."

"Lazybones." The soft, gently teasing tones were like a caress. "Kent?"

He forced his eyes open, squinted at Georgia looming above him. "Go 'way, Georgia. I'm dead. Sleep is what this old body needs."

"Well, I need a walk. I can't sit around; I have to do something to work off lunch. Hey, how about wading in the creek?"

Kent kept his mouth shut, pretended to doze. He almost smiled at her harrumph of disgust.

"Honestly, anyone would think you two were a pair of stodgy old seniors halfway through retirement."

Kent opened one eye, winked at Christa.

"Bye, Georgia," they said in unison.

She flounced away, her long legs carrying her through the wild-flowers, over humps and hillocks until she was at the creek. After she spent a few moments crouched over the water's edge, Kent saw her slip off her sandals and smiled at her squeal of protest on contact with the cool water.

"You don't have to keep staring. She won't disappear."

"What's wrong, Christa?" Kent sat up and forced himself to wait. "I thought you wanted to come out here, but now you seem irritated. Did I say something? Is it the perfume?" He tried to think of some other way he might have offended her.

"No, everything is lovely. Really. I appreciate it."

He wished she would take off her glasses. Perhaps then he'd have a hint as to her unhappiness. "Then . . ."

"I don't know what's wrong with me. I just got to thinking about what the rest of my life holds, and I couldn't come up with one single thing. What is my future, Kent?"

"What do you want it to be?" he asked, afraid to hear the answer.

She twisted her head, allowed the glasses to slip to the end of her nose. Her eyes were brimming with tears. "I don't know," she whispered. "The things I once wanted seem impossible now."

"What things?" For longer than he'd dared hope, Christa had

been upbeat, energetic, excited. Was that due to John's arrival? Or was he simply a diversion that had given her a respite?

"Think back, Chris. When you were training, back when you say you could hardly wait to get out of here, where did you want to go? What did you see yourself doing?"

"Designing," she answered promptly.

Where had that come from? "Clothes?"

She shook her head.

"What then?"

"I'm not sure. Some kind of creative design, using textiles and colors in a new way."

Kent had no idea what she was talking about, but maybe, if he pursued this line, it would spark something inside her. "Furniture? Interior design? Architecture?" He lay back on the blanket.

"Maybe." For a long time Christa said nothing.

That was okay with him. Let her think about the future. It couldn't hurt.

"Kent?"

"Hmm?" He felt the edges of sleep crawling over him again.

"Something's wrong. Georgia—she's not moving."

He bounded to his feet, peered into the sun.

"Kent, it's a bull. It's going to charge!"

Georgia was inching her way back up the creek bank, her feet bare. She glanced over her shoulder, then yelled, "Get Christa to safety!"

The bull pawed the ground.

His heart in his mouth, Kent could only pray as he scooped his sister into his arms, then raced toward the camp van.

John met him there, puffing hard as if he'd run. "Put her inside." John waited until he'd slid Christa into the van, then slammed the door. "We've got to distract it."

Kent ran back and scanned the picnic area for something—anything—to wave. The tablecloth! He yanked it free of the picnic supplies and swung it through the air as John called out something unintelligible.

The bull paused as if puzzled by their antics.

"Keep calling. I'll try to move nearer." Kent had intended to place himself between Georgia and the bull, but she was too far away, and the bull was losing interest in him. Georgia's bright red sundress was far more to his taste. He snorted, pawed the ground, then bellowed.

"Run, Georgia!"

She turned and fled across the meadow until she found a sturdy maple. With an agility he hadn't known she possessed, she swung herself onto a branch.

The bull galloped a few steps, looked around, then bawled his frustration. Evidently the tree's foliage hid enough of Georgia's dress that he couldn't find her. Disgusted with the two men, he swung his head around several times, then turned tail and trotted across the creek, stepped daintily over a fence, and made his way to greener pastures.

"Just stay up there for a moment, if you don't mind," Kent ordered, blood pumping in his veins like a jackhammer. "I want to check something. John?"

"I see it."

They walked across the creek toward the fence without saying a word. Kent bent, picked up the broken wire, and matched it to the other end. It was a perfect fit.

"Seems strange it would break today at that particular time while she was in the creek." John's eyes, clear and innocent, met Kent's as he spoke.

"Very strange," Kent agreed. "And how does fence wire break like this? Clean through, no fraying."

"You're saying you think it was cut? Deliberately?"

"That's what I'm saying." Kent kept his eyes on his new handyman.

John tipped his head to one side. "But why? Who would want to hurt Georgia?"

Could a tone like that be faked? "I don't know." Something in the grass reflected the sun's glare. Kent dropped the wires, moved his hand in the grass, and brushed against the coolness of metal. "Here's how they did it." Using a handkerchief, he picked up the wire cutters. They were his own from the camp. "Do you mind not saying anything to the women?" Kent asked. "I don't want them to worry."

"Of course." John followed him back through the creek, watched as he slid the cutters into the picnic basket, along with the other articles. "Shall I go help Georgia?"

"If you don't mind." Kent deliberately waited until John was at least twenty feet away from him. "By the way," he added, trying for nonchalance, "how did you come to be out here? I thought you had a headache."

"I did. Ralna gave me something she said always works for her. I guess it worked for me too. So I thought I'd come and help celebrate Christa's birthday. I walked over."

Some celebration.

As he drove the quiet group home, Kent's focus remained on John. He knew nothing about the man, had no knowledge of his history, and even less about him personally other than that he was a good worker. And yet, he'd listened to Rick, let John virtually move into the camp, even welcomed his help. How dumb was that?

Kent parked the van by the side of the house, watched John help Christa out while Georgia scurried off toward her cabin.

Dear Lord, what is going on here?

He rubbed the aching bands that held his neck, trying to relieve the burning pressure there as he surveyed the thickly forested area surrounding his home and separating it from the rest of the camp.

Just as he felt separated from God.

I'm doing something wrong. I must be. What is it?

Nothing.

John could be the stalker. But Georgia's still a problem. If she weren't here.

New pain dragged at him, a different kind of pain, hidden under his chest bone, away from prying eyes and public speculation. If Georgia MacGregor left, she'd take a part of his heart with her. The vine had taken root.

Kent opened the van door and stepped down, lips firming with decision. There had to be a way to stop this, some method to find out who was perpetrating these attacks. He reached in the picnic basket and pulled out the wire cutters. This was the first step. There would be fingerprints. Whoever had cut those wires needed to get away fast. He'd dropped the cutters in his haste to leave.

That was his first mistake.

Covering the cutters with the red-checked tablecloth, Kent climbed the stairs and went into the house.

Christa waited inside, her face blanched white. John stood behind her.

"What's wrong now?" Kent set his package on a nearby shelf.

"The suits," Christa whispered, holding out the phone. "Head office. They're here. They came to see how we handle registration."

And he'd been absent.

Kent suppressed a groan, took the phone, and told Ralna he'd be right there.

Just how much worse could things get?

CHAPTER TWELVE

Y ou're going to have some overtime coming."

"Overtime?" Georgia glanced up from the pastry she'd just rolled out, watched Harry Perkins tug at the collar of his shirt. "Oh, hello, Mr. Perkins." What did he want with her?

"I noticed you were here before six this morning."

So he'd been up poking around even then? Well, she supposed it was his job as an executive, and he was only doing it the best way he knew.

"I don't get overtime. I don't want it. I like being a part of Camp Hope, knowing that in some little way I can make a difference in kids' lives."

Truth as a defense? My, what progress you've made, Mrs. MacGregor. She ignored the mocking voice inside her head.

"Huh." He wiped his handkerchief over his beet red face.

"This might not be the best place to wear a suit," she said. "And of course, you would pick my baking afternoon to chat. I'm afraid it gets a little warm in here with the ovens going. You should do what I do."

"Besides lose sixty pounds, what are you suggesting?" His skepticism was obvious.

"Chew ice. It helps keep you cool. I keep some trays on the go all the time." She jiggled her glass as a demonstration. "With this heat, it's difficult to ship ice cubes out here, not to mention way too expensive, but we try to make sure the campers' drinks are well chilled. I have a private stash of ice cubes."

He peeked over the rim of her glass at her ice chips. "That keeps you cool?"

"That and my after-lunch swim." She could almost see his ears perk up. "Ralna comes with me. Never swim alone, you know."

"I know." He checked out the storeroom, the freezer, the coolers. "Can't you turn up the air-conditioning?"

"Not if I want those doughnuts to rise." She lifted one of the tea towels, delighted to see how quickly the yeast was working. "Sometimes heat is good."

Mr. Perkins nodded. "I guess. And I shouldn't be complaining. It's not nearly as hot in here as it was last year. Almost passed out then." He stared at her. "Nice of someone to kick in the money for air-conditioning. We should send them a thank-you letter."

"I don't think you can, but check with Ralna. I understood the donation was anonymous." She forced herself to keep slicing the peaches into her piecrusts. "There are compensations for working in the kitchen, Mr. Perkins." She winked at him, then poured a tall glass of iced tea, added some of her precious ice cubes and a slice of lemon, and chose two of her best butter tarts. "Try this."

"Why, thank you." His bushy eyebrows stretched to his hairline after the first bite. "You're wasted out here," he said.

"Wasted?" She shook her head at him. "Surely God doesn't waste anything, Mr. Perkins." She paused, trying to remember the words she'd so often spurned. "God has a plan for everything; we just have to allow Him to show us that plan."

"Hmm."

Georgia didn't know whether he was agreeing or not. Maybe she'd said too much. She'd do better to cook and keep her lips sealed. That way she wouldn't ruin anything for Kent.

"My grandmother used to make peach pies."

"Oh?" She fluted the edges of one of the pie crusts, basted the top, then set it inside the oven before moving on to the next pie. Someone newly returned from the fruit valley had donated three cases of peaches to the camp. Most she'd turn into peach cobbler, which she'd bake tomorrow evening and serve hot with ice cream. But she'd set aside some of the best fruit to make pies. They were supposed to be a surprise for the head-office gents, a blatant attempt at winning approval, if the truth were told.

"She always put in a hint of cinnamon, said it brought out the flavor." Mr. Perkins seemed lost in the past as he sipped his iced tea.

"My mom did the same. And I follow her tradition." Georgia slid the last pie into the oven, then checked her heating oil. "It's a good thing you were able to stay till now. This is doughnut afternoon. In about three-quarters of an hour this place will be brimming with starving campers. Would you mind giving me a hand?"

It was a daring thing—to ask an executive to pitch in with kitchen duty. Georgia waited for him to decline.

To her surprise, Mr. Perkins took off his jacket, rolled up his sleeves, and donned an apron her helper had left behind earlier. "I'd be delighted. Just tell me what to do."

"Well, thank you! If you can manage the dipping, I'll fry in three pots instead of two." She set three glazes before him, handed him a pair of gloves, and demonstrated her method.

After several Doughnut Wednesdays she'd perfected her technique. Now the golden brown doughnuts slid off her slotted spoon onto the cooling racks much faster than Mr. Perkins could dip, especially since he seemed frozen in place.

"With the numbers we've got here," Georgia explained, "we really need a deep fryer, but this works in a pinch. Of course, when the fall camps take off, we'll have to add some equipment."

"Fall camps?"

Uh-oh. Why had she brought it up? It was Kent's job to explain. "Oh, didn't Kent mention that?" She pointed to the glazes, watched Mr. Perkins's work, and nodded. He'd do. "We've had some requests to conduct several camps in September and October. Two biology classes from the university doing research on local flora, a men's retreat, and—what else?" She shrugged. "I've forgotten, but if you ask him, I'm sure he'll explain."

The long johns and jam busters she always fried last.

"Don't glaze these, please. I always stuff them with filling. We have public swimming tonight, and we offer coffee and doughnuts. Kind of a little outreach to the community."

"Indeed." Mr. Perkins nodded, obviously deep in thought.

Since he remained silent, Georgia didn't bother trying to make small talk. Instead she concentrated on her work, delighted with the progress she'd made. If she was lucky, she could get cinnamon-bun dough ready for tomorrow morning's breakfast. That ought to impress Mr. Perkins, at least.

Finished with the frying, Georgia donned her own gloves and began dipping, moving him to the task of adding the sprinkles and colored decorations the kids loved. When that job was completed, she demonstrated how to arrange the cooled glazed doughnuts on huge trays, one tray per table. Back and forth he went, placing pitchers of juice, cups, and napkins on each table.

"We're ready. Thank you very much, Mr. Perkins. You've been a wonderful help." She saw his eyes stray to the trays of extras she always kept back for the counselors' late-night meetings. "Go ahead; you've earned it. I want to get my chicken fingers ready for dinner."

"You have a great ministry here, Mrs. MacGregor. I agree with you. God does have a plan for you to be here. Thank you for spending your afternoon with me."

She grinned at him. "Well, it isn't a day at the beach, but some days it's just as much fun. I appreciate your help." Should she brag about Kent's hard work, tell him the hours that had gone into making the camp shine?

No. If they couldn't see for themselves that Kent Anderson was the best man for this job, then he wasn't the man they deserved.

The doors to the dining room wrenched open, and children flooded inside, somehow managing to find their correct places at each table. A short grace was offered; then began the arduous task of choosing the right doughnut.

"Just like locusts," Mr. Perkins remarked ten minutes later as the group filed out, staring at the empty platters, drained pitchers, and sticky piles of napkins. "All that work, gone in minutes."

"That's a good thing," Georgia teased. "If they left them, I'd wonder what was wrong."

The back door opened, and her three volunteers for the evening shift marched in. She told them her plans and they set to work.

"I'm in your way. I'll leave." He rescued his jacket, but he didn't put it on. "I'll see you at dinner, Mrs. MacGregor."

"It's Georgia. Yes, see you later." Distracted by the oven timer, she checked her pies, lifted them out, then glanced at the clock. Whatever advantage she'd had, had now disappeared. How was she going to serve dinner on time tonight?

"Taco salads tomorrow at noon, Irma. Can you start on that? Monique, I need you to slice potatoes for dollar chips."

Whatever happened to Kent now was out of her hands. But it was a good feeling to know that she'd done all she could to find the way to the heart of one of these head-office men, even if she used food to do it.

"I have never seen three men of that particular age enjoy themselves so much while being practically drowned." Kent could barely control his excitement. "I think I misjudged them, Georgia. They're not the stuffed shirts I always thought."

"Their loss of dignity might have had something to do with Christa's knocking them into the pool." John's droll tones sent everyone into a new round of laughter.

"I didn't do it on purpose!"

Christa's cheeks still burned with embarrassment, but whether it had to do with the accident or with her debut into a group other than the usual one that included only himself, Georgia, and John, Kent didn't know. Nor did he care. She'd come out of her shell a little farther. Bit by bit Christa was getting used to being around people. Tonight, for the first time in ages, he was glad to be the director of Camp Hope. Tonight he had hope.

As long as he didn't think about Georgia leaving.

"John and I are going to the office. He's going to help me surf the Net for something." There was a certain light in Christa's eyes as she spoke that made Kent wonder exactly what they were searching for, but Georgia's prodding reminded him of the guests he had waiting at home.

Once they locked the gates, Kent and Georgia hurried back to the main house, where Georgia dished up her peach pie and blushed at the accolades from the head-office men.

"I'm delighted to tell you how pleased we are with your work here, Kent. Camp Hope has gone beyond the usual ministry to young campers and seems to be reaching into the community." Mr. Perkins refused another slice of pie. "That young man—the one who helped your sister in the pool?"

"John Riddle." Kent supplied the name with the slightest hesitation, noticed Georgia suck in her breath.

"Yes. He's an able fellow. But he seems a bit old to be spending his summer at camp. What do you know of him?"

Kent explained what history they knew.

"I see. Well, the Lord certainly provided help when you needed it. He was showing me his work on your Web site. I must say, it's a vast improvement. Putting the applications on-line saves a lot of time for your office people, and you can respond easily, without the cost of snail mail. And the bulletin board to let campers talk about their experiences is obviously a great selling tool."

Kent risked a sideways glance at Georgia. John had told him some of what he'd planned for the Web site, but he'd been busy with something else and had paid little attention. By the bemused look on Georgia's face, she knew little more than he.

"That Herb fellow seems very competent at what he does also. You've done well choosing your staff."

Something about Mr. Perkins's tone alerted Kent, and he studied the other man for some clue to his meaning. "I'm very fortunate that so many people have donated the time and effort to help us out," he responded quietly, refusing to take credit for something that had not been his doing.

"Camp Hope has certainly made a remarkable turnaround." Mr. Perkins nodded. "It's something to think about. And now, Kent, Mrs. MacGregor, I think it's time we retired for the night. I, for one, am not used to so much activity." He winced as he rose. The other two men quickly followed. "Thank you for that pie. It was every bit as good as my grandmother's."

Kent didn't understand the reference, but Georgia did. She smiled and watched as the three left the room, then began collecting dishes.

After Kent helped load them into the dishwasher, he touched her arm. "Want to go for a walk?"

"Sure." She followed him out the door, down the steps. "I think that went well."

"Better than well." He waited until they'd cleared the house and were hidden by the little vale of trees that separated his house from the main camp buildings. Exuberance bubbled up inside, a new well-spring of hope that could not be quenched. He picked her up and swung her round and round. "We did it! We did it, Georgia!"

"I think so too."

The quiet gravity of her voice signaled him, and he gently set her feet back on the ground, withdrew his arms. "I'm sorry. I guess I got a little carried away." He walked staidly beside her, but even her solemn stare at the ground couldn't stop the effervescence inside him.

"Don't apologize. I'm very happy for you." She slowed when they came to the bench in front of the chapel and sat down. In the distance the sound of children's giggles as they tore through the meadow playing their night games echoed on the breeze. "I think your promotion is secure."

"Maybe." Why didn't she sound happy about that?

He sat beside her, gazed up into the sky, searching for whatever held her attention so raptly.

"My husband used to love watching the stars. I gave him a telescope one Christmas."

"It's a hobby of mine also," Kent admitted, hoping she'd say more about her past. "I don't have a telescope, but sometimes I sit out here and just watch the show. Sometimes it's the northern lights, sometimes shooting stars. Sometimes it's only a solid black canvas with pinpricks of light dotted all over it. But no matter what I see, it all seems like a miracle."

"Miracle?" She echoed, frowned.

"A very wonderful miracle." He clasped her hand in his, felt a wiggle of delight that she didn't try to pull away. "Don't you see? I was chosen to participate in this world that God created. Me. Why was that? I don't have anything special to offer. I'm nobody. But here I am, alive, healthy, in a country where I can pray and worship, and nobody tries to stop me."

"Well . . ." Georgia didn't sound convinced.

"There's another miracle—who am I that God would allow me a personal relationship with Him? He's God of everything, and I'm permitted—no, encouraged—to call Him Father, to ask Him for things, to be part of His family."

Silence now.

Obeying her unspoken directive, Kent waited beside her on the bench and watched the slow ascent of the moon. A long time passed.

"This place—it's different somehow. There's a peace at Camp Hope that I've never experienced in other places."

"You've made a difference here, Georgia. God has used you. Your work here, nursing the kids, preparing meals especially for them, suggesting we get more involved locally." He tilted her chin upward, peering into her eyes. "All of these things—these possibilities—you turned them into reality. Every day I thank God that He sent you here. I can't imagine Camp Hope without you."

She moved her chin, focused on the ground. Had he said too much?

"I didn't do it for you." Her voice barely carried. "I didn't do it for God either. Or for the camp." She faced him. "I did it for me, to keep me from thinking about the past. As long as I could keep going, keep my brain concentrating on some problem here, I didn't have to think about what I'd lost."

"Your husband. And your child." Would she tell him now?

"Evan loved Tyler, was so proud of his son." From her pocket, she slid the picture he'd seen before. She lifted her hand from his, brushed the tips of her fingers over the beloved features. "They died when our house burned. I left for only a few minutes. I remembered we were almost out of diapers, and I decided to make a quick trip to the convenience store. They were asleep. I knew they wouldn't notice." She gulped, voice tortured with memories as her entire body shook.

"It wasn't your fault." Kent wrapped his arm around her shoulder, hugged her close. She seemed not to hear him.

"When I got back, the whole house was on fire, blazing like an inferno. How could it have happened? How could everything be fine when I left and totally destroyed twenty minutes later?"

"They couldn't get Evan and Tyler out?"

She jerked at the sound of their names but finally shook her head. "No one could get in or out," she whispered. "The fire chief said they would have died of smoke inhalation. He didn't think they even woke up, but I always wondered." Her eyes blazed in remembered anguish. "They suspected me for a while. As if I would hurt my own family!" Glints of anger flashed in her eyes. "I loved them."

There were no tears; no sobbing sounds emerged from her throat. In clear concise tones, she described the whole ghastly scene as if it were a nightmare that never quite dissipated. She was still blocking the pain, he realized.

"Evan and I trusted God," she said, voice hoarse with emotion. "We believed He'd take care of us. We'd dedicated our child to Him. And He did this. Why?"

"I don't know, Georgia. I can't understand the mind of God. I only know that in coming here, you reached Christa when nothing else could have. You opened her eyes, expanded her world, helped her think about more than herself." He swallowed. "I know that can never make up for Evan's and Tyler's lives. Nothing can. But good has come out of your tragedy."

"So you think God planned it all? To get me here?"

"No!" He scrambled to explain what he'd only begun to fathom. "But He can take the ruins and make something beautiful from them. Because He's God."

Georgia stared at him for a long time, obviously mulling over what he'd said. Kent silently prayed that something he'd said would help heal the scars of her life.

"I think you don't practice what you preach," she said.

"Pardon?"

She put her picture back in her pocket, stood, and walked a few steps away before turning to face him. "If it's true for me, then what about you? Christa's accident?" she prodded. "Tell the truth, Kent. Weren't you eyeing a job up the ladder even before Christa got hurt? Weren't you planning your career moves even then?"

In a flash the old charts and schemes he'd put into proposal form washed through his brain. He'd first come here to get a feel for the operational side, but once he'd achieved his goals, he'd never intended to stay at this level. Once Christa was on her way, he'd expected to focus on his own future, on the knowledge he could use from Camp Hope to streamline things throughout the organization.

Which had come first—the idea of promotion to advance his ideas or promotion to help Christa?

"If you really believe that God makes good things out of bad, why are you still trying to get away from here?" Her gaze brushed his, settled on the open collar at his neck. "I've seen that chart in your office, read all the notes you put on it for creating a kind of camp template. You want to generalize your ideas from here to other camps. But Camp Hope isn't other camps. It's unique. The work that gets done here is special because of you. Can't you see that?"

Was she right? Camp Hope had become special to him, but he'd always believed Christa had to leave the camp to get the help she needed. And yet it was here that she'd opened up to Georgia, here she'd befriended John. He blinked at the implications of his own conclusions. Was he supposed to stay here? But Christa would need money to pursue the education she'd once spoken of. Camp directors didn't earn that kind of money.

"Kent?"

He nodded. "Just thinking. Maybe you're right. Maybe Christa is supposed to be here; maybe I'm not supposed to move on to head office. The truth is, I don't know anymore. It's all I can do to keep things floating here. The future worries me. I'd like to see some of my ideas tried elsewhere. Why not? The manual I was working on—that could be helpful for anyone who's trying to rebuild, as we are."

"Of course it can. And maybe that will happen. I don't have any more answers than you do. Maybe we're both supposed to wait so God can show us what's next." She shrugged, began walking toward the barn. "Come on. I'll go with you while you do your grounds check."

He matched his steps with hers, not entirely satisfied that she'd managed to change the subject—again.

"Georgia, about the fire—I don't want to make you dwell on it, but I was wondering how it started. Did you ever find out?"

She shook her head. "I didn't want to know. Not then. It hurt so much, I just wanted to forget." She stopped, frowned at him. "I think Doug told me once that they suspected arson. Maybe that's why they thought I did it. But I don't think anything was ever proven." She surveyed his face. "I could ask him to check it out, but why? What difference does it make? It's over and done. There won't be any traces now."

"That's true." He opened the barn door, walked inside to check each stall, smoothing a hand over questing muzzles as he moved. Everything looked secure. "It's just that I was thinking about these things that have happened to you. Let's start with your flat tire. I probably should have told you before now, but that tire was slashed. It didn't just go flat; someone cut it." He hurried on before she could interrupt. "That night you said someone was out there, that someone spoke to you."

"'An eye for an eye.'" She whispered it, face blanching.

"Then there was the incriminating newspaper article that I just happened to find beneath your window. That fall into the pool. The bull."

"The bull was an accident." She peered at him more closely. "Wasn't it?"

He hated to frighten her further, but if someone was after her—and he felt certain someone was—she would need to be on her guard. "The fence was cut. I took the wire cutters to the police, but the fingerprints they lifted were inconclusive."

"And the pool?" She sucked in a breath.

"I found a piece of wood behind the pool. It had blood and hair on it."

"But what you're saying is—someone is deliberately trying to hurt me?" Georgia asked.

"Yes."

"But . . . why? What did I do to hurt anyone?"

She sounded betrayed, as if he'd deliberately said these things to hurt her. Kent couldn't hold back any longer. He stepped toward her, wrapped his arms around her, and hugged her, his heart aching to ease her pain.

"What did I do, Kent?" The forlorn whisper stabbed his heart.

"Probably nothing."

"Then why . . . ?" She lifted her head, her eyes brimming with pain. "You think someone killed my husband and child because . . . why?"

"That's what we have to figure out." Unable to hold her without kissing her, and knowing that this was neither the time nor the place, Kent set her gently away, took her hand. "Come on. We need some coffee."

In the camp kitchen, he dug out a filter, found the coffee beans. She took over, more, he suspected, to have something to do than through any urge to show up his lack of skill.

"Why?" she repeated when they were perched on two kitchen stools, sipping from their mugs. "No one would choose me out of the blue. There has to be a reason."

"Yes, there does." He concentrated. "Tell me about your life. Before the fire. What did Evan do?"

"He designed software. He worked from home a lot of the time, but he had an office downtown. Every two months or so he had to go out of town for a meeting with a client. He'd gotten a big promotion when we moved to Calgary. One of his committee's designs won the company a huge contract."

Kent mulled it over. "Any of the team upset with him?"

"Good grief no." She laughed, shook her head. "They all got substantial bonuses for their work on the project. They were delighted."

So her husband hadn't been the target. Who then—her? He didn't know what to think. "And you were working as a nurse?"

"Actually, I'd been off work for a while."

"For the baby?"

"No, after that."

Kent watched closely, sensing there was something she didn't want to say.

Georgia drew a deep breath. "I was suspended for a few days. Standard procedure when a patient dies unexpectedly. After an investigation and a coroner's hearing, I was cleared of any error or misconduct. They knew I didn't do anything wrong." Her voice faded. "But it's very hard to lose a patient."

Kent was growing frustrated. No matter how he tried to puzzle this out, there just didn't seem to be answers. "What about coworkers? Any problems there?"

"Not up to that point." Her fingers intertwined. "Certainly nothing after, because I didn't go back. I couldn't."

"Why?"

She looked at him, her heart in her eyes, and he knew she still felt guilty in spite of her vindication. "The case made the headlines. I was 'that nurse.' You saw a piece of an article about it, remember? A reporter on one of the local papers was trying to make a name for himself. He made me sound psychotic. Mad Nurse Georgia." She laughed, but there was no mirth in it. "My name, my picture, our address—all of it was splashed all over the newspaper. I couldn't go back there."

Her voice dropped to a whisper. "My patients, the other nurses, everyone would always carry a suspicion. In the backs of their minds they'd wonder if maybe I'd known, done it deliberately. I asked for leave and stayed home with Ty."

Kent tried to understand, but something still wasn't quite right. "Why would anyone think that, Georgia? What reason would anyone have for believing you would willingly hurt a patient? Something doesn't make sense."

She didn't answer. Why? Was she hiding something?

"I have to know the truth, Georgia. Help me understand."

Still she remained silent.

"I believe someone is deliberately trying to hurt you. If that's the case, it could affect our camp, the kids, the people who work here—potentially all of us. Please tell me what I need to know to help you."

When she finally spoke, Georgia's voice was so low he had to lean close to hear it. But as the facts emerged, he reared back in shock. "The woman died." She looked up at him, her face set in stiff lines of sheer pain. "And I was the one who administered the poison that killed her. Now do you understand?" Her cheeks blazed a bright pink.

"But—but you were cleared."

She nodded. "Yes, they said it wasn't my fault. That someone had switched things, that I couldn't have known." Her lips curled. "Do you think that helped? She and her baby were dead. Because of me."

Kent watched Georgia straighten, school her features. Inside his gut, his stomach tightened at the guilt she carried. A flash of insight provided his next words. "And you think that's why your husband and child died—because of that? That God took some kind of retribution for something that wasn't your fault?" He shook his head. "No! It isn't true."

Kent scrambled for the right words, wondering as he did if this feeling of guilt underlaid her inability to let go of the past and accept her loss. "Georgia, God isn't like that. What you're accusing Him of—He would never do that."

Where were the words? How did he explain it? *Lord, this woman is hurting, carrying a burden that isn't hers. Help me.*

"Accidents happen, Georgia. Things we don't understand occur every day, things that hurt us and others. That doesn't mean God is punishing us. It's the result of living in a world that doesn't obey His laws. Your family died. But not because you did something wrong. It was an accident."

A loud crash reverberated from outside the kitchen, as if something had hit the wall, jarring the metal shelves that stood against it.

"What was that?" Georgia asked.

Kent's instincts went on high alert. He peered through the window, saw a shadow disappearing into the trees behind the chapel. At least he thought he'd seen it. "I don't know, but I intend to find out. Stay here."

Georgia seemed shocked, as if transported to another world.

"Do you hear me, Georgia? Do not leave this building until I come and get you."

She looked into his eyes. "Be careful," she whispered, reaching out to touch his hand with her own. "Be very careful."

"I will. It would help if you could pray. Can you do that?" His fingers tightened around hers. He needed her touch, needed to feel that she was there with him in spirit.

Finally she nodded. "I can pray," she said, a faint smile touching her lips. "I'm just not sure anyone's listening."

He bent, brushed his mouth across hers. "That, my dear, is where you are dead wrong. 'Before they call, I will answer.' All you have to do is call." He delayed one minute more, searching her eyes for a response to the tender concern that coursed through his own veins. Then he realized that if someone had been outside, the person was now getting away.

Without another word, he sprinted out the door and into the bush, every sense on high alert.

≈◆≈

He pasted himself against the wall of the craft shack and held his breath, though his lungs begged for release.

Moments later his pursuer's footsteps crashed through the underbrush, barely four feet away. He saw him pause, glance around, then continue his search more slowly, trying to track a trail that wasn't there.

Still he hid, waiting until the man returned, reentered the kitchen, escorted *her* back to her cabin. He checked his watch, the faint green glow easily readable in the pitch darkness: 2:45. He was safe.

His knowledge of the area was imprinted on his brain. It took barely three minutes to find the main house, to check that all the occupants were in bed and asleep. That was good. He wanted no witnesses.

Not yet.

He moved into the cover of the trees, his mind casting back to what he'd heard. So she thought the fire was an accident, did she? Or surmised that God had sent it? Fury zipped through him. How stupid she was! Yet more proof that she should never have been allowed to care for those who needed help.

He wanted to do something—anything—to discredit her. Anger took over as he cast about for ways to reveal her untrustworthiness.

"Georgia is such a wonderful cook."

"Oh, this pie is heavenly."

The kitchen was never locked. It was there he'd show them. He crept inside, studied the area, then approached the cooler.

Small towns were filled with gossip. If just a hint of something out of the ordinary got out, a scandal would erupt. He could almost hear the comments: *"Food poisoning!"* The camp would suffer because money talked. When campers started canceling, they'd realize that *she* was to blame. Then they'd get rid of her. And he would be waiting.

He worked swiftly, silently, the gurgle of the bottle barely audible, even in the silence of the night.

Then, when the moon slid behind a cloud, he sneaked away from the building and into the dawn.

They would see. They would all see.

CHAPTER THIRTEEN

Kent? Can I speak to you for a minute? Privately." Georgia tried not to blush when Ralna winked at her, easily reading the older woman's thoughts. Thankfully, the rest of the lunch crowd weren't paying them any attention. Just Ralna.

She thinks we're up to something romantic. Georgia almost laughed. How she wished it were true. But this conversation would have nothing to do with romance.

"What's wrong?" Kent followed her outside the dining hall, glanced around to ensure no one was near. "I can see it on your face—something's happened. Tell me."

"Kent, I think I should quit."

"What?" The word burst out of him, indignant, disbelieving. "Now? But . . . you can't!"

"I think it's best if I gave you my resignation and got away from Camp Hope." She couldn't look at him, couldn't endure watching his frustration. Neither could she bear to have anyone else hurt because of her. And that was exactly what would happen.

"Come with me." He led her into his private office and shut the door. "Now what exactly is this about?"

She couldn't tell him the truth. Georgia knew he would talk her into staying, talk himself into believing he could handle this, along with whatever came next.

But she'd spent most of the morning thinking about the right thing to do. Kent believed someone was behind her flat tire, the newspaper clipping, the charging bull. When she remembered that voice whispering a threat in the dead of night, she knew he was right.

But whoever it was had brought her problems into the camp. Now this person was endangering others. No one else must be allowed to suffer because of her.

"Georgia?"

"I told you from the beginning that I wouldn't be here for the whole summer. I warned you that I would only stay until I felt the time was right to move on." She licked her lips, swallowed. "The time is right."

"Why now?" He paced back and forth across the office like a caged tiger. "What makes this particular day the one when you decide to leave?" He stopped, turned, frowned. "Is it me? Is it something I've done?"

She shook her head. "It has nothing to do with you. It's me. It's time for me to go. I'm giving you one week's notice, starting today. I'm sorry but that's the best I can do." And even that was too long. Who knew what could happen in a week, how many innocent kids could be hurt because of her?

"I don't accept your resignation. I won't." He glared at her.

"You have to because I will leave. One week from today, Kent." She moved toward the door, hating herself for doing this to him but knowing there was no other way. "I'm sorry."

"Are you?" he asked, eyes blazing. "Then stay. Things are going so well. We've made huge strides, begun to see the fruits of our labors. You're the one who instigated so many of these changes. And now you want to walk away?" He raked a hand through his hair. "This makes no sense."

"It does to me," she whispered. It made perfect sense. He just didn't know it. And never would, if she had her way. "By the way," she murmured, holding the door open with her toe so she couldn't change her mind, "we've had some pranks in the kitchen, the cooler to be specific. It's bumping up our food costs. I wonder if you would ask Fred to finish those locks for the cooler that I asked for. In fact, I think the entire kitchen should be locked when it's not in use."

That was as close to the truth as she was willing to go.

Kent nodded, but he didn't answer, so Georgia left. He was probably right. What else was there to say?

Wednesday—Doughnut Day again. But today the work had lost its fun. She forced herself to cut the dough, mix the glazes, prepare the creme fillings. As she worked, she went over the past week's events once more, hoping she was wrong.

Once might have been an accident, and she'd thought it was just that when she'd smelled the bathroom disinfectant in the cooler that first morning. The bottle was on the floor, its contents spilled over the carrots and watermelon crates. She'd made sure both were thoroughly washed, then for added measure, peeled the carrots. A taste test, first by her, then by her helpers, had convinced Georgia that no aftertaste remained. As far as she could determine, none of the chemical had touched already prepared food.

The who of it was a mystery. The night before it happened, she and Kent had shared coffee right here. The floor had been clean, and the bottle had not been in the cooler. She would have smelled it when she put the cream back. Georgia had put it down to a freak accident.

Until Friday.

She'd planned waffles as a special treat, prepared tons of them well ahead, and frozen the stacks so she merely had to reheat them. But when she'd reached for the bowls of whipped cream, a faint odor made her check the contents. Someone had topped the topping with shaving cream.

It was an expensive prank, one she'd been determined no one

would repeat. Fred had agreed to make locks for the cooler and freezer doors, but the influx of new campers had him scrambling to find enough beds.

Georgia had spoken with the maintenance crew, posted signs, and even moved things around so it was more difficult to enter the walk-ins after hours. She'd checked and rechecked, just to be certain.

Everything had seemed fine. Until this morning.

There was no way bleach could mistakenly be added to the sealed gallons of orangeade. Not possibly. And by now she knew it was her the intruder was targeting because of the note: "Leave before someone dies. Again." It lay in her pocket still, its message chilling even in the warmth of this day.

"Georgia? The office said you called." Rick Mercer stepped inside the kitchen, closed the door carefully behind himself. "Is this a good time?" he asked, glancing into the dining hall.

"It's fine." She slipped the note in its plastic bag out of her pocket and handed it to him. "I need your help." As quickly as possible she explained the past week's events. "I scrubbed the cooler down last night, and I've kept everyone out of it today. Only my prints should be inside. The containers and the juice are still in there. I didn't know what kind of tests you'd have to do."

"I see." Rick's grim face told her he was worried. "And you didn't tell Kent. Why?"

"Because he thinks he can stop whoever this is."

"And you don't believe him?"

"I can't take the risk." She looked Rick straight in the eye. "You know what happened at the hospital. You know that someone has already died because of me."

"Yes." He held her gaze. "I also know that you were cleared."

Her face burned with shame, but she pressed on, determined to make him understand. "But they never found out how the switch occurred. In the crowd of public opinion, I am still a suspect. This is exactly the same."

Rick shook his head. "Not quite. Don't forget I've been watching you, Georgia MacGregor. I've seen you work twenty-hour days in this camp. I've watched you interact with John, seen you bandage cuts and kiss bruised knees better. I know how hard you've tried to help Kent make this place a success. I'm not prepared to believe you'd hurt anyone, let alone a child."

Tears welled in her eyes. "Thank you for your confidence."

"You've earned it. Now show me the cooler."

While he investigated, she told him every unusual occurrence she could remember since she'd come to Camp Hope.

"Some of this I knew, of course. Kent told me. But this business—" he motioned toward the cooler—"puts a new light on things. I'll speak to Kent about having the place locked up when you're not here. In the meantime, I have enough fingerprints to get started. I'll dump this orangeade out, shall I?"

He lifted the huge pail over the sink and began pouring, faltering only once, when the door opened.

John poked his head inside. "Oh, hello, Officer." He stared at the orange liquid going down the drain. "May I have some of that? I can't seem to quench my thirst lately. I think it's the pills."

"I'll get you a drink," Georgia cut in, pouring him a glass of the iced tea she'd prepared for lunch.

"Thanks." He sipped the tea, made a face.

"What's wrong?"

"Nothing really. I just prefer the orange. I'm sorry if you had to make more. I drank about a gallon of it last night before I went to bed."

"You were in here last night?" Rick set the empty pail on the floor, his voice very casual.

Georgia pretended to be busy watching her oil heat for the doughnuts. John liked orange drink. She remembered the can in her room. But that was before he'd showed up. Still—he could be pretending amnesia. Could John be the person who was threatening her? Somehow she'd never thought of him as the culprit. Even now, looking at him, John seemed an unlikely candidate.

"Yes. About midnight, I think it was." He turned to Georgia. "You gave me that pill about—what? Ten o'clock?"

She nodded.

"Then I'd say midnight. It always seems to happen about two hours later. I get an intense thirst. I don't know why." He peered into the sink. "What's wrong with this stuff?"

"What makes you think anything's wrong with it?"

John snorted. "Nobody throws perfectly good juice down the drain when there are two hundred thirsty kids outside."

Georgia opened her mouth, but Rick beat her to it. "It wasn't perfectly good. That's why we had to throw it out, John."

"Oh." He shrugged, handed over his glass. "Well, back to my mowing. I don't think I've ever sat on anything for as long as I've spent on that tractor. Funny how soft you get working in an office. I used to work out for an hour every day, but mowing the grass with a push mower is a far better workout. I shouldn't complain. The tractor is a nice change. I should get one. I could do the neighbors' yards. The Browns would love to see me pushing a mower." His chuckles echoed around the room as he walked to the door and pulled it open. "See you, Officer. Georgia."

"See you, John." Rick waited until the door was closed, then looked at Georgia.

She nodded. "I heard him. He lives next door to the Browns. He works in an office. He works out for an hour a day. Either he's weakening as an actor, or his memory is coming back."

"Uh-huh. I also heard him say he was in here last night around midnight." Rick stood at the window, watching as John climbed on his mower and rode it out of sight, then glanced back at her. "Maybe it's him?"

"I don't think John's doing this. Besides, the tire—that was before he showed up."

"I know." Rick looked at her as if willing her to understand what he wasn't saying. But did he mean that John had *followed her* here?

"What was all that about his pills?"

"Making him thirsty, you mean?"

He nodded.

"I wondered the same thing. They're supposed to relax him so he can sleep. I've never heard of thirst as a side effect. That doesn't mean anything, though. People react differently to medications."

"Where do you keep them?"

"All the campers' medications are locked up in the nursing cabin. John's are with them."

"Can I see them?" He sounded worried.

"Of course." She turned off the gas under the oil, shifted the pots where it was cooler, then untied her apron. Suddenly she paused, glanced around. "What about the kitchen?"

"My cruiser is parked right outside. I think that might deter someone for the few minutes it will take to walk there and back." He smiled at her reassuringly. "I think your criminal only works at night, when everyone else is asleep."

"Okay." She placed tea towels over the few trays of doughnuts that wouldn't fit into the ovens to raise, then followed him to the door. "I can't be too long. Those need frying."

"We'll hurry."

And they tried. But Rick insisted on looking inside each bottle of medication, checking each inhaler, examining the syringes she'd been given for a diabetic girl.

"I thought maybe they'd been switched, but John's medication looks like the same stuff the hospital gave us. Does he use it every night?"

"Oh no." She shook her head. "He usually tries to go without, but sometimes I think he overdoes physically, and that makes it harder for him to rest. That's usually when he asks me for a pill."

"Hmm."

By the time they returned to the kitchen, Georgia's helpers were there, busily working on preparations for supper. She motioned to Rick, then moved to the corner where they couldn't be overheard.

"I appreciate your help, Rick. And thank you for volunteering to tell Kent. I just couldn't. Maybe if he hears it from you, he'll realize that I have to leave."

"You're quitting?" Rick frowned. "Why?"

"Why? Because if I leave here, these . . . attacks will stop; that's why. I won't risk any more people getting hurt because of me."

"We're not going to let that happen," he assured her, watching as she lifted off the tea towels, set the oil on the element, and turned it on. "Can I have one of those after I've talked to Kent?"

"Sure." Georgia picked up a tray, paused, then set it back down. "Did either of you touch these?" she asked her helpers.

They glanced up from their work and shook their heads.

"We've got more than enough to do. Besides nobody makes Georgia's doughnuts like Georgia." Their teasing grins took away any sting the words might have had. "We wouldn't dare interfere."

Rick moved closer to Georgia. "What's wrong?" he asked.

"I don't know." She stared at the pale disks, trying to identify her concern. "There's so much flour. I try to use as little as possible because it turns the oil dark." She shrugged. "Put it down to paranoia."

The first doughnut had almost hit the hot oil when Rick grabbed her arm. "Wait. Can you smell something?" He sniffed the air.

Georgia did the same, touched the doughnut, then rubbed her fingers together. "Baby powder?" she whispered.

Rick didn't answer; he merely slid a doughnut into a zipper bag he pulled from his pocket. "All of them?" he asked, standing so her helpers couldn't see what they were doing.

She checked each tray resting on the table. "Yes, all of these." Then she bent, removed a sheet from the oven. "I don't think he touched the ones in here." She showed him.

"Fry one. I'll try it. If it tastes okay, you can go ahead and serve the good ones. The others will have to be dumped, I imagine."

She nodded.

"Guess I get my taste test sooner than I thought," he teased, accepting the browned delicacy she offered.

"I could put glaze on it."

"No. I want to taste the doughnut." He bit into it, chewed it thoroughly, finished it. "Nothing wrong with that, except that I want more."

Between frying, Georgia counted the remainder of good doughnuts. "I won't have enough for the community activity tonight," she mumbled, trying to think of something that she could substitute.

"We've got all that ice cream. Why not have a sundae night?" One of her helpers walked into the storeroom and returned with a couple of large food-service cans. "We have plenty of toppings, and it's certainly hot enough."

"That's perfect. You're a genius. Do we have any of those disposable dishes left?" From the corner of her eye, Georgia saw Rick leave. He put the plastic bag inside his car, then drove around to the office.

For better or worse, Kent would soon know the reason she could no longer stay at Camp Hope. Maybe then he'd understand.

>—◆—<

Kent forced himself to remain in his chair and hear out the constable who'd become a close friend. "What do you want me to do?"

"I want you to stop thinking you can handle this person. Whoever is doing this has stepped beyond simple frightening tactics and has escalated his maneuvers to where they could endanger others, not because he tries but because he wants to get to Georgia." Rick's face mirrored the anxiety of his voice. "Hear me, Kent. Whoever this is isn't going to give up. At least, that's my take."

"I realize that. But to use food . . ." Kent blanched as the scope of the possible repercussions filled his mind.

"He knew Georgia would notice. The smell, for one thing. Bleach and disinfectant are pretty powerful odors. She's a nurse, trained to notice details. He would have counted on that." Rick grimaced. "I don't think the powder on the doughnuts would have stuck once they hit the grease. And I doubt if it would be deadly." He took out a pad and began to scribble on it. "Get locks on the cooler and freezer doors immediately. In fact, get locks on the kitchen so no one can get in or out without a key. That means you'll have to find a way to secure the pass-through into the dining room. Maybe you should lock it too."

"Fine. No problem." Kent made himself a note. "Fred, Georgia, and I will have the only keys."

"And I want that window in the nursing cabin barred. I don't want anyone tampering with medications."

"Done." Kent paged Fred on the radio and told him what was needed. "Anything else?"

"Yes." Rick frowned, his face thoughtful. "You need to find some way to convince Georgia to stay."

"Make her stay?" It was the opposite of what he'd expected. Kent shook his head. "I don't think I can. She was adamant. Why? You just said it's risking the entire camp for her to remain." Confused by the request, he watched his friend's head shake. "It's not risking the camp?"

"Not necessarily. He only cares about discrediting her, trying to make her look bad. No one else has been injured, have they? No camper attacked, locked in, that kind of thing?" He paused and nodded. "I didn't think so. For some reason Georgia MacGregor is the target. If she leaves, this perp goes with her, and we'll never find him. I believe the chances of our stopping him drop as soon as she sets foot off this land."

"But that means . . ." Kent gulped, stared at Rick. "By keeping her here, we're deliberately risking Georgia's life!"

"No more so than by letting her leave. Here she has people

around her constantly. They can check, notice strangers, watch for the unusual. The moment she leaves, she's on her own."

Kent knew what Georgia would say to that. "She'd rather put herself in danger than allow anyone else to suffer," he explained. "I'm sure that was the reason for her resignation this morning."

"Then you make her see reason. Or find someone who can. I don't much care which. I'm not about to let this guy just walk away so he can try something somewhere else." Rick's mouth tightened. "I've got a few things to check out. I need to get going. Keep me posted." He wheeled toward the door, dragged it open.

"Rick?"

"Yeah?"

"Thanks." Mingled with the worry, a blessed sense of relief that he could share this burden with someone else filled Kent with gratitude. "I don't know what we'd do without you."

"Neither do I." Rick grinned, stepped outside. "By the way," he added, unlocking his cruiser door, "I forgot to tell you. You've got a two-hundred-and-fifty-pound donation of pork coming. You could probably use it for family camp, right?"

Kent caught the twinkle in Rick's eye. "How do you happen to know about our donations?" he asked solemnly.

"Community service work. Cops know everything that's going on in a place this size." He waggled one hand, started the motor, then drove away.

"Make her see reason or find someone who can."

Kent walked back into his office, turning the idea over in his mind a hundred times before he finally reached for his phone.

"This had better work," he muttered to himself as the phone at the other end rang. "Hi, this is Kent Anderson at Camp Hope. I wonder if you can help me."

CHAPTER FOURTEEN

Doug?"

The joy on Georgia's face was worth watching, Kent decided, even if it was there because of another man.

Georgia dropped the towel she was holding and raced across the pool deck to throw herself into the tall blond man's arms.

"Hey, kid! You're getting me soaked."

But Doug didn't let her go, Kent noticed. If anything, his arms tightened around her, hugging her close, his earlier glowering face now transformed by a huge grin that matched Georgia's.

"What are you doing here?" At last Georgia pulled away, dashed the tears from her cheeks. "Not that I'm complaining. It's wonderful to see you. But this is a long way from the Calgary tower."

"Ain't it the truth?" Doug looked around. The astute gaze Kent had come to recognize on the drive from the airport mentally catalogued every detail of Camp Hope, at least what he could see in the semidarkness. "So this is your hideaway, huh? Not bad. Not bad at all." He gave Kent a thumbs-up.

Kent nodded, forced himself to remain smiling. This was

Georgia's friend, he reminded himself for the hundredth time. Her *childhood* friend. It was only natural they'd be excited to see each other. That didn't mean there was anything else involved.

"I don't see the Vette. How did you get here?" Georgia glanced behind him at the parking lot.

"I took a plane to a quaint little city—I forget the name of it. Then I phoned your Kent to see if someone could come and pick me up. And here I am."

"Your Kent." Kent liked the sound of that.

"You got Doug?" Georgia was looking at Kent with that funny light in her eyes, the one that made his stomach do weird things.

It was all Kent could do to nod.

"Actually, I think *you* called *him*, didn't you?" She obviously took the guilty look on Kent's face as agreement. "Thank you," she whispered, tears welling once more. "Thank you very much. I could use a friend right now."

So what am I—the enemy?

She didn't notice his chagrin. All her attention was on Doug. "How long can you stay?" she demanded, then shook her head. "No. Don't tell me—just the weekend."

Doug nodded and chucked her chin with his fist. "Long enough to find out what you're up to."

"Five-nine or five-ten, same as always." Georgia giggled at her own joke.

They were like an old married couple, Kent decided, watching the nonverbal interplay between them. Doug was asking if she was all right; she was trying to pretend she was fine.

"If you've had enough swimming, maybe we could go to the house and get some coffee?" Kent noticed Christa and John waiting in the background. "I'm sorry. I should have introduced you to Christa. Chris, this is Georgia's friend Doug Henderson. Doug, this is my sister, Christa, and our friend John Riddle."

Christa shook hands with Doug, then turned to Georgia. "You're right. He does remind me of a beach bum," she remarked, loud enough for everyone to hear.

"Christa!"

"What have you been telling her, Georgia?"

Kent met Doug's shocked stare and shrugged. "My sister is too old to send to her room," he apologized.

"That's okay. So's Georgia. I'd forgotten her tendency to um . . . make fun of my good looks."

Behind them, the two women didn't even bother to smother their chuckles.

Within moments, Georgia had everything arranged. They walked back to Kent and Christa's house, leaving Kent to close up the pool, which he did with a minimum of fuss. He wanted to hear exactly how Doug intended to persuade Georgia to stay when Kent hadn't succeeded in two days of pleading.

An hour later, when John had left and Christa had gone to bed, he got his chance.

"So what is this I hear about your leaving?" Doug plopped down beside Georgia, took her hand in his. His tone was gentle. "Are you nuts? This is the best place you could be. Look at you. You've lost that starved-waif look, you've got a tan, your eyes are bright. You look good, Georgie."

"Starved-waif look? Huh! Thank you—I think." Georgia glanced sideways at Kent, bit her bottom lip. Her golden head tipped to one side. "But you don't understand, Douglas. I can't stay."

"Why? Because some crazy person is after you?"

"No." She shook her head, her chocolate eyes darkening with worry. "I don't care about me."

I do. I care a lot about you, Georgia MacGregor. Knowing he was telegraphing his feelings just by looking at her, Kent felt overwhelming relief that the other two were too involved in each other to notice him.

"It's scary, I know, Georgia. And you'll have to take precautions—"

"No," she insisted, more loudly this time. "This is about the kids.

What if one of them had drunk—?" She closed her eyes, drew in a deep breath. "I couldn't bear it if another child was hurt because of me, Doug. The only way to make sure of that is if I leave."

"What will that do?"

"Draw him away from here." She frowned at him. "If it's me he's after—and it seems obvious now—he won't stay here if I'm gone. Kent can finish out the camping season without worrying that something will spoil his shot at that promotion he wants."

Kent almost blurted out that he couldn't care less about the job right now, except that it would release Christa from the camp.

Doug's eyes widened at her response. "But that's no answer, sweetie. What if he follows you?"

She shrugged. "I'll handle that when—no, if—it happens."

"How?" Doug was relentless in his questioning.

Kent was beginning to wonder if it had been such a good idea to ask this man to help. He didn't like the way Doug, no matter how good a friend, kept hounding her. Georgia looked confused, lost.

Kent decided to intervene. "Maybe—"

Doug silenced him with a black look. "There's no *maybe* about this." He turned back to Georgia. "This is serious business. You're familiar with Camp Hope, you know the routine, you notice when something is out of place. You know who you can call on for help here." He grimaced when she glanced at Kent.

Kent allowed himself a moment's satisfaction that she'd turned to him when the word *help* was mentioned.

Doug ignored him, kept pushing. "But out there—" he jerked a thumb over his shoulder—"he's got you at his mercy. There's no predictability, no way to prepare."

"I could go home," she whispered.

Doug shook his head. "You can't live the rest of your life in a bubble, kid. Isn't that why you left Calgary?" He covered her hand with his. "Besides, you'll never know who he hurts along the way in trying to get to you, who he'll try to go through to get to you."

Georgia stared at him, her face white, strained. "Then what? I-I don't know what to do." She looked at Kent. "Camp Hope is my primary concern, but I don't want to ruin things for you either. What if this person does something here, something so bad that it causes the head office to fire you? How would you and Christa manage?"

Kent knelt in front of her, covered her free hand with his own. "Listen to me, Georgia. Long ago I asked God to be in charge of my career, to send me where He wanted me, where I could work for Him. I think it's about time I let Him do the leading, don't you?"

He waited a moment, then continued. "You always argue when I say I think God led you to Camp Hope. But this could be one of the reasons He did—to stop this person. We're isolated here. We know who comes and goes; we can tell if something's out of place."

That wasn't exactly true. Obviously, whoever was taunting her had been moving at will in and out of camp property. But she had to admit it was still safer for her here among friends than alone on some country road.

"Stay, Georgia. Keep doing what you've been doing. We've only two more weeks left until the summer camps end. Then we get a break. Stay just two more weeks. Please?"

He wanted her to stay a whole lot longer than that. In fact, it burned deep inside to think of this place without her. But he wasn't free to say that. Not now, not with Christa dependent on him. Not with this madman lurking in the shadows.

"You're sure?" Georgia searched Kent's face for answers. Her lips twisted into a crooked smile. "The next time I get conked on the head, you won't regret it?"

He inclined his head to one side. "There's no way I can answer that and win, Georgia."

She thought it over, then grinned. "I see what you mean. Never mind. I assume the correct answer is no." She drew a deep breath, straightened her spine, and nodded. "All right. I'll stay."

Kent heaved a sigh of relief as he rose and stepped back. She was strong, stronger than both of them perhaps. But she wouldn't have to be. He would be right there if anyone tried to harm her.

He wanted to hug her, to tell her how delighted he was that she would be here, for however long God gave them. But Doug was watching him with that eagle-eyed protective glare that projected a warning.

"Two weeks more, then I'm leaving," she said, glancing from one to the other. She blinked. "You know, I only ever planned to stay two weeks in the first place."

Kent hid his grin. "God works in mysterious ways."

"Amen." Doug grinned at both of them. "Now that's settled, where can I bed down? I'm exhausted."

"Here. We've a spare room just waiting for you." Kent was aware of the sharp look Georgia directed his way, but he ignored it—for the moment. Time enough to explain about Doug's sudden arrival when they were alone.

>>—◆—<<

So she was staying.

Well, it didn't matter. He'd made up his mind long ago. The where and how of it weren't important. It was justice he craved, justice would fill the hole in his life that *she'd* caused.

He crept back through the oversized ferns he'd planted last week around the northern perimeter of the house. Beyond that he'd arranged ten of the wild rosebushes so prolific in this area.

He was sick of this place, sick of waiting, hiding. Most of all he was sick of smiling, of pretending that everything was wonderful, that he was here as nothing more than some kind of slave labor. Not that he wanted to be paid. He wouldn't have touched their money.

No, satisfaction would be much more costly than a few paltry dollars. A life for a life. That was all the pay he'd need.

He was used to the walk back to his camper now—it seemed like a short stroll. In the past few months his body had become hardened, toned, ready for battle. He'd learned to read the ground for signs that someone had been poking around his place. Tonight he had plenty of warning. The white police cruiser was clearly visible in the evening light.

"Hello. You've been camping here for a while, haven't you?"

He nodded, watched the Mountie scan the area.

"You're not sick of the place yet? Don't long for your own home? You've been away quite a while."

"I like roughing it." He strolled over to the table he dragged into his area, poked the fire into life, and added a few chips. Soon the flames licked up the crumbs he offered and demanded more. He set a log in the middle, watched the bark catch alight. "Besides, sitting out here after dark is restful. Kinda private here. Which is a good thing. I'm not much around kids, you know. Never had any of my own. I like the peace and quiet of this place."

"Kids can make you crazy all right. Always a constant stream going through the camp in the summer." The Mountie rested one foot on a log, put his elbow on his knee, his eyes on the fire. "You like a van better than an RV?"

"Way better when it comes to gas prices around here." He laughed, pretending this was an ordinary conversation. "Not much more than a bed and a chair in there, but they said I could use the camp showers. And I get all my meals free. Didn't think I needed much more than that." He added another log.

"The woman they have cooking there this year sure knows her stuff. Had me some doughnuts the other day." The cop shook his head. "Sure tasted like heaven to me."

Did the guy think he was stupid? That he wouldn't know he was laying a trap? He almost laughed out loud. "I wouldn't know. Don't eat much of that kind of thing."

"You're kidding?" The cop looked amazed. "Don't know how you can help it. She's always got something sweet on the go."

"Guess I'm just more of a health-food person. I like fruits, vege-tables."

"So you're a vegetarian?"

He laughed jovially at that. "Oh no. I like meat. But in modera-tion. Everything in moderation, the good book says." He smiled, relaxing even more. These juvenile questions were so stupid. Two could play this game. "Say, I have some real nice trail mix in the van. Dried lentils, carob, seeds, and nuts. You want some?" He pretended to rise.

"No, no thanks. I had a really big dinner."

As expected, the Mountie waved off his offer, tried to conceal his grimace of distaste. That was the problem with cops. Too soft.

"Well, if you're sure. I always go for a walk after dinner. Helps settle things for the night. That's where I was when you drove up. I saw your lights, but I was too far away to call. Awful rude of me not to be home when guests come to call." He chortled at his own joke and watched the flames flicker in the slight breeze that stirred the leaves overhead, as if to remind him that someone was watching. "I like it here. Real peaceful."

"It isn't peaceful where you're from?"

He chuckled. "Not so's you'd notice. A hundred guys tromping around a bunkhouse isn't quiet."

"Where you from?"

Ah, he'd been waiting for that. "Came off a stint up north. Heavy oil upgrader. You heard of them?"

"Heard of them. Never knew anyone who worked there. Except you." As expected the Mountie feigned interest. "What's it like?"

"Lots of work for anyone who doesn't mind the shifts and spend-ing long winter nights among a bunch of men. Usually six weeks in, a couple out. Some of the guys get real lonely for their wives and kids during the winter. They think it's boring up there. I usually offer to take their shifts. Real good pay for that." He grinned. "Socked up a nice little nest egg for myself while I was in and a whole mess of vacation time. The company wouldn't let me carry the days over till next year though. Said I had to use 'em or lose 'em. So I'm using 'em."

"You have a lot of days left?"

"Another month. But I'm not staying here that long. I suppose I'd better tell Kent I'll be leaving next week." He scratched his head, then peered at the cop. "Got a trip to the Maritimes planned. You ever been to the Maritimes?"

"No."

"Supposed to be something else. All that Anne of Green Gables stuff, you know. And lighthouses." He closed his eyes, thought about it. "Whole lot of things to see in the Maritimes. I've got a book about it. I could lend it to you if you got it back to me before I left."

"That's kind of you. But I think I'd better pass. I'm back on regular shift next week, so I won't have much time for reading. I hope you have a good trip though."

Dumb cluck probably couldn't read above a fifth-grade level. That was the problem with the justice system—they let anybody in, even stupid small-town hicks like this one. It was a joke!

Apparently the constable had seen all he needed to. After a couple more minutes of chitchat, he straightened, dusted off his pants, and pulled out his keys. "Guess I'd better get going." He deliberately took the long way around, stopping at the rear of the van. "Man, this thing is covered with mud. What happened?"

"Saw the funniest thing in the newspaper last week. You ever hear of mud drags?" He waited, feigning excitement.

The cop nodded. "We have them here in the late fall."

"You're kidding?" he asked in disbelief. "I must be behind the times then, because it was news to me. I drove to the city yesterday to see how it worked. Whooee! It was a mess, I'm telling you. Mud flying everywhere."

"Yeah, it gets pretty messy. Did you enter?"

He laughed as if it were a huge joke. "Me? No way! I never drove in stuff like that. For sure not with a van. Guess I parked in the wrong place, though, because by the time I was ready to leave, this thing was plastered. Got talking to a guy about those modified four-by-fours with the lift kits. Real monster trucks. Realized later I'd parked beside their practice pit. Dumb. Really dumb."

He shook his head like the idiot the cop thought he was, then scraped a finger through the encrusted mud. "Gotta get this thing to a car wash," he muttered. "But I just haven't had the time. I suppose I could have stopped in the city, but I don't like driving after dark. Too many deer on the roads around here."

"I wondered why I hadn't seen it for a few days."

He felt the blood rush to his cheeks. So they were watching him, were they? Well, let them. He was too smart to get caught by these hick cops. "Guess I was a little ashamed," he said, pleased that he'd infused the words with just the right inflection of embarrassment. "I suppose it seems a little childish for a man like me to be interested in kids' stuff like that."

"I like the mud drags myself. Nothing wrong with a little mud." The cop listened to his crackling radio, pushed his cap back, and headed toward his patrol car. "I have to be going. See you."

"Anytime. Kinda nice having a visitor." He twisted his mouth into a fatuous grin and waved, remaining in place until the car had disappeared in a froth of dust.

One week. One more week was all he would waste on her. In the meantime he'd plan her surprise, one the cop and other people around here wouldn't soon forget.

It was a sad thing when you couldn't count on the law. But he'd manage. He'd see justice done, no matter what.

CHAPTER FIFTEEN

I'm bushed." Georgia let every muscle go limp as she floated in the water. "I don't even have the energy to swim tonight."

"Nobody does. Don't worry about it. It's always like this after family camp, and it's not just the increased numbers. Anyway, you've been going at this heavy all summer. I don't know how you do it." Christa paddled back and forth, from one side to the other, the inflated armbands around her upper arms gleaming in the glare of the overhead lights. Her version of laps.

She seemed fine, but ever since yesterday morning, Georgia had sensed a reserve between them.

"Have you heard from your friend since he left here?" John's watchful gaze never left Christa, though he allowed himself to float away from her.

"Doug?" A pang of regret washed through Georgia, but she quashed it ruthlessly. "He's phoned several times. Working, as usual." She missed him terribly, but it had been wonderful to see him, even if only for a weekend.

"The two of you seemed awfully close."

Startled by the tone underlying her words, Georgia turned and met Christa's gaze. "We *are* close. We have been for many years."

Christa looked . . . upset. Why? "He's like my brother, honey. Doug and I go way back to kindergarten."

"I just don't want Kent to get hurt." Christa turned her back, began paddling the other way.

Ah, she was worried about her brother. She'd seen the attraction growing between them and assumed Kent had been dumped. It was the first time Georgia had seen this very protective side of Christa toward Kent, and it touched her heart to know she really cared about him. So often it had been Kent who'd shielded his sister. From the little she'd learned while being at Camp Hope, Georgia had concluded that Christa's main interest was to get away from him.

"Kent's a different kind of friend than Doug. But I care about them both." Would that suffice for now? It was hard to explain to someone else when her own feelings were so confusing. "We've been so busy, we haven't had as much time to talk as I'd have liked, but I wanted to tell you how much I appreciated your help with things."

Silence.

"I'm sorry we got behind in our Bible study," Georgia said.

"It's okay. I finished it yesterday."

"Really? Good for you. I'll have to catch up on my own then." Georgia tossed the idea around for a few moments, then decided to plunge ahead. Knowing Christa, she'd make no bones about telling her if she didn't want to talk. "You never did tell me about your accident," she said, wondering if this was the right time. "We were talking that day, and then something interrupted us. We could talk now if you want."

When Christa didn't answer, Georgia wondered whether she should press her. Something about that event had colored the relationship between brother and sister ever since. Maybe, before she left Camp Hope, she could at least help them mend the past.

"I'd like to understand what happened, why Kent feels so responsible."

"I don't think I can explain that. You'd have to ask Kent about his feelings." Suddenly Christa was stroking very strongly. Water splashed up in a huge wave, drenching her red face. "It wasn't him. He didn't force me to go. I did that all by myself."

"You went swimming the night of the storm?" Georgia saw her nod. Her breath snagged in her throat. "Christa, why? You must have known how dangerous it was."

"I wasn't thinking about that. I was angry, I was hot and fed up, and I wanted out of here."

For a moment she looked like the recalcitrant person Georgia had first met flailing in the pool. Then Christa's expression changed, a rueful look replaced the sour one. "You want the truth? I was acting like a spoiled brat," she admitted. "I felt like I had no control over my life, that I had to take a stand or get flattened by Kent's roller-coaster plans for Camp Hope."

"But I thought—"

"That I hated it here? I did. Some days." Christa shrugged. "Other times I felt just a little bit smug that I was the director's sister, that I could swim at odd times, ride horses when I wanted to, that kind of thing. I was a teenager. My moods vacillated like the wind."

"And that night you decided to go to the pool?"

Christa nodded, head turned away. "I was showing off earlier that afternoon, jumping Daisy over the creek. Daisy is the kind of horse that gets nervous when the weather's off. Thunder and lightning terrify her. She balked a couple of times and that made me even madder. When I struck her, she stumbled, rolled. I was thrown. It was an embarrassing thing for someone who's ridden as much as I have."

Christa stopped, paddled around for several minutes.

Sensing that she needed the time to deal with her memories,

Georgia grabbed a flutterboard off the deck and concentrated on her underwater kicks.

It wasn't long before Christa moved beside her. "Fred saw me. He came to me after I got home, bawled me out in his own gentle way. He said if I ever struck a horse again, he'd tell Kent I had to be kept away from the barns. He insisted that the horses belonged to the camp, not to me personally. I was damaging their investment, but more than that, he wouldn't allow cruelty to animals. He made me feel about three years old. I made up my mind then that I would get out of here as soon as I could."

The picture was clear now. Georgia could understand a young girl's frustration. With no mother to talk to and everyone seeming to order her about, she must have felt terribly alone and confused.

"It wasn't bad when I sneaked into the pool. The wind was blowing, but the storm was way in the distance. I'd been swimming laps for about fifteen minutes when Kent must have noticed something. He always did his rounds about then. I knew that and I'd timed it so he'd see that I wasn't slacking, that I'd more than made up my shortfall in time."

Georgia held her breath. She could almost imagine what came next, but for Christa's sake, she kept silent. Sometimes not saying a word was the best way of offering comfort.

"I had the blocks in place, ready for me to jump off. I wanted conditions as close to a race as I could get them. I waited until Kent was close enough to see me; then I climbed up, got in position. He yelled something at me, but the wind had picked up and I couldn't hear. I didn't want to hear." She grabbed the wall, her fingertips white as she clenched it.

John had left them together and was now sitting and leaning against the fence, his legs stretched out on a towel. He looked totally at ease, but Georgia knew he was listening to every word.

"I'm not sure exactly what happened next. Later Kent said there was lightning, but I didn't see that. I dug my feet in, prepared to push off. The block moved. I hadn't bothered to secure it, thinking that by putting it right next to the board, I'd be safe enough. Of course I was thrown off balance. I hit something."

Christa paused, grasped for control. Her face was pale, her breath short, gasping. Georgia almost intervened, but Christa resumed her speech. "That's the last thing I remember until I woke up in the hospital, paralyzed from the waist down. They said my spine had been damaged. That I would never walk again. And I haven't." The last three words came out on a stifled sob.

Christa turned away, made a big production of splashing, no doubt to hide her tears. "So here we are. It wasn't Kent's fault. It wasn't anyone's fault—except mine. 'I am the master of my fate.'" She pretended to laugh but instead burst into tears.

"Oh, Christa." Georgia abandoned her flutterboard and gathered her into her arms, squeezing as tight as she dared. "It's all right."

Christa's tearful gaze met hers. "But it isn't. Don't you see? I ruined Kent's plans, ruined camp for all those kids, gave the place a terrible reputation so that parents were afraid to send their kids. I did that all because I was a spoiled brat." She shook her head, the tears falling faster now. "I've tried and tried to apologize to Kent, but he won't listen. I wrote a letter to the head office, told them I was to blame, not him. They sent a get-well card." Her eyes flashed with frustration.

"Christa, Kent understands. He knows you didn't mean to cause problems for the camp. It was an accident."

But Christa would not be consoled. "He doesn't understand. There's like this . . . this chasm between us. He holds back all the time, treats me like I'm made of glass, like I might break if he yells at me or tells me to stop being a drag on him." Her sob hiccuped in the night stillness. "He's so patient, so gentle, so accommodating. I hate that!"

"He's been trying to help by not pressuring you, by giving you time to deal with everything."

"Don't you think I know that?" Christa sighed. "I wish, just once, that he'd lose his cool and be my big brother again. I need him to be my brother, not my parent. I need him to stop doing things for me and start seeing that I'm not that stupid kid anymore. Why can't he do that, Georgia? Is it because Kent hates me for wrecking his life?"

"Of course not." Georgia didn't know what else to say, so she just kept hugging.

"Christa, you should get out now. It's cooled off quite a bit." John had moved to stand above them, his face inscrutable.

"Yes, I want to get out. I'm cold." She held up her arms and let him hoist her out of the water. "Thank you," she whispered as he wrapped her in a towel, then set her in her chair.

"You're welcome." He sat back down, leaving her to towel dry her hair and don the sweatshirt she always brought.

Georgia stayed where she was, replaying the conversation in her mind. Something wasn't quite right, but she couldn't think about that now. This was a time for honesty, for helping Christa face the future. But how?

The truth. She knew it was the only way.

"Christa, Kent thinks he has to get that job at head office because, if he does, he'll make enough money for you to live on your own. Is that what you want?"

Christa shook her head, then frowned, stared into the shadowy bushes to the west. "You want to know the truth?" She turned back to Georgia and smiled. "The truth is, I don't know what I want. The truth is, in the city I'd be able to build a life, meet friends, get away from him. He wouldn't have to waste his life hovering over me, paying for my mistake."

"But?"

"But then there's you."

"Me?" Georgia blinked. "What have I got to do with this?"

"Everything. I look at you dashing from here to there, full of plans to change this, talking to that camper, making special night treats for a cabin of little boys who miss their moms, and I remember the plans Kent and I had for this place." She closed her eyes, leaned her head back against the wire fence. "We were going to accomplish so much here, Georgia. Most of all we were going to teach kids about God. We'd sit around a campfire every so often between camps and make plans about what to do next."

"You could do that again." Georgia ordered her brain to forget the flicker of hope that wavered in the breeze of Christa's words. It would be only the two of them. She wouldn't stay. How could she?

"Could I?" Christa seemed lost in her own thoughts. "I wonder."

In the shadows of the shower house next to the pool, Kent froze, his sister's words slamming into him like bricks falling from the sky.

He'd failed her. He'd been trying to live up to his father's wishes, to be the parent she'd lost. And instead he'd made himself into some kind of overbearing ogre from whom she felt alienated.

How had it come to this? Why hadn't he seen?

All at once Kent realized he no longer knew or cared about the hows, whys, or whens. The time had come to change things.

With a whispered prayer for guidance, he walked around the building, determined to find out exactly how he could make amends. Christa was physically crippled because of him. But as long as he was able to change, she would not become emotionally crippled too.

"Did I hear someone talking about plans for Camp Hope?" He ignored Georgia's quick in-breath.

"Yes, I was." Christa met his gaze squarely. "What happened to my idea for a climbing wall?"

"Money, time, board approval." He sat down on the diving board and only then realized how emotionally weary he was.

"Oh, the board." Christa swallowed. "I forgot about them. I don't suppose they're too willing to allow such a risky sport after—"

"Extreme sports seem to be all the rage with teenagers. I expect you could offer quite an interesting camp if you featured cross-country biking or something like that. Those things typically cost a lot more than regular camp, so you charge accordingly, thus improving the bottom line." The words seemed to flow out of John's mouth.

Everyone stared at him.

"Additionally, you could run the extreme camp while the others are operating, in a sense doubling your revenue."

Christa blinked. "Wow! You seem to know a lot about this, John. How come?"

"My niece . . ." He frowned, his brows joining in a furrow of concentration. "I don't know," he said at last.

"Those bikes—they'd be expensive to buy. We'd have to have some here for kids who don't own their own. That means we'd have to repair them. I'm not sure . . ." Kent shook his head. It was a nice idea, but even with a good year like this one, they couldn't afford the kind of expensive bikes John was talking about.

"Let's just keep thinking with open minds. We won't discard any ideas yet." Georgia grinned at Kent. "We'll do ways and means in the next session."

The others chuckled.

"Okay, extreme sports." Kent nodded, wishing he'd kept quiet instead of dampening their enthusiasm. "What else?"

"Go-carts."

They all looked at Georgia.

She looked right back. "You heard me. Go-carts. You know—you build a track, get some go-carts, and let kids drive round and round. Go-carts." Her narrow shoulders lifted. "I admit I don't see the attraction myself, but in Calgary the kids line up for hours to get a turn on those things."

"We could never afford go-carts, Georgia."

"Now who's nay-saying?" Kent grinned at his sister. "Ways and means later, remember? Number two on the list—go-carts. What else?"

"Which reminds me, what have you been doing all evening? Why didn't you join us earlier, Kent?"

He was hoping no one would ask. He didn't want to admit to the nervous twitch in his stomach, that niggling feeling that he'd missed something, that there was something he should have done.

"Kent?"

They were all staring at him. He grinned. "Sorry. I had a few things I needed to check on." He saw immediately that Georgia understood what he hadn't said. She studied him, eyebrows raised. He nodded, just once. *Everything is fine.*

"Let's get back to our brainstorming. What kind of things were you thinking of, Christa? After all, you were the one who got us started on this."

"I'd like us to hold camps especially for kids with handicaps."

Christa's idea surprised him. "But . . . how could we do that? What would they do out here?" Did that mean she wanted to stay? Why? What had changed? Kent opened his mouth, thought better of it, and clamped his jaws together. He glanced at Georgia, hoping she understood his unspoken plea for help.

Apparently she did. Georgia winked. "Describe the kind of camp you visualize, Christa. Where would we start?"

"The paths, of course. We'd have to pave or cement them. Or at the very least, make boardwalks so kids on crutches or wearing braces or in wheelchairs, like me, could get around more easily." Her voice grew more earnest. "It's okay when it's nice, but if there's rain, it gets mucky in places and I get bogged down. Even after all this hot weather, I can't make it to the barn."

"You think the kids should *ride?*" Kent gulped. Neon signs flashed *lawsuit* in red and green letters across his brain.

"Why not?" The glitter in Christa's eyes dared him to say no.

"With the proper teaching and the right equipment, some could ride very well. Kids and horses are a natural."

When had she learned this? What had she been reading? Kent sat silent, content to listen as Christa laid out a complicated program that would allow even the most physically challenged child to enjoy some aspect of Camp Hope.

Finally Georgia announced, "I'm hungry. Let's go build a campfire and roast some hot dogs." She glanced around. "Anybody interested?"

They rose as one, a group of weary adults consumed by the possibilities in the future.

Before the others had changed clothes and returned to his yard, Kent had the fire burning, the food laid out, and hot chocolate to ward away the late evening's chill.

As he worked, he thought about Georgia. She had sounded like a partner—positive, interested, and planning for the future. He pretended she was inside the house, getting things ready, preparing for a party they would host together. Suddenly he realized that he loved this woman. Maybe if he spoke up, let her see how he really felt, she'd realize that she cared for him too, that she wanted to stay. To be able to stop hiding his feelings, to be open and freely caring for her—he couldn't imagine life much better than that.

Kent arranged the chairs around the fire, his mind busy with plans. Tonight. He'd tell her tonight. After the others had gone. They could spend all day tomorrow talking things through.

The others arrived. They talked and ate, sipped and talked well into the night. Ideas began to emerge that would allow the camp to make the modifications Christa suggested in the least expensive ways.

"You know, Herb could make wooden walkways with the trimmings from the mill. They get rid of loads of odd-sized pieces. That would cut costs."

Kent waved a hand, swallowed his drink, and winced as it scalded all the way down. "Not Herb," he told them, inhaling to cool his throat.

"Why not?" Georgia frowned. "I think he's doing a wonderful job around here."

"He's leaving tomorrow. Today was his last day."

Georgia glared at him. "I wish you'd told me. I'd have made a special cake so we could all thank him. He's given so much—it's the least we could have done." Her annoyance showed in the snap of her expressive brown eyes.

"I'm sorry, Georgia. But he specifically asked me not to tell anyone. Said he didn't want a fuss, that he'd enjoyed his time here and was glad to help." Kent looked at John, who shrugged and avoided his eyes. "Herb is an unusual man. He did a lot of work for us, and I appreciate all of it, but he never did really open up. Some days it seemed like he disappeared into thin air. I always wondered if he sneaked off for an afternoon sleep." Kent shook his head. "But he always got the jobs done—well done. Of course, John may have another opinion."

He waited to see how John would explain his impressions of the enigmatic handyman.

Unaccustomed to being the focus of attention, John looked surprised by the group's scrutiny of him. "I don't know what to say. He asked a lot of questions." The words seemed pulled from him.

"I suppose it's natural to be curious." Kent moved his chair closer to Georgia's, delighted when she didn't move away.

"What kind of questions?" Christa leaned forward, her face glowing with a slight tan in the flickering firelight.

"Mostly about Georgia. He thought she was very attractive." John offered Georgia a funny smile. "I didn't tell him anything."

And what was it, exactly, that John Riddle thought he knew about Georgia MacGregor? Kent wondered curiously.

"He didn't sleep in the afternoon. He went for walks. I used to see him on the gravel road," John ventured.

"I didn't even ask where he was staying." Georgia's chagrin was obvious. "When he didn't ask about housing, I assumed he was staying with friends. Now I really feel awful."

"But why? He enjoyed his time here; now he's going on to something else." John cleared his throat. "I think we should start on Christa's ideas without Herb. I'll look into getting the wood." He rose. "If you'll excuse me, I think I should go to bed. I have that appointment in the city tomorrow. The doctors are going to do tests. Again."

He sounded resigned to never learning his identity. Kent felt a rush of compassion for the man. So many times a prick of memory had bubbled up to the surface, but never enough to explain his past. It must be a frustrating way to live, yet John never complained.

"Constable Mercer is coming to pick me up at eight-thirty tomorrow morning. Good night."

He glanced at each of them, but Kent noticed that his gaze rested longest on Christa. It wasn't a lewd or suggestive stare. Just a contemplative look full of unspoken questions. He was a little surprised to see that Christa seemed to understand.

"Good night, John. I wish you well at your tests tomorrow." Christa reached out, clasped his hand in both of hers. "Will you be late returning?"

"I don't know." That confused look washed over his face again. "We may have to stay over. I guess it will depend on the constable and the doctors." He looked at their joined hands, then gently drew his away. "Good night."

He'd barely moved beyond the firelight when Christa turned her chair and pushed the button that would ease it up the ramp. "I'm going to bed too. Good night."

"She's tired," Kent said once she was safely inside the house. "I think she probably overdid it tonight."

"It was a big night for her." Georgia kept her voice low, but she stared directly into his eyes. "Christa told me about the night of her accident," she murmured. "Did you hear her?"

He froze, felt the hairs on his neck stiffen. The clarity of her stare made him realize he couldn't pretend. "I overheard part of it." He wove his fingers through hers, relishing the touch of her silky skin, still smooth despite her hours in the kitchen.

"She thinks you're shutting her out, that you've been acting differently toward her ever since the accident." Georgia's hand squeezed his. "She's hurting, Kent. She wants to recapture that closeness you used to share, but she can't because you won't let her. Why is that?"

He'd known this moment would come. Truth to tell, he'd expected to be confronted before this. The fact that he hadn't was both a source of relief and ongoing tension.

"You've always intimated that you've been to blame for the way Christa is now. But tonight I heard nothing in her story that would indicate you were in any way at fault, other than caring too much." She squeezed his hand again. "So what guilt are you hiding inside, Kent?"

The moment he'd dreaded for two years was here. Now the truth would come out, and Christa would hate him for it.

Worse, Georgia MacGregor would understand that he'd lived a lie. She'd know him for the fraud he was. Would she think that discredited anything else he said?

"What's the big secret you've kept bottled inside that drives you to constantly make restitution, Kent?"

CHAPTER SIXTEEN

Restitution?" Kent laughed, a harsh bitter sound in the silence of the night. "I wish I could. How many times I've stared at those stars and prayed that I could somehow go back, not to that night but before that. If only—"

"You can't do that, Kent," Georgia said. "You have today. Maybe tomorrow. Yesterday's gone."

He hung his head. "I know."

Her fingers slid away from his. He didn't blame her. When she heard the truth, she'd probably want to run as fast and as far from him as she could get. His hopes for a relationship died.

Then her palm cupped his cheek, and she nudged his head up to face her. "Just tell me. I'll listen, I promise."

He twisted his head, pressed a kiss into her palm. Then he drew a deep cleansing breath and began the horrible story. "I was so proud of her."

"Christa?"

"Of course." He smiled, remembering. "She was so much younger than me, the most beautiful child I'd ever seen. We spoiled her, I suppose. It was so easy to do, and she never took advantage. I doted on her as much as my parents did. My father's last words to me were about her. 'Take care of your sister.' So that's what I tried to do."

"You raised her?"

He nodded. "After our parents died, yes. From the time she was thirteen. We got along so well together. She aced everything in school, joined the glee club, the band, and then the swimming club. Just as a summer hobby at first. Right after she finished her swimming lessons."

Kent felt Georgia shift. "You didn't teach her?"

He shook his head. "No. A friend of hers had a pool. She taught her the rudiments, but Christa insisted on knowing more, always more. She finished the levels sooner than she was supposed to, but nobody could say she hadn't earned it." He tried to modify the pride that seeped through. "She was like a fish. Everything about the water intrigued her, but speed swimming was her favorite."

"I suppose she has the medals to prove it." Georgia's nudge encouraged him to continue.

"My parents' insurance paid for me to go to college. There was some left, but I wanted Christa to have an education too, and I wasn't sure it would be enough for whatever she decided to do. I knew I had to get a good job to pay for all the extras. The coaching, the pool time—it all cost a fortune."

"I can imagine."

She probably did. Georgia had done some training of her own. She'd know how quickly the money drained away.

"When the job here came up, I was delighted. Not just because I'd always wanted to run a kids' camp but because I'd be able to use my thesis to map out the steps I'd take to make such a camp first in its class."

Georgia was frowning.

He forced the next words out. "I'd factored in the money, you see. Christa would have all the pool time she'd need, and it wouldn't cost a dime. If you want the truth, I was hoping that maybe she'd take to camp life and we could make our names together. I was a little worried because, other than swimming, she had no plans for the future."

"At her age, that's natural."

He closed his eyes, remembering. "Maybe it is. At first it worked. She loved the kids, loved teaching them, loved thinking up new and better ways to do things."

"She is analytical, Kent. She gets a picture in her mind and then hunts out the ways and means to do it."

Kent nodded. "I know. It happened that winter. I was taking my last few classes and she was in training. She won every meet she'd ever entered. Her coach said someone important had seen her race. People started talking Olympics and gold medal. I wasn't so sure it was possible and I didn't want her to be hurt, but Christa had no doubts. She knew she could do it."

"But then you came back here."

"Yes. And she fell in love. Or at least that's what she called it. The gold, the camp—she was willing to throw it all away for a punk with no goals." Even now he could hardly believe how easily she'd been willing to give up on her dream.

"So you stepped in."

"I had to. I'd promised my dad, and I intended to keep my promise to him." He almost smiled at the stupidity of it. "I suppose I was jealous."

"Probably. So she rebelled and had her accident. I know all that." Georgia stood in front of him, hands on her hips. "What else, Kent? Tell me all of it."

He licked his lips. *Please understand.* "That night—she slipped, turned, hit her back on the diving board, and fell into the water." He heard the cold emotionless tones of his own voice and wondered where the control had come from. "I couldn't believe it. I expected her to roll over and scream at me, but she didn't. She wasn't moving.

I raced across the compound, wasted time searching for my key because she'd locked herself in. Then I realized she hadn't moved at all, that she was still floating facedown in the water."

He couldn't go on. To do so would be to throw away every connection he'd made with Georgia; everything they'd shared would be tainted by his confession. But to stop now would exclude her, just as he'd done with Christa.

Suddenly he realized that he loved Georgia as he'd never cared for anyone in his life. He wanted to know everything about her, to be there when she was afraid, to help her get past the hard parts. He wanted a life, a future with her.

Did she want the same? If she did—and he fervently hoped she did—they'd never have it unless she knew the truth about him, all the truth. Secrets had poisoned his relationship with Christa. He wouldn't allow them to ruin what he might have with Georgia.

"She was lying there in the water, and I couldn't reach her." There, he'd said it. The words came faster now. "I knew there was only a certain window of time in which a person can go without oxygen before the damage is irreversible, but it was slipping away and I couldn't get to her."

"But—"

He hurried on, anxious to get it said. He couldn't look at her, couldn't watch the horror on Georgia's face, so he stared into the fire. "I hung on the end of the diving board as far as I could. She was too far away. Finally I remembered the pole. I got it, snagged her suit, and dragged her closer. It seemed like hours before she was close enough that I could turn her over."

"You couldn't swim."

The quiet condemnation of those whispered words hit him like stones from an angry mob. "No." Admitting this cost his pride, but what did pride matter now? He pushed on. "I grew up scared stiff of the water after a kid named Billy Edwards dunked me. I was seven." He dragged a hand through his hair, pulling at it as if to ease the pain that radiated from his soul. "Every single time she got in the pool, every time we went to a meet, every time she took a header off those blocks, I cringed inside. I could feel what it was like not to breathe, to have the water choke you until you thought you'd die, and I relived it every time."

"Oh, Kent." Georgia moved toward him.

He held up a hand. "Wait. I have to finish." She nodded and he drew enough air to fill his lungs, hoping it would release the tension that held his neck in an iron grip. "So that night Christa was lying there and I knew she was dying, that she didn't have any oxygen, that she wasn't breathing. But I didn't know what to do."

He looked at her then. "Do you understand? I was supposed to look after her. I was in charge, and I didn't know what to do!" He gulped, then shuddered at the memory.

"Go on."

"Fortunately, Fred had seen the whole thing. He sent one of the lifeguards to me while he called the ambulance. If that boy hadn't done artificial respiration—" he cringed—"she could have died! I stood there, looking down at my beautiful sister and knew that it would be my fault if anything was wrong. I was in charge. I was supposed to protect her. Instead I drove her too hard, and she hurt herself. And all I could do was stand and watch."

"But I've seen you, Kent. You do laps every day."

"She was unconscious for three days. I made a promise then that if God spared her, I would *never* allow that to happen to another person again. Nobody was going to die in a pool because of me." He breathed out on a rush of remembrance. "In between visiting hours, I took swimming lessons." He grimaced. "I failed beginners' class four times because I couldn't stand my head under the water."

"You never told me that, Kent. Not once in all those long days and nights. You never explained." Christa sat in the doorway, tears pouring down her cheeks. "I thought I'd embarrassed you, ruined your dreams, your career, your goals. I thought you resented giving up everything for me, and I felt so terrible. I didn't understand why you would do it. I never imagined you felt guilty, that you couldn't swim."

"You . . ." He couldn't come up with the words.

"How helpless it must have made you feel to see me lying there and not be able to help. And then to see me in that bed, sitting there day after day. Knowing you, I can imagine the guilt that festered." Christa's quiet sobs broke the night calm. "But it wasn't your fault. It was mine. I'm sorry, Kent. I'm so sorry."

He had to go to her, gather her into his arms, and rock her as he'd done when she was still a tiny girl who looked adoringly at her older brother, one she'd thought could do no wrong.

"Oh, Christa, I'm so sorry. I've let you feel guilty when it was my fault. But I couldn't tell you. I was afraid you'd be ashamed of me. It wasn't you I was trying to avoid all this time; it was me. My conscience. If only I could have jumped in and saved you."

They wept together, gradually shedding the past with all its hurts and pain.

Christa held on tight, hugging him as she shushed his condemnation. "I could never be ashamed of you, Kent. You're my big brother. I love you."

I love you.

The words were doubly precious now because for so long he'd yearned to hear Christa say them as she had before—when she'd looked up to him as the big brother she adored.

"I love you too, Christa. I'm sorry I failed you, that I didn't trust you enough to forgive me for not helping you when you most needed me. I'm sorry I couldn't keep my promise to Dad."

"You did keep it, Kent. I'm alive. Dad would be proud."

She forgave him and he forgave himself. At last it was as if the chasm between them had been bridged, the past put where it belonged. Once more it felt as if they were a team, ready to face the future together.

"Dad would have said that something good will come out of this,"

Christa murmured, resting her head on Kent's shoulder. "I don't know what, but I'm certain that God can make things work together for good." She smiled at Georgia. "Our Bible study reminded me of Dad."

"Did it?" Georgia was staring at Kent.

Kent brushed away his tears, feeling no shame for them. They were the kind that cleansed, renewed. He wished he could do the same for Georgia, that she, too, could be free of her past.

"Maybe this is a good time to think about what those good things could be." Georgia glanced at Christa, lifted one eyebrow. "Any ideas?"

"Not yet. I have to think about it a bit more. I don't want to leave here though. Not right away at least. I'm kind of intrigued with the idea of Camp Hope as a place for disadvantaged kids to find healing."

"So that means you'll be around for a while." Georgia winked at Christa. "You have any problems with that, Kent?"

"I don't know." He tested it out, found relief in thoughts of staying here, watching Christa's ideas come to fruition. In fact, he had a few ideas of his own he'd always wanted to try out, all of them including Georgia. "I can't imagine what the future holds. I may not be around if head office decides I should move on."

His sweet Georgia, however, was a little more pragmatic. "Oh, for goodness' sake! You belong here, Kent. This is where you shine. You have a knack for creating a place that welcomes anyone who steps through the gates. I recognized it the first day I came here."

"I do?" He did?

"Of course. Who realized Ralphie the brat was a problem child because he couldn't read? Who spent hours talking to a boy who was afraid God wanted him to become a missionary and was scared stiff about telling his parents?" Georgia spread her hands. "This is what you do, Kent. You're not a pencil pusher. You're not an office man. You do your best work right here, one-on-one, with whomever God sends your way. Do you know how rare a gift that is in today's world? After hours of physical labor, not everyone is willing to take the time or spend the energy listening because they care about the soul of a child."

"But Christa—"

"Is a big girl who needs to grow up and decide what she wants to do with her life." Christa grinned at him as he eased her out of his arms into her wheelchair. "And I will, but I think I'll need a little time. And if you two don't kick me out, my old room to do it. Is that okay?"

"More than okay," he said, his heart filled with gratefulness.

"So you're going to stay on here?" Georgia fixed him with what he privately termed her granite look—sharp, hard, and piercing. "You're not going to run away?"

"I didn't think I was running away," he muttered. "But I did rather like the idea of building camps around the model I'd constructed."

"Forget the model!" Georgia threw up her hands. "Don't you get it yet? This is hands-on work that can only be done by you. It doesn't follow any preconceived pattern. That's why you're good at it. You meet people where they are and you go from there."

"You really think so?" He felt bemused by her generous praise.

"Of course she does. Because Georgia does the same thing. Sees a need, fills it. You two make a good pair. What one doesn't think of, the other does. A matched set." Christa winked at him, then turned to Georgia. "But of course, you'll be leaving. Heading back to your life in Calgary. What will you do—go back to the hospital? That would certainly be fulfilling."

What was Christa doing? Kent didn't want Georgia to go anywhere. He needed her right here with him. There was no way he could do it all himself. Georgia was the one who kept him on track, helped him assess the value of what they were doing, and filled in his weak points.

"I suppose you'll reopen your apartment, won't you? That will certainly be a change from living out here. I don't know if I could do without the trees and the openness of this country. Still, it's your life. You have to decide." Christa yawned, patted a hand over her mouth. "I'm going to bed. Good night, brother dear. I love you."

He leaned down, brushed his lips against her hair, and thanked the God who could restore for this night of reparation.

"Those are the sweetest words I've heard in a very long time," he whispered in her ear.

"You should try repeating them," she whispered back. He opened his mouth obediently, but Christa interjected. "Not to me, silly. Look around. I'm sure you can think of someone else you want to say that to."

He froze, then opted for humor. "Right now I'm saying it to you. I love you." He hugged her. "Now go to bed and stop sticking your nose into other people's business."

She giggled, whirring away as she wished Georgia good night.

Turning, Kent saw that Georgia had resumed her seat and was now staring into the fire. He sat beside her and took her hand in his. "Thank you, Georgia."

She looked up at him for a moment, then shook her head. "I didn't do anything but encourage you to tell the truth."

"Maybe. But suddenly I feel like a load has been lifted from my shoulders. It's a good feeling."

"I'm glad. Christa's tougher than she looks. You should have explained to her long ago."

"I guess I should have." Before things had progressed from bad to worse between them, he realized. But Christa wasn't his primary concern at the moment. "Georgia, a moment ago we were speaking about your leaving." He took a deep breath. "Do you have to? I mean, you've become such an integral part of Camp Hope that I can't imagine not seeing you every day."

"But—" she peered at him, a helpless look on her face—"I have to go. The summer camps are finished next week."

"Yes, but we have things planned for fall."

"You want me to cook for the fall camps? But I thought—"

He shook his head, refocused. "I'm not saying this well, and I'm sorry." *Please, God, if this isn't right, stop me.* "What I really want to say . . . Georgia, I love you. I've never said that to any woman, and it's a little nerve-racking, but it's the truth. I'd like it very much if you wanted to stay here with me, help me build Camp Hope into what it could be. I'm . . . I'm asking you to marry me."

"Marry you?"

The shock in her voice made him wince. But at least she hadn't run away.

"You were right, you know. This is where I belong. I realize that now. And you were the reason for that. I think this is where you belong too. Together we could make something of those plans we had, turn them into reality. I can't imagine another summer here without you to talk to, to bounce ideas off, to depend on to set me straight when I get offtrack."

Still she said nothing.

"Is it too soon, Georgia? Do you need time to think it over?" The rush of words would not be stopped. "Because if that's what it takes, that's what I want you to have. In my own mind I'm certain that you're the only woman I will ever love. But I want you to be certain too. Are you?"

⟫⬥⟨

Was she?

Georgia couldn't think while looking at Kent, so she turned her head and stared into the fire, trying to decipher the truth.

Loving Kent, that wasn't a betrayal of Evan. He'd been her first love, and he still held a special place in her heart. She would always love Evan, but he was part of her past.

Her heart had grown, expanded, changed. At last she faced the truth. Love for Kent had taken root in spite of her attempts to keep him at bay. Time and again she'd told herself she was leaving, that this was a temporary phase, a time and place beyond her reality.

But it had become more than that. Camp Hope had become a place of hope for something she'd never imagined she would feel again—love. She cared about Kent, cared deeply about his future and his dreams—because those dreams had expanded hers. There were a thousand possibilities here that only lacked completion.

What Kent would do with Camp Hope mattered to her, not only because she yearned to see him succeed, but more than that, she longed to be part of his success, to encourage him when money was tight, to be there when he wanted to talk about his problems and share his successes. Together they could expand this camp so it would reach out and comfort those who were hurting, as it had for her. Camp Hope would become a place that would matter, not just now but far into the future after they'd gone.

Strangely enough, it was Evan's words that flooded her mind now: *"I like the idea that their legacy will live on because they've laid up treasure where it counts."*

He'd been speaking about her parents. But it was every bit as true of him with his legacy of the air-conditioning as it could be of her.

If she stayed.

"Georgia? You've been quiet an awfully long time."

"Have I?" She searched his eyes. They were dark with concern, that mysterious green holding a hint of uncertainty. "I'm sorry."

"Don't be sorry. Just tell me I'm not the only one with these feelings. Please?" That lopsided grin was back, though not as full of teasing as usual.

"Kent, I . . ."

"I was afraid of this." He pulled back, crossed his arms over his chest, and stood. "I'm sorry. I shouldn't have said anything. I didn't want to pressure you. Let's just forget it, all right?"

He took two steps back. Georgia saw the pain flicker across his face, though he tried to hide it. "I . . . um . . . I think I'll say good night. It's been a long day."

"Will you please stop talking and listen to me!" Exasperated, Georgia grabbed his arm and tugged him down into the chair next to hers. "I'm trying to tell you something."

"And I'm trying to save you the embarrassment." He pulled his arm free. "You don't have to break it down, Georgia. I get it, okay?"

"No you don't." Frustrated beyond words, Georgia leaned forward and pressed her lips against his, shocked by how much she wanted to kiss him.

He froze for about two seconds. Then his arms were around her, and she snuggled close, his lips caressing hers. It was a long kiss, full of questions and answers. Georgia slipped her arms around his waist, relishing the strength that enfolded her, a promise of protection. Content to drift in the magic of the moment, she held him, feeling his fingers threading through her hair and easing it free of the clip she'd used.

Oh, God, is this of You? Is this why You brought me here? Please, don't let me mess up. Don't let me make a mistake that will hurt him.

Dare she dream?

Maybe she could have a full new life—if she dared.

"I care about you too, Kent," she whispered. "I care so much."

"Thank you for saying that." He cupped her cheeks in his hands. "Do you know how many times I've dreamed of this, then awakened to find it wasn't true, wanted so badly to go back to sleep, to live the dream again?"

Georgia shook her head, amazed to hear these words from him— the most self-sufficient man she'd known. He needed her. "This thing between us, it's like those wild grapevines in the woods, twining itself around my heart until I couldn't get free of the thought of you. Actually I don't want to be free."

"If you can't stay here," he said, his lips millimeters from hers, "I'll understand. We can ask God to use us somewhere else."

She brushed her fingers across his lips. "God wants you here. I've never been as certain of anything as I am of that. It would be wrong of me to try and change His leading, even if I wanted to." She saw his surprise and nodded. "That's the surprising thing—I don't want to, Kent."

"You want to stay here?" he asked.

She nodded. "I've seen the difference this place makes—*has* made—in my own life. I don't think He's finished with me yet, but I . . . I want to be part of it. Whatever it turns out to be."

He hugged her tightly. "Thank You, God."

When he finally drew away, Georgia drew deep breaths of air into her starved lungs, delighted to find that her passion matched his.

"It's late," he whispered, his hand smoothing the tendrils he'd mussed. "You've been up since dawn and you should get some sleep. Come on; I'll walk you to your cabin." He stood, then held out his hand.

Accepting it, Georgia let him draw her upward. His gaze was warm, tender. She could have stayed wrapped in it forever. But he was right—it was late. And though they had no camp until Sunday night, and she wasn't scheduled to make breakfast tomorrow morning, she would not sleep in. Habits were hard to break.

As they walked slowly through the darkened grounds, Kent whistled a tuneless sound that bore no resemblance to the love song she knew he was imitating. She only hoped he didn't wake someone. Where the yard lights didn't provide enough illumination, Kent waved his flashlight. From time to time he tugged her close, pretending there was something in her way, but using the opportunity to kiss her. Georgia made no protest. She couldn't. She wanted him to kiss her, to reassure her that this love was real, that she hadn't dreamed it all.

When at last they came to her cabin, Georgia was breathless and giggling and happier than she'd been for many months.

"At some point before too much longer, you and I are going to talk about getting married," Kent warned her, his hands resting on her shoulders. "And it's not going to be a long discussion."

"Yes, boss," she teased, saluting.

"I mean it."

"Yes, boss."

He tilted his head to one side and frowned. "Are you always going to be this amenable?"

"That depends on you." She grinned, stood on tiptoe to kiss his nose, allowed one last embrace, then pulled away to unlock her door.

"Good night, Kent," she whispered, knowing her face telegraphed everything in her heart. *Beloved.*

"I love you, Georgia."

She smiled, blew him a kiss, and closed the door.

Outside she heard the low timbre of his voice through the thick plank door. "Good night, sweetheart."

She couldn't say it yet. But soon, God willing. Soon she would have the courage to tell him what he wanted to hear. It was just a matter of time.

———◈———

The flames were white-hot. Their tongues darted out to lick up the space between her and Kent. Her skin felt parched and dried by the heat, yet she couldn't reach him.

"Move back!" she screamed, trying to make him see that danger lay all around.

But Kent didn't see, didn't notice that the sap-loaded evergreens around him were incinerated like tinder, that the air whooshed up around them as flames cut off his escape route.

"Kent!" She had to stop it, had to keep it from happening again. But how? They were alone. There was no one to help, no one to call on, no one to stop the inferno. He was going to die!

A tree crashed to the ground, flaring as the wind sucked the flames closer to him. Now sparks littered the shoulders of his blue flannel shirt like tiny stars. Smoke, thick and white, billowed up, obscuring his face for long minutes. The wind was blowing the hot breath of the monster closer toward him, eating up the distance like a raging tiger. It was all around him now, fiery orange fingers tugging at the hem of his jeans.

Not again. Please, dear God, don't let it happen again.

But it was. And there was nothing she could do to stop it. Once more the wind whipped the clouds of smoke. This time she could see only his face, agony distorting his features. Then the fire totally consumed its prey and Kent was gone.

"No!"

She woke, sitting straight up in bed, the repugnance of it far worse than before, still clinging to her though she fought to shake it off.

Then she remembered.

She wasn't free to love him; she would only hurt him. Besides, she'd loved once. And she'd lost everything. What if the dream was a vision—a foretelling of the future? What if God once again took away one whom she loved?

She wouldn't live through it. Georgia knew that as clearly as she knew the day and the hour. It had taken every ounce of strength she possessed to fight her way free of the depression, to leave the familiar and venture outside her safe place. She could not do it again.

Georgia poured herself a drink of water from the carafe she kept on her dresser. As she sipped, she saw the orange soda can, still waiting to be returned to the recycle bin. A shiver of fear tickled up her spine, a feeling of powerlessness, of evil.

"Please, God. Please." She whispered the words over and over until a measure of control returned.

With shaking fingers she checked the door, ensured the dead bolt was in place. Then she dug around in her purse until she found her cell phone. She clicked it on, breathed a sigh of relief that it was working.

For the next four hours, Georgia huddled on her bed, wide-awake as she rehearsed her speech. Camp Hope had been a nice dream, a temporary place to regroup. But Georgia would not find peace here.

It was time to make plans to leave.

———◆◆———

He trod the familiar paths one last time, just to check, to ensure that nothing would alter his goal. His plans were made. There would be no going back.

Yes, the others had all left for the weekend. Only the three remained.

Tomorrow night, under the cover of darkness, before anyone returned, while the crippled one lay asleep, he would mete out his justice. If the man Kent got in the way, he would pay also. There was no other choice.

At last he would finish what had started more than two years ago. Then he would leave this place with its talk of God and mercy and forgiveness. Perhaps God could forgive; he could not. Would not.

He hoped for a sense of peace, of relief in knowing that it was almost over. He felt none of that. But it would come. Later.

She would pay for her sins. When she realized that he'd caused her pain, stolen from her as she'd stolen from him, she'd understand why she had to die. Then he would be free. He would go on with his life, knowing that justice had been served.

It will not bring Justine back, a voice inside his head taunted.

Nothing could.

CHAPTER SEVENTEEN

She couldn't leave—not now!

Last night he'd tasted heaven. Now, to have it grabbed away—
Kent tried everything he could think of, prayed harder than he'd
ever prayed, even neglected some much needed chores to spend
a few precious hours in the chapel asking God to make Georgia
reconsider.

The camp was empty, virtually deserted except for Christa,
himself, and Georgia. The counselors had left last night to spend the
weekend in the city and to watch a play. Fred and Ralna had gone
with them, claiming that they needed to pick up some of Ralna's
heart medication. It sounded good, but Kent knew Fred had play tick-
ets in his pocket. Fred loved a good comedy. John had left with Rick
for his doctor's appointment.

He and Georgia could have spent all day together. In fact, Kent
had wasted time this morning trying to help her understand that
God's plan for them was still unfolding. That what she feared might
never happen.

"I want to be here with you, no matter what. Don't you understand? That's what love is! We face whatever happens together. And we depend on God."

"You don't understand. I can't do it again, Kent." Her eyes had glassed with tears. "I care about you, truly. But someone is behind these things that keep happening to me. You've said it; Rick has said it. And in my heart, I think I've always known it. I've been here for months, and we haven't come close to catching him. Who knows how long this could go on?"

He'd tried to reason with her, but she'd shaken her head. "I should never have said what I did last night."

"Why? Wasn't it honest? The truth? Were you lying when you said you cared?" It stung to say it, let alone think it. But he had to ask.

"No." She wouldn't look at him. "I do care about you. And for a time I believed that would be enough. But it's not. That's why I'm leaving. I can't go through that kind of loss again, Kent. Not ever again." Her voice dropped to a whisper. "The next time I might not survive."

There was no argument he could offer to counter the wealth of pain he heard in her voice. He could only imagine the grief and suffering of knowing your child and your husband had been taken. Doug had provided some insight into the depths of her despair, of the treatment she'd had, of her near hospitalization.

But oh how he wanted her to say that she believed in him, trusted him, would cling to him. And then he remembered that this wasn't about him—it was about her faith. Hadn't she all but told him that when she'd first arrived?

Week after week she'd puzzled through her understanding of God—the one she blamed for taking her loved ones. As he'd watched, listened to her with Christa, found himself the object of her affections, he'd come to believe she'd resolved that issue, but last night's nightmare had reminded her too clearly.

"If we were together, if I stayed here, and then God took you as He took Evan, I'd die, Kent," she'd said, one golden tendril caught in her golden lashes. "I have no reserves, nothing left to sustain me. I feel like I'm taking baby steps, barely walking, getting through the days without looking ahead. I just . . . I can't do it. And it's not the way to start a marriage."

"But—"

She'd shaken her head. "Marriage is for partners, strong partners. I would feel like you were propping me up, always watching out for me. You and I both know you'd soon grow tired of that. You are a strong person. You've had to care for Christa and run this camp. I'm a wimp. I'm afraid to trust, afraid to depend on the God who let me down so badly. I know that's wrong, I know it's stupid, and I know it isn't worthy of a Christian. In my head, I know all that."

She waited a moment, but Kent remained silent. She needed to say this so he waited.

"But in my heart—" tears washed down her cheeks in rivers, and one hand touched her chest—"in here, I'm just hanging on by my fingertips, waiting for the next catastrophe to happen. I don't want to feel like that, but I do. Knowing that, I can't stay here, be with you. I won't marry you. I'm sorry."

Every word was like a knife, but Kent had clung to the promise he'd claimed long ago. He made a decision in that moment to demonstrate his own faith in God. "Listen to me, Georgia. 'For God has not given us a spirit of fear, but of power and of love and of a sound mind.' That's His promise to you and to me and to all of those who turn to Him. He will be there for us."

She had gulped, as if to speak, but he shushed her. "If you have to leave here, if you can't stay, I'll understand. Because my faith is big enough for both of us. You didn't come here by chance. God led you. Christa's accident was awful and hard to get through, but God can use that. I don't understand why Evan and Tyler had to die. I probably never will. But I have faith that God has already and will continue to use their deaths to further His own plans—plans that you and I know nothing of."

"What do you mean, has already?" she'd sniffed.

He'd held her hands in his, delighting in the soft, pliable skin, the smooth nails, the tender strength. "Because you were the air-conditioner benefactor, weren't you?" He smiled at her surprised look.

"How did you know?"

"You appeared and we had cool. It wasn't hard to put two and two together." He lifted the tendril from her eyes, smoothed it back. "And that's only one small thing God has used from your time here to impact the world for good."

"You think God took Evan and Tyler so I could . . ." Her eyes were like saucers at the thought of it.

"So He could use you?" He shook his head. "No. What I am saying is that something bad happened. But God can take bad and turn it into good if we let Him."

"Maybe." She looked unconvinced. "How do you mean?"

"Well, think about it. Either God is in control or He's not. If you know something about the qualities of God, you know that everything that happens to us passes through His hands. That doesn't mean He causes it. It means He's a miracle God who can use bad for good."

"I can't stay, Kent." Her voice had brimmed with pain. "Please don't ask me to."

"I'm not going to. I'm going to pray that God will show us His way in this. Because I do think He has a plan for us, Georgia. We just have to wait to see it." He'd leaned down, brushed her temple with his lips, then smiled. "Maybe if we both pray, we'll get a quicker answer."

She nodded, but her face was sad.

He'd wanted to rant and rave, to argue until she saw his side. But Kent knew he couldn't fight her fear no matter what *he* said. It was too big, had grown bigger because of the things that had happened here. He'd done his best. Now it was up to God.

"I'm sorry," she'd whispered. "I never wanted to hurt you."

"I know."

It had cost him a lot to walk away, to finish the chores he'd begun, to ready the camp for the final summer session. Several times he simply stopped, closed his eyes, and talked to his heavenly Father about it.

Christa called him for lunch on his radio, but it was a silent meal among the three of them. His sister seemed to sense the undercurrent running between him and Georgia. She sent surreptitious glances to both of them, commented on the fresh rolls and wonderful fruit salad, and babbled about life in general until Kent finally excused himself, pushed away from the table, and left.

Someone had forgotten to put away a volleyball. Kent grabbed it, slammed it into the big net that contained the others. But he found no relief in the action.

Last night he'd stayed awake, planning, dreaming, celebrating. Too soon, it seemed. Today, as quickly as his joy had arrived, it was gone, torn away by bad memories and fear of the future.

Believe.

The voice inside his head was quiet, clear, and definite. He knew the advice was heaven-sent. The time had come to put his money where his mouth was. Either he believed God would work it out, or he didn't.

"What is faith? It is the confident assurance that what we hope for is going to happen. It is the evidence of things we cannot yet see. God gave His approval to people in days of old because of their faith. By faith we understand that the entire universe was formed at God's command, that what we now see did not come from anything that can be seen."

The Scriptures his counseling staff had chosen for their summer ministry echoed through his mind. How right, how appropriate their selections.

"It is impossible to please God without faith. Anyone who wants to come to Him must believe that there is a God and that He rewards those who sincerely seek Him."

"Without faith," he whispered, ruminating on the words. "It's impossible to please God without faith."

The next step was clear. Georgia's future—and his own—was out of his hands. There was only one thing to do: trust God, believe that He would work it out. Kent had been dispensing advice about trust all summer. It was time to walk the walk.

——≫•◆•≪——

With still only the three of them for dinner, Georgia had little to occupy her afternoon. The time weighed heavily on her. Once she would have sought out Kent or Christa, but all that had changed.

One week more—that's all the time she had left at Camp Hope. Then she'd be gone.

How would she fill her days? What reason would she have for rising? There would be no crafts to plan, no doughnuts to make, no children needing her to reassure them that they'd feel better in the morning. In fact, there would be no one. No one at all.

That latter thought halted her walk past the chapel. She'd been in here before, of course. Many times. But today was different. Today no one watched her enter or saw her sink onto a hard cedar bench. No one knew or cared that she simply sat there and stared at the big carved cross at the front. Now there was nothing to block out the confusing whirl of her mind and the unanswered questions that would not be silenced.

Kent had made it sound like a choice—that he *chose* to believe that God would do what was right. Was that what she needed to do—to ask Him to help her and then wait to see what He did? Was that faith?

It sounded too simple.

And too hard.

Wait for what, the next bombshell?

Round and round she chased the argument, growing more frustrated by the moment, until she caught a glimpse of several posters laid out across the front of the chapel, ready to be hung as the theme for next week's teen camp.

She stood, walked closer, read the words. *"We are pressed on every side by troubles, but we are not crushed and broken. We are perplexed, but we don't give up and quit. We are hunted down, but God never abandons us. We get knocked down, but we get up again and keep going. Through suffering, these bodies of ours constantly share in the death of Jesus so that the life of Jesus may also be seen in our bodies. . . . That is why we never give up. Though our bodies are dying, our spirits are being renewed every day. For our present troubles are quite small and won't last very long. Yet they produce for us an immeasurably great glory that will last forever! So we don't look at the troubles we can see right now; rather, we look forward to what we have not yet seen. For the troubles we see will soon be over, but the joys to come will last forever."*

"Don't look at the troubles we can see, but look forward to what we cannot see," she whispered, allowing the words to percolate deep. "God never leaves us."

Over and over she read the verses, imprinting them on her mind. And each time, a new truth seemed to glimmer from a particular passage.

It seemed too personal to simply be a verse that anyone could read. The counselors had chosen this particular Scripture—was that part of the plan Kent insisted God had? Was this God that everyone but her seemed to know so well—and was He communicating to her?

She sat down on the edge of the dais, awed at the thought. Had God really arranged this especially for her? More importantly, was she correct in understanding that God actually wanted her to respond to Him, that all she needed to do was believe?

"We are pressed on every side by troubles, but we are not crushed and broken."

"That's me, God," she said softly, her eyes on the cross. "Troubles all around. I know I haven't talked to You for a long time. I'm not sure I even know what to say now. But I'm here. Waiting."

The waver of gentle calm dropped over her spirit like a featherlight duvet, chasing away the shadows. As petals of a flower unfurl, she could feel her heart opening to accept that longed-for comfort.

"I don't understand what any of this means, God. I thought—" she stopped, cleared her throat, began again—"I thought You took Evan and Tyler from me, that You were punishing me. And I didn't understand. Can You help me understand?"

It felt funny to speak aloud in the silence of this place, but somehow it was easier to speak from her heart if she actually said the words aloud, like a conversation with someone you knew, someone who didn't care if you made mistakes.

"I love Kent and I know he loves me. But I'm so afraid."

"We get knocked down, but we get up again and keep going."

"If my coming to Camp Hope was part of Your plan, as Kent keeps saying, then I guess You know how to work this out for me. So I'm asking You—please, let me stay. Let me learn more about You. Make something good out of this."

When she paused, she felt the drag of her old nemesis fear and knew she had to get rid of it. "I'm afraid, God. Not for me but for Kent. I don't want him to suffer because of me."

She made her decision. "So here's where I put it on the line, God. I'm making the choice to believe that You are good, that You haven't left me hanging, that You are at work for me, that You hear and respond." The words sounded foolish in her own ears, but Georgia ignored that. "I'm putting my faith in You, God. Please hear me. Please answer."

Georgia was a little worried when she opened her eyes and found that nothing she could see had changed. But then she reread the words. *"We look forward to what we have not yet seen."*

Words were one thing. Now she had to get her mind focused on what she couldn't see. God was there. The problem in communicating wasn't Him; it was her. It would take practice to keep turning to

God, to keep believing. No one knew how long it would take for God to work out the situation, or if He'd work it out the way she wanted.

But she had a hunch that God wasn't interested in half measures. Either she had faith in Him or she didn't. As long as she did her part, she could depend on Him to care for her. The knowledge was a sure, steady fire deep within.

She rose, walked to the back of the church, and tugged open the door. The slant of the sun told her that it was late, far later than she'd realized, so she hurried across to the dining room, determined to hold her thoughts close until she'd sorted through them. Her decision was between God and her. Until she left Camp Hope, she'd savor each moment while she waited for God to teach her.

"Hey!" Kent came racing across the compound, his face strained. "I've been looking for you. I was worried when I couldn't find you anywhere."

"Sorry." She smiled at him. "I was in the chapel—doing some thinking. I guess I lost track of time."

"You want me to make dinner?"

She made a face at him. "Ah, no. Thanks. I want you to make another campfire for us to sit around. I've got a picnic all ready."

"Are you sure? Your nightmares last night—"

She shook her head. "That was last night. Make the fire, Kent. I'll start hauling stuff over."

He studied her for several moments, his eyes swirling with doubt. Finally he nodded, turned on his heel, and strode toward his house.

It wasn't until she'd loaded her supplies into the basket that Georgia realized the kitchen door hadn't been locked. Nor had the cooler.

She checked each container she'd been about to put into the basket. As far as she could tell, they all seemed normal. Everything in the cooler looked as she'd left it. With only one full week of camp to go, she'd deliberately kept her stock small, and just yesterday she'd cleaned the entire cooler from top to bottom. It was easy to take inventory. Nothing seemed awry. Relieved but still curious, Georgia repacked the basket.

A few minutes later, Kent walked through the back door. "Ready?"

She nodded. "Kent, were you in here this afternoon?"

"Yes. Why?"

"The door wasn't locked. Nor the cooler door."

His face blanched. "Is anything—?"

"It looks fine," she said. "I checked."

"I wasn't in the cooler." His eyes darkened to a troubled eddy of turquoise. "I was in the pantry."

They turned their heads in unison, saw that the pantry padlock hung secure.

"That was about three. I know I locked the door then because my key stuck. I had an awful time trying to get the thing out. It's funny—I never had a problem with it before."

"Did you come back?"

He nodded, his face sheepish. "When I couldn't find you anywhere, I wondered if you'd gotten locked inside. You weren't here and I was a little frantic. Maybe I forgot to lock it again."

"Maybe." She waited for him to pick up the basket, then followed him out, locking the door securely behind her.

It could have happened just as he'd said. She had no reason to doubt it. Except that Kent was a creature of habit. He had developed a routine, and in the time that she'd been here, Georgia had seldom seen him deviate from it.

Christa was by the fire when they arrived, poking a stick into it and watching the blue-red sparks shoot upward. "Hi, Georgia." Christa smiled, but her thoughts seemed elsewhere. She glanced at Kent. "Do you know what time John is supposed to return tomorrow?"

He looked surprised by the question. "I have no idea. I suppose it depends on what the doctors tell him, on the tests they want. Why?" He frowned as if he too noticed something unusual in her manner.

"It's nothing. I just wish he were here, that's all." She poked the fire again.

"Christa?" Georgia squatted in front of her. "Something's bothering you. Please tell us."

"I saw . . . well . . . I *thought* I saw someone out here this afternoon when Kent was working in the office."

The three of them looked around the yard.

Georgia saw Kent glance at his sister. "Probably shadows," he said. Georgia knew he was anxious to reassure Christa that she was safe.

"In the middle of the afternoon?" Apparently Christa wasn't buying his attempt at reassurance. She shook her head. "I was sitting over there reading." She pointed toward her usual spot on the screen porch. "It was hot and I kind of dozed off. Something woke me up. A squeak, like a door opening, I think. I'm almost positive I saw someone go into the toolshed."

"It was probably me." Kent blushed. "I broke something in the office and I needed a hammer."

Christa frowned, seemed to reconsider. "Have you changed clothes since then?"

He shook his head, glancing down at his worn jeans and dust-covered boots. "No."

"Then it wasn't you. The person I saw wore black. I don't think he knew he'd been seen." Her eyes were huge with fear. "I thought maybe . . ."

Georgia hoped Kent would call his police friend after Christa had gone to bed. Then the two men could go over the area inch by inch at first light. Until then, she knew Christa would be safe as long as her brother was nearby.

"There's nobody out here now but us, Christa. So let's enjoy our picnic," Kent said.

And they tried. But it seemed as if a pall hung over the camp. No doubt everyone was tired from the night before. Of course, that wasn't the only reason. Georgia felt the thin line of tension swimming between her and the other two. Kent had no doubt explained to Christa about what had happened between them this morning, because Christa no longer made her teasing remarks. In fact, she barely spoke at all.

So they sat in the silence of the evening and watched the fire as the rising wind whipped the flames into a fury.

"You missed your swim today." Kent knocked the pile of half-eaten logs down, lowering the fire so it became mostly coals.

"Yes." Georgia peered upward, noticed the clouds skimming across the sky. "It's really cooling off. I wonder if we'll get rain."

He too looked up, watching as the moon ducked into hiding. "I don't know."

That was the thing—no one knew what would happen tomorrow. Except God.

"It's almost the end of summer," Christa whispered. "Soon everything will change again. I wish—" She didn't finish the sentence, choosing instead to swing her chair toward the ramp. "I'm going to bed. Good night, Georgia. Kent?"

"I'll do one more round and then I'll be there, Christa."

"Good night." Georgia watched her maneuver the ramp, listened as the bang of the screen door reverberated through the silent forest. "I think I'll go to bed too. Tomorrow everyone will be back. It's bound to be busy."

He nodded, then walked beside her until they reached her little cabin. "Georgia?"

"Yes?" She faced him, studied his rugged features in the yellow wash of the yard light.

"You said you'd been doing some thinking. In the chapel." He hesitated, and his hand reached out to touch hers. "Does that mean . . . ?"

She shook her head. "Nothing's changed, Kent. I still feel I have to leave here at the end of next week. I'm carrying a lot of baggage from the past, and I need to deal with that."

He looked so sad she had to offer him some hope. "The good news is that I'm going to trust God to show me His way." She threaded her fingers through his hair until they rested at the back of his neck. "I don't know how everything will work out, Kent. But if God is who and what you say He is, then He knows what's in our hearts. All I know is that my heart will remain here—at Camp Hope." *With you,* she wanted to whisper. But it wasn't the time.

"Okay," he mumbled, his breath whooshing out in a huge sigh. "That's enough for me to hang on to." He lifted her other arm, draped it around his neck, and formed his own circle around her waist.

"God is in control," she heard him whisper just before his lips met hers. He kissed her so tenderly, as if she were infinitely precious, adored, loved beyond words. And she kissed him back, hoping he'd interpret what she was trying to say without words.

At last he drew back, feathered his fingers through her long hair, his eyes on the bouncing curls. "Sleep well, Georgia. I love you more than life."

She touched his cheek, felt his lips graze her palm; then he was gone, striding into the night.

After unlocking the door, she stepped inside and slid the dead bolt home. There was enough light from outside so she didn't turn on the light.

Minutes later, as she lay in bed, she thought about Kent's words. *"More than life."*

She prayed it never came to that.

CHAPTER EIGHTEEN

The wind tore at her, forcing her to use every muscle to keep her chair on the path. Christa fought back, her fears escalating as the shadows around her danced, and whooshing branches swooped overhead like vultures waiting to land. Her biggest fear was reality now, and she was helpless.

In the recesses of her mind she could hear John's voice: *"You're stronger than you think."*

Maybe. But where was Kent?

Once more she stopped, pulled the radio from her pocket, and called him. "Please, Kent. Answer me. I'm afraid. Where are you?"

A few crackles were the only response.

Christa rounded the corner of the dining hall, anxious to get to Georgia. They could search together. But something was wrong. Georgia's cabin sat there, all right, but smoke billowed from it and flames licked at the sides.

"Georgia!" She screamed as loud as she could, but the wind captured her words. A droplet of rain splashed on her face, but it was not enough to drench the hungry fire. She pressed the Forward button down hard, sped her way to Georgia's door, then stopped, knuckles pressed to her mouth.

The door was locked—from the outside.

What did she do now?

"You're stronger than you think."

"Georgia! Wake up, Georgia!"

Overhead the rumble of distant thunder smothered her voice. What to do?

The garden hose lay coiled up beside the dining hall. She rolled her chair over, grabbed the nozzle, and twisted the tap to full. The combination of sprinkling rain and the gushing nozzle made it diffi-cult to negotiate the wet sand, but Christa ignored that and pressed on.

She directed the hose to the door first, where it seemed to make little difference to the devouring flames.

"Georgia—fire!" Over and over she called, praying that her friend had not taken one of the sleeping pills she knew she sometimes used when her nightmares were bad. "Georgia, you've got to get out. Now!" She whacked the end of the hose against the window, smash-ing the glass with the metal end. "Georgia, wake up!"

"Christa?" The groggy voice barely penetrated the howling wind.

"I can't find Kent. Your cabin is on fire. You've got to get out." Christa kept the hose on the wood below the window so when Geor-gia climbed out she would not be burned.

"I can't get the door open."

"It's locked. Someone locked the padlock from the outside. Use the window."

"Locked? I'll have to use the chair to reach the window."

Satisfied that her friend would soon be safe, Christa studied the situation. The rain was a steady shower now. Why didn't it stop the fire? She frowned, moved slightly closer. The wood wasn't on fire— at least not much. The flames were feeding on something else, some-thing that smelled like the gas they used for lawn mowers.

The man she'd seen going into the workshop!

This was no accident. Someone wanted Georgia's cabin to burn.

"Come on, Georgia!" Christa heard a scrabble at the window and looked up. Georgia crouched inside. Then suddenly she was gone. "What's wrong?"

"Nothing. Just getting my pictures." She was back, squeezing through the window. She dropped lightly to the ground. She moved to Christa and wrapped her arms around her. "You saved my life."

Christa held on tight. At least she was no longer alone. Then she remembered Kent. "We have to save the cabin. Quick! Get the fire extinguishers from the office."

"I left my keys—"

"Break the window if you have to! And hurry."

———◆———

Strangely enough, the office was unlocked.

"Kent?"

No one answered.

Georgia grabbed the two extinguishers and raced back across the yard. She handed one to Christa. "You work on the door. I'll do around the bottom. What's that smell?"

"I think it's gas."

She saw the truth in Christa's eyes. Deliberately set. Georgia turned and began spraying, glad that Christa was able to do the same. By the time the canisters were empty, the flames were out.

Christa leaned back in her chair, her eyes on the padlock. "It was deliberate," she whispered. "Someone locked that door on purpose. But why?"

"I don't know." Georgia lifted the metal cylinder and smashed it down on the lock, hitting it over and over again until it finally broke. Images of a house fire from over two years ago replayed through her mind. She glanced at the lock she'd just broken. *I unlocked the door when I came in and put the padlock on my dresser. It's still there. This is a new lock.* Someone had gone to the trouble of finding a new padlock to keep her from escaping.

"Christa."

Christa turned her head and blinked.

Georgia shoved her cabin door open, beckoned. "Come in. We've got to get you in some dry clothes."

Christa made no protest as Georgia helped her put on a long denim skirt and a thick sweater. Then she handed Christa her raincoat. "Put this on," she ordered. "Then we have to find Kent."

"I've been calling him on the radio for ages, but he doesn't answer."

Georgia changed her own clothes as swiftly as she could. "Call him again," she said, tying her soaking hair into a ponytail.

Christa tried, but there was still no response.

"Okay, let's go."

Georgia's thin windbreaker would be little protection against the dashing droplets, but that didn't matter. Kent mattered. Where could he be? What if he'd seen the person who set this fire—no! She couldn't let fear dominate.

Christa was urging her chair over the doorstep.

"Wait a minute," Georgia said. "When did you last talk to him?"

"I was reading in bed. He radioed, said a gate was open, that the horses were out. He was very worried about the damage they could do if they got into the neighbor's fields. Paying for that grain would cost an awful lot." Christa's eyes met hers. "What do we do?"

Reality hit. They were two women, all alone in the camp. If Kent was hurt or unconscious, they had to find him.

"We get help. My cell phone is in here somewhere." Georgia dug through her purse, then remembered that she'd called Doug with it this morning. And left it . . . she rushed toward the night table, opened the drawer. The cell phone lay inside. "Good. Now if it will just work." She flipped it open and stared. Someone had pounded a nail through the receiver. Her phone was useless.

"What's wrong?" Christa's voice edged upward, her fear obvious. "Georgia?"

"It doesn't work." She put the phone back in the drawer, pushed it closed, not wanting to add to Christa's worries. *Someone's been inside my cabin.*

"Stay here. I'll try the office phone." She raced across the now muddy area, shoved the door open, and grabbed the phone off the counter. No dial tone. In Kent's office she had no better luck. Was it deliberate, or part and parcel of this storm and the lightning that now ripped through the sky?

She ran back to her cabin. "Phone's not working there either."

"Could be the lightning."

"Yes." Georgia debated on how much to say. "I could go to the dining hall."

Christa shook her head. "No outside line," she reminded Georgia. "You can only take incoming calls. It's so no one phones long-distance without permission."

Georgia deliberated only a moment, then hunkered down until she was level with Christa. "Listen. I think something's wrong. I think that right now it's important we find Kent."

"So do I." Christa's eyes blazed. "And don't even think about it. I'm going with you. I love him too."

Her defiance was a good sign. Georgia grinned. "Okay. We go."

They managed to travel only about two hundred feet before they both realized it was impossible to continue.

"There's too much rain," Christa yelled over the storm. "My wheels are getting bogged down in the mud, and I'm not strong enough to turn them manually."

Georgia nodded her understanding. "I could push."

Christa shook her head. "Takes too long," she puffed. "Think of something else."

All of Georgia's thoughts were on Kent. Where was he? Was he hurt? dead?

She did a slow three-sixty trying to come up with a place, a sanctuary where she could keep Christa safe while she searched for Kent herself. The danger was clear. Someone intended to hurt her. There was no reason to believe this person wouldn't hurt anyone else who stood in his way.

Evan and Tyler. The fire.

Two fires? The hair on her neck stood up straight. It couldn't be coincidence. This was no game. Someone was endangering others because of her. What she'd feared most was happening.

But Christa was not going to die in a third fire. Not if Georgia could help it.

"Come on. I've got an idea." Georgia gripped the handles of the wheelchair and pushed while the motor strained to carry Kent's sister over the mucky ground.

Once inside the dining hall, Georgia dragged the door closed, then explained her plan. "That lock on my door—it's something to do with another fire, Christa. One from the past." She gulped, then explained. "Two years ago, my husband and son were burned in a house fire. My cabin was lit on fire tonight. I believe both were deliberate."

"I think so too. Oh, Georgia." Christa reached out, squeezed her hand. "I've wanted to say this for so long—I'm so sorry about your family."

"So am I. But the thing is, I've got to find Kent and stop this madman. And I want to make sure you're safe while I do. So here's my plan. Come with me." She led her to the walk-in cooler. "This thing vents to the outside. It draws its air from there. It has good seals. Even if someone lit the dining hall on fire, and I don't think that's going to happen, you would be perfectly safe in here."

Georgia stopped and stared at the padlock swinging open. Someone had been here. Putting a finger to her lips to shush Christa, she grabbed a rolling pin, then yanked the door open. There was no one inside. In fact, it looked like nothing had been touched. Was someone trying to make a point—that he could come and go as he pleased, and there was nothing she could do about it?

"I-I don't want to be locked in there, Georgia. I'm scared." For the first time Christa's voice wavered.

"I am too, sweetie. But we have to do something. We can't let him win." She smoothed her hand over Christa's hair, pushing back the hood of the raincoat. "You won't be locked in. You'll be locking someone out. Come in here and I'll show you."

She waited until Christa was inside the cooler with her, then showed her how to bar the door so no one outside could open it. "You'll be the one who decides when you come out. And if you stick this shelf bracket in like so, wedge it so there's just a crack of space, you can hear if anyone is coming." She shifted, looked into Christa's frightened eyes. "Can you do it?"

"You're sure no one could lock me in?"

Georgia shook her head and pointed. "I turned the hasp in—see? They'd have to get the door open, bend it back, and lock it, but they can't if you've got the bar there."

"I thought you could never get locked inside this cooler." Christa frowned.

"You can't. But you can make it so nobody else can come in unless you want them to. My dad had one like this years ago when he renovated the restaurant. Doug and I made it into a secret house, complete with password and everything. I've done this a hundred times."

Christa inspected the arrangement, then twisted to look at Georgia. "You've led a very . . . unusual life," she said at last, a smile quirking up the corners of her mouth.

"I know." The need to hurry was like an ache inside her, nagging her to move on. She had to find Kent—and fast. "Christa, I have this feeling that Kent needs me. Will you be okay in here?"

"Yes." Christa made up her mind quickly. "If you'll hand me a stack of those towels and aprons and stuff, I'll pack them on myself to keep warm." She grinned. "I'm glad I have your sweater. It's warm as toast."

Georgia swathed Christa's feet and lower body as well as she could with whatever linens she could find. "Now, when I go, you fix the door exactly as I showed you. Okay?"

Christa nodded.

"Be warned. I'm going to try to open it, so make sure it's secure. And don't open it for anything until I tell you to. Got it?"

"Yes. Now go and find my brother."

"I'll try." Georgia bent, hugged her close. "I love you, Christa."

"I . . . love you too."

They shared one last look; then Georgia stepped out of the cooler and swung the door closed. She waited two minutes, then tried to open it. But there was no way she could budge the cooler door.

"Good girl," she whispered. "Please, God, keep her safe."

She turned and raced out the door, heading for the barn. She chose the shortcut, even though the path wasn't well lit and the land was rougher. It was the path Kent preferred, and she knew he would have come this way. Each building that she passed, she checked for signs of him. Each patch of ground she trod, she scoured for something, some clue that would tell her his whereabouts.

She found nothing.

The nearer she came to the southeast end of the grounds, the more she heard the horses, nervous, no doubt, with the lightning flashing. Free of the bushy undergrowth, she stepped into the clearing, only then realizing that the horses were outside the barn, not safely tucked inside as they were supposed to be.

Her heart raced as she slipped through the gaping barn door. "Kent?" She waited for an answer.

There was none. Something was very wrong. She could feel it in the chilly fingers of fear that crawled across her shoulders. The stalls were empty, as was the tack room. The gate was closed and secured, so he'd been here. But he would not have left those poor horses outside, not in this storm. So where was he?

Knowing the frightened animals would probably not respond well to someone they didn't know, Georgia left them loose in the corral and continued her search. Trying to see through the sheets of rain and alternating slashes of light and dark, she picked her way through the gloom of the shadowy underbrush, heading back toward the main buildings.

Panic waited to overwhelm her, so she whispered the words she could remember from the verses she'd read in the chapel. "We don't look at what we see, but at what we cannot see."

I can't see You, God. Help me. Please.

How could she go back and tell Christa that she hadn't found Kent, that she had no idea where he was?

Georgia sagged as terror reached out and gripped her stomach. What if she couldn't find Kent? What if she was all alone? Who was doing this? And why?

She had no answers. Where was God now? Did He hear her prayer? Would He answer?

Tears of frustration, anger, and worry obliterated her view for a moment. Her foot caught in a tree root and she stumbled, falling to her knees.

"We get knocked down, but we get up and keep going. So we do not give up."

Oh, God, I'm asking You to help. I can't do this anymore. I don't know where Kent is or how to help him. But You do.

The truth flooded her as if a veil had been lifted from her mind. *She* couldn't do this anymore!

Of course not. She'd been trying to carry on under her own strength, depending on her own abilities to understand and deal with the pain in her life. But true surrender meant leaning on God. Humanly speaking, she couldn't deal with this situation. She had neither the physical resources to search the entire camp nor the mental stamina to confront whoever was trying to harm her.

God knew that. And He didn't expect her to do it alone.

As she sat on the soggy ground, the dampness soaking through her clothes and chilling her skin, her soul warmed to the knowledge.

She was not alone. God was there, had been there all along. She didn't have to handle this alone. She could take this situation and leave it entirely in His hands if she wanted to. Or she could hang on, rant and rave about the injustice of life, and never allow Him to show His willingness to help.

"I get it, God," she whispered, tears rolling down her face, mingling with the rain. "I'm not supposed to handle all this, am I? I'm supposed to lean on You." She took a deep breath and handed her burdens over. "I don't know what the future holds; I don't understand why this happened. And I don't need to. Just show me what to do next. Please?"

She was so intent on praying she almost didn't notice when the wind died down.

But the voice—oh, that dear, blessed voice—carried on the night air like a cowbell. It was Kent's, louder than normal, as if he knew someone might be nearby listening.

The words weren't clear, but she knew the sound all the same. Slowly she rose, stepped through the bushes, thankful the rain had dampened the underbrush enough that it barely crackled when she walked.

After several tense moments, she came to the path that led to the pool.

"Why do you want Georgia?"

The answer made her blanch. "She has to die."

She stepped closer, careful to keep herself hidden by the canopy of branches but close enough to distinguish the figure of a man she'd accepted as a friend, a man who'd worked alongside all of them.

"Someone got her out of the cabin. Where is she now?"

"What cabin?" The desperation lacing Kent's voice hurt her heart. "What are you talking about?"

"I set a little fire." The hate-filled voice laughed. "Much smaller than the one in Calgary, but enough to do the job." Anger took over. "But she got away. It won't happen again. She has to pay. You will not stand in my way. No one will."

Georgia caught the glint of steel when Kent's flashlight moved. The man had a gun, and he was pointing it at Kent's head.

She allowed herself one moment for a heaven-sent plea, then stepped forward. "Are you looking for me, Herb?"

He wheeled around, then backed up, eyes flashing back and forth, keeping track of Kent and her. He waved the gun. "You'd better get over here before I finish off your boyfriend."

She walked forward, crossed the compound, and entered the swimming area. "Why would you want to do that, Herb?" She moved closer to Kent, met his eyes, and felt a surge of relief that he seemed fine. "I thought your grudge was with me. You've certainly tried to harm me often enough. Would you mind telling me why?"

"Why?" His whole demeanor changed. The meek, quiet helper had been replaced by a man so infuriated he could barely speak. "You stole everything I had!"

"But I've never even met you before." She frowned, tried to remember. "I'm sure I'd never spoken to you until you came to Camp Hope."

He smiled, but there was no mirth in it. His thin lips curled, baring his teeth. "I followed you here. From Calgary. You missed out on my first little party, but I wasn't worried. I knew I'd get another chance."

"Your first—" She stared at him. "You killed Evan and Tyler," she whispered, the horror of it made far worse because now she knew he'd done it deliberately, planned each step, and executed it as if she were a criminal.

"Yes. I thought you were inside with your husband and child." He moved nearer, his gun waving wildly through the air. "You should have died then too."

"But . . . why?" To have planned it all out, ruthlessly organized the deaths of innocent people—she couldn't wrap her mind around it.

"You killed my wife and my baby girl. You had to pay. Justine demanded it."

The simplicity of those words and the awful penalty they carried hung suspended in the air. Though the storm had moved on, flashes of lightning still speared the sky, illuminating the hate in his eyes.

"Justine Willows," Georgia said. The puzzle came together. "You were her husband?"

"We were going to be married." His face tightened into a mask of anger. "I was the father of our child—the baby you killed."

"But I didn't!"

"Have you forgotten so soon?" Herb shook his head. "Some nurse you are. She was under your care. She was in labor. You put a mask over her face. A mask filled with poison. My wife and my baby died because of you. Now you have to die. 'An eye for an eye.'"

That soft whisper reminded her of the voice in the hills the night she'd had the flat tire. "That was you in the woods?"

He nodded, exulting in his explanation. "I've been here all along, watching, waiting." He sneered at her gasp of shock. "You locked yourself up in that apartment in Calgary, and I got myself a job. I watched the whole thing, you know. The pretense to find the truth. But no one wanted to know the truth. The hospital wanted to cover it up, pretend it wasn't their fault, that you weren't their employee, that you hadn't murdered a woman and her child with your carelessness."

"But I didn't do it on purpose. It was an accident!"

"Oh, I heard that. They bought your little sob story, didn't they? Poor little nursie, rushed off her feet, had no chance to check the tanks."

"We never checked them." Even as she said it, Georgia knew he wouldn't believe, wouldn't really listen. His eyes were wild with anger. But she had to try. "The company contracted to take the empties, bring in the full tanks of Entonox, and hook them up. We'd never had a problem before. It was just—"

"An accident?" He laughed—a harsh bark of fury. "You think that telling me my wife and child died because someone made a mistake and put poison in a tank is good enough? that I can accept that? Could you accept that your husband and kid died for no reason?"

"No," she admitted, the magnitude of what he'd done overwhelming her. "But I didn't deliberately set out to hurt Justine or the baby. I was trying to help her. She was having such a difficult time. The doctors felt—"

Herb threw back his head and yelled, "The doctors! I don't care what the doctors felt. *You* killed her. *You.*"

Georgia almost wilted under the impact of his accusation. It was true. She'd put the mask over Justine's face and told her to breathe. And she watched life leach away. But she hadn't done it deliberately. "Herb, listen."

"No! You listen. I waited until the investigation died down; I was certain the whole world would know the truth. But you covered it up. You must have known the time would come for justice." He lifted the gun and aimed it at Kent. "You care about him, so he'll die first."

"Wait a minute!" *Dear God, help me.*

"Wait? I've waited over two long years. No more waiting." He turned toward Kent.

Georgia rushed into speech. "Where were you when Justine went into labor?" she demanded. "Why weren't you there with her?" She could see him falter, noticed the gun wobble as he turned from Kent to her. "She never listed any husband. I asked her over and over if there was someone who could come and be with her while she had the baby. She said no one cared."

"I-I . . ."

"She was all alone, going through agony to have your child. So where were you, Herb? If you loved her so much, where were you when she needed you?"

His head swung from side to side as if he were searching for an answer. "I had to work, to support us. I took extra shifts, scrounged and saved every dime so we could have a better life."

"Really? Or did you keep working because *you* wanted the money, wanted to impress her?" Georgia tried to remember exactly what Justine had told her. "She didn't care about money much. She told me she'd learned that doing without some things was easier if you had someone beside you to share the good times with. But she never talked about you. You weren't around much, were you, Herb? She went through that pregnancy without you."

"I was there! I came home every three months. I brought her gifts and enough money that we were supposed to buy a house after the baby was born." His jaw thrust forward in belligerence. "I was there and I loved her."

"But not enough to marry her," Kent interjected. He stared at Herb, piecing the information together. "This woman you loved so much, this woman who was going to have your child—you didn't legally make her your wife?"

"I had to get the money—to make sure we'd have a future!"

"But she didn't care about the money." Georgia studied Herb, watching as the impact of her words hit home and forced him to realize his mistakes. "Justine was overdue when she went into labor. You must have known the baby would come soon; you should have been there for her."

His chin drooped forward onto his chest. He looked at his feet. "I was coming home," he whispered. "I just needed one more day. I'd talked to her two days before. Nothing was happening with the baby. I thought it wouldn't matter if I took one more shift. It was an easy one, night shift. Nothing but a watch-keeper's shift."

"So you sat around cracking jokes with the boys while Justine went to the hospital by herself?" Georgia watched him closely, thought she saw him weakening. "Justine would have found it easier if you'd been there to help her through the pains," she murmured. "She was alone and scared. I tried to keep checking on her, but I had two other women in labor that night. I couldn't stay. You should have been there for her."

From the corner of her eye, she saw Kent move, positioning himself in a better place. She knew he'd try to grab the gun.

"She loved me," Herb said, the agony in his voice reaching her. "Justine was the only one who ever loved me enough. I could hardly wait to see her, to show her the down payment. But when I got there, they told me she'd died. And the baby with her."

There was nothing to say. His self-condemnation must be overwhelming. Georgia couldn't add to it.

She didn't get the chance.

With a snarl, he turned on her, the anger raging across his face. "She would be alive, our baby would be too, if you hadn't interfered. You went home to your husband and your cute little boy, and I was left with nothing. Not even a house we'd shared." He pulled his hand from his pocket, flicked a lighter in Georgia's face. "Wasn't it fitting that you should be left with the same? You killed them."

She had to do something. "I didn't kill Justine and the baby. But I understand your anger." She'd felt the same bitter fury eat at her soul, had come so close to where Herb was now. Like him, she'd blamed the wrong person. God was not the cause of Evan's and Ty's deaths. Herb was. "Why involve Kent? He hasn't done anything to you. He's innocent."

"So was our baby. But she died." He turned to Kent. "I tried to warn you. I left you a newspaper clipping to show she was no good, that she hurt people. But you kept on letting her be with those kids, feed them, give them medicine. You had a murderer in your precious camp and you let her stay."

Once again Herb lifted the gun; this time he pointed it at Georgia. Murder was in his eyes. "Go and get in my van, Mrs. MacGregor. We're going on a little trip."

She stared at the highly polished gun barrel, felt the terror all the way to her soul. *God?*

"She's not going anywhere with you." Kent surged forward, trying to knock Herb off balance.

Everything happened in slow motion. Georgia watched Herb's arm swing in an arc until he'd centered his aim, not on her but on Kent. A sneer twisted his lips. "You should have listened to me."

A blast echoed through the air. Kent faltered, his green eyes expanded in shock. Then he tumbled headfirst into the pool, sank to the bottom, and stayed there. A thin trail of red crept up through the water, spinning a web as his life force trickled away.

He'd killed him.

For the second time, Georgia would lose a man she loved.

Where was God now?

CHAPTER NINETEEN

I *am with you.*

A flash of lightning cracked across the night sky, shooting lethal daggers into the distance.

Now!

The order came from inside her head and dissipated the inertia that held Georgia transfixed. She'd asked; God had answered. It was time to trust.

She reached out, grabbed a fin from the basket of pool supplies, and swung it at Herb, using every bit of force she could muster. She caught him broadside. He stumbled, slipped on the water Kent had splashed on deck, and lost his footing. As he went down, his head made a loud thud against the unforgiving cement.

Georgia crept closer, checked his vitals. He was unconscious. She kicked the gun into the pool and saw Kent still lying in the water. The blood trail was getting darker.

In that second the truth of her feelings overwhelmed her. She loved Kent. God had led her here, given her a new beginning. But He had not caused her problems; Herb had. God was not the cause of her misfortune. But He'd been there to help her get through it. He would be now.

"We set our eyes not on what we see but on what we cannot see."

Georgia could not see God. But a certainty lay deep inside her. He was there. She only had to ask. *Please help Kent.*

She stepped out of her shoes and dived into the pool. Two strokes took her to the bottom. She grabbed Kent's collar and tugged him upward, then towed him to the steps in the shallow end.

It took a matter of moments to crouch over him, place her lips on his, and breathe into his lungs. She repeated the action several times.

Finally, he coughed, blinked, then stared at her. "I'm in trouble, aren't I?" he rasped.

She frowned at the angry, bloodied mark on his forehead. How badly was he injured? Concussed? He certainly wasn't making sense. "What do you mean?"

"Swimming alone, fully dressed, at night, during a lightning storm, bleeding into the pool." He shook his head. "I've broken every rule I ever made."

Joy filled her. "Yes, you have. I love you, Kent Anderson," she whispered.

"I know. I love you too." He accepted her helping hand, sat up, his fingers probing his forehead. "It's just a graze. I'm fine. It made me woozy and I lost my balance. Must have bumped it on the bottom." He frowned. "Where's Herb?"

"Over there."

They both looked at the unconscious man.

"We'd better tie him up."

The plastic rope that anchored the pool cover to the big roller had not yet been untied, which was probably the reason Kent had come to the pool in the first place. That rope was perfect for the job. It took several minutes to secure Herb.

"There. He's not going anywhere." Kent wrapped his arms around her waist. "I'm glad Christa's out of this."

"Christa!" Georgia slapped a hand over her mouth. "Oh no! We've got to go get her, Kent. I left her—"

"In the cooler." John finished the sentence as he pushed Christa's chair toward the pool. "She's fine." He glanced at Kent's forehead, nodded, then grinned at Georgia. "I couldn't find anyone, but I noticed the towels you'd folded last night were all missing. One was on the floor in front of the cooler and that little red button that signals the cooler light is on was lit but the door was closed. I figured something was funny." His face was serious. "I must compliment you on your excellent hiding place. There's no way that madman could have caught her in a fire locked up in there."

"Original, that's for sure." Fred walked out of the darkness behind John. "Guess maybe you could use a hand here."

Ralna appeared too, her mouth working. "What in the world has been going on?"

Georgia felt Kent's glance on her, then smiled at him. "It's a long story that I'll be happy to share tomorrow. But right now I think we should call the police."

Fred nodded, his eyes on Herb. "Rick just dropped John off. He's headed back to town, but I'll get ahold of him, ask him to bring some others. You two—" he pointed to two of the senior counselors who had just appeared—"watch this guy. The rest of you go to the dining hall and wait. I imagine there'll be some questioning and such."

The entire camp staff was staring at them. "You all came back?" Georgia asked.

"I finished those medical tests this afternoon," John said. "Rick wanted to show me around town, but I had a funny feeling that something wasn't right. Then I remembered that I'd seen Herb's van in town. He was supposed to be long gone. Rick left to issue an APB on the guy."

"Ralna left her medication behind. The storm shut down the water park so the kids all voted to come back early. Not that we were needed." Fred glanced at Kent's arm wrapped securely around Georgia's waist. He winked. "I see you managed just fine, son."

Georgia moved from Kent's arm to hug the older couple. "You two are always needed."

"So are you, sweetie," Ralna whispered before tugging her husband toward the dining room. "Come on. We'll make some hot chocolate."

"Is it okay if John takes me home? I'm cold." Christa grinned at Kent and raised an eyebrow. "Besides, you two probably have stuff to talk about. Maybe you want to clean up that wound while you're at it, Georgia."

Christa didn't wait for permission but turned her chair around. Then she paused. "By the way, John, you need to get working on those paths. I had quite a time tonight. Mud up to my ears."

"I'll start tomorrow. If it's okay with Kent." John moved alongside Christa.

"It will be all right. Trust me. Kent has other fish to fry," teased Christa.

Kent winked at Georgia. "Fish?" he repeated.

"Listen." Georgia hushed him.

"I'll see you home, Christa. But I can't stay long. I need to do something."

"Hmm, that sounds . . . odd, don't you think?" Kent peered after the disappearing couple. "Do you suppose John remembered something?"

"The way tonight is going, it could well be." Georgia stared up at his dear face as praises poured from her heart. "But I thought your sister said you had other fish to fry."

"So I do. Very pretty fish." His arms wrapped around her waist. "Thanks for rescuing me."

"You're welcome." She waited but he kept staring at her. "Is something wrong?"

"No." He shook his head, tucked her head under his chin, and hugged her close. "Everything is just fine. At last."

"Then would you mind kissing me?"

She heard his chest rumble with laughter. "Can't."

"Why not?"

"Company." He motioned to the two counselors watching Herb, then turned her in his arms in time to see the RCMP cruiser come racing into camp, lights flashing. Rick slammed on the brakes and got out of the car.

"Hey, Rick. How are you?"

"Oh, just peachy. Yourself?" Rick glanced at Herb, who was now conscious and struggling to get free. "This the guy? He looks like—" He hunkered down, took a second look. "Didn't he just spend his summer working here?"

"Yep." Kent grinned.

"Oh yeah." Rick's gaze moved to Georgia. "I see you finally got the girl. Smart move, though it took you long enough." Rick snapped his handcuffs on Herb, then removed the rope. "Good thing she's a nurse if you're going to go around whacking your head like that. How'd you do it, anyway?"

"Oh, I forgot," Georgia said. "There's a gun in the pool."

Rick blinked, looked at Kent. "A gun." He sighed. "Well, Kent, since you're already wet . . ." His meaning was clear.

Kent chuckled. "Sure, make me break more rules." He climbed into the pool. "Got an evidence bag?"

"Right here. Don't touch it, okay? Use the bag to pick it up." Rick held out the plastic container.

They watched as Kent retrieved the gun, handed the sopping wet bag back to Rick.

"I don't suppose you saw where the bullet went?" Rick shook his head in pretend disgust. "No, I didn't think so. Too busy looking at each other, I suppose. Come on, Herb. You and I need to have a little chat about a fire."

"Two of them," Kent growled. "He tried to torch Georgia's cabin tonight."

"Busy boy. Well, you'll have lots of time to rest where you're going."

"Wait a minute." Georgia stepped forward and stood in front of Herb. "I need to say something."

"I don't want to hear anything you have to say. Murderer."

Tears welled. "I'm sorry about Justine and your daughter, Herb. I never wanted to hurt them. I was only trying to help. I'm truly sorry for your pain."

He glared at her, then looked away.

Two other cruisers pulled in along with an ambulance.

"What did you call them for?" Kent demanded.

"To make sure you're in your right mind." Rick grinned. "Since they're here, let them take a look at your head. Then my guys are gonna want statements from you two. Separately."

Kent leaned over, brushed his lips against Georgia's ear. "I guess the fish will have to wait," he whispered, "till later."

"Later," she agreed.

It was a long time later when Georgia sat on the picnic table outside the pool area. The area around the pool had been taped off with yellow police tape, which Rick had insisted would be gone long before the last batch of campers arrived.

She turned her back on it and stared to the east, where the horizon had begun to send tentative fingers of flamingo into the dark sky.

Even if she'd had another cabin to go to, she wouldn't have been able to rest. There was too much to think about.

God had answered her prayers. Answered her—Georgia MacGregor. A web of warmth spread outward through her body. She was loved. God cared for her. Even though she'd blamed Him, He'd still been there.

What kind of love is that?

She thought of Herb, his anger and guilt mixing in his mind until hate had taken over. What if God hadn't drawn her to Camp Hope? What if she'd allowed the pain to fester until she'd become like him, clinging to the past? trying to get revenge to ease the pain?

She slipped the pictures out of her pocket and stared at them, one fingernail gently tracing the roundness of Tyler's squirrel cheeks. She'd had him for such a short time, but she'd loved him with all her heart. He was safe now, running through heaven's playgrounds, the angels watching him chase the birds he'd loved to watch.

And Evan. She gazed into his solemn eyes and knew he would wish her to move on. He'd hated waste of any kind; he would neither have wanted nor expected her to mourn him forever. He'd have liked Kent; she knew that. They were as different as night and day, but they both loved God.

In her hands she held the ashes of her life. But from these ashes God had worked something new and wonderful. She could find a future filled with love if she was willing to depend on Him to lead.

"I still don't understand why," she whispered, tears rolling down her cheeks, "but it's okay. You know and that's enough."

Once more the awning of peace she'd felt that very first day she'd come here settled over her. The prickle of fear, the nebulous worry, the dark cloud of depression—they were all gone, diminished and extinguished by the power of a love that wouldn't quit. God's everlasting, enduring love.

"I thought I'd find you here." Kent sat beside her on the table, but he made no move to touch her. "I didn't thank you for saving my sister. And me. Thank you."

"You're welcome." She watched the fingers of light move upward, expand, saw the sky lighten as a new golden glow grew.

"I'm sorry he hurt you, Georgia."

"So am I. But he hurt himself far more."

A long silence yawned between them. She knew Kent wanted to

say something important, but for once, she felt in no rush. God had given them both time.

"You were looking at your pictures again," he said.

"Uh-huh."

"Do you . . . I mean . . . will you ever be free of the past?"

Georgia smiled. She admired the beloved faces one last time, then slid the tattered photos into her jeans pocket.

After a moment's hesitation, she turned and placed her hands in his. "The past brought me here," she said, staring into his mossy green eyes. "I had no hope. I'd lost faith in everything, even God. And then I met you."

She smiled through the tears, willing him to understand what she was saying. "I had to go through this, Kent. But I couldn't have learned to trust and rely on God without your help. You showed me how to trust God with my future." She paused, regarded his beloved face. "Don't begrudge me my past. It's part of who I am."

His hand cupped her cheek. "How could I begrudge you anything? I love who you were, who you are, who you're becoming. All this time you've been searching for hope. I'm glad you found it here."

"Camp Hope," she whispered, unable to suppress her joy. "Where all things are possible with God."

"Speaking of possibilities—will you stay, Georgia? Will you marry me, help me make this place into what it could be to others, what it's been to us—a place where God changes lives?"

The words were so precious, so filled with hope, with possibility. And with love.

"Oh, Kent," she said softly, amazed by this gift from a God she was only beginning to know. "How could I go anywhere else? This is my sanctuary, my home. And home is where the heart is. Mine's right here." She lifted her hand and tapped his chest. "I'm not going anywhere."

"I love you." His lips moved over hers while her arms slid round his neck. As the eastern sky bloomed with the freshness of a new day, a new promise was made in two hearts that had passed through fiery trials and found God faithful.

An eternal promise.

A NOTE FROM THE AUTHOR

Dear Friends,

Thank you so much for taking the time to read Dangerous Sanctuary. I pray the book touched your heart and led you closer to our wonderful God.

For each of us there is a place we can go, a sanctuary to run to when life overwhelms—it lies in the Father's arms. Only there do we receive strength that can sustain us through the worries today brings and a renewal of hope for tomorrow. May you find that place.

Watch for Forgotten Justice, book 2 in the Camp Hope series for the continuing story of Christa and John. In the meantime, I look forward to hearing from you. My prayer for you is for abounding love, rich joy, and unquestioned peace.

Blessings,

Lois

ABOUT THE AUTHOR

A former human-resources manager for a national chain, Lois now lives in a small Canadian town with her husband and two sons. After delving into the entrepreneurial realm, Lois settled down to full-time writing. It's a job she loves in an environment most would envy. The perks of working in her home office while the birds chirp outside her window, coffee breaks on the patio, and the chance to chat with fans around the world make this a career she wouldn't trade.

This prolific author of seventeen inspirational romances (including *A Time to Remember*, June 2004) has also penned a novella titled "From Italy with Love," January 2004. *Dangerous Sanctuary* is her first foray into romantic suspense, one which she hopes to continue for many years. Lois enjoys making pottery, singing with a local group, and traveling, but her favorite activity is swimming.

You may contact Lois by writing to her in care of Tyndale House Author Relations, P.O. Box 80, Wheaton, IL 60189; or via her Web site at www.loisricher.uni.cc.

Turn the page
for an exciting preview of book 2
in the Camp Hope series

Forgotten Justice

Available winter 2004

ISBN 0-8423-6437-4

www.heartquest.com

FORGOTTEN JUSTICE
Excerpt from Chapter 1

Christa finally found him in front of the camp's computer. "John?"

He seemed not to hear her. His fingers lifted onto the keyboard, and he began entering rows of numbers.

A Web page burst upon the screen—a page that scared Christa.

"There's something I was supposed to do," he mumbled. "Something that means life or death . . . to someone. But I can't remember what it was."

She reached out to touch his shoulder, but her hand froze in midair. A deep sense of foreboding filled the room, warned her to wait.

John stabbed the screen with one finger.

October 20, Christa read.

"That's a little over two months from now." His voice was sharp, tortured. "Two months until a deadline that will cost someone his or her life."

"Whose life?" Christa felt as if evil had moved into the room. "John, what is the threat?"

"I don't know," he whispered. "And I have no idea how to stop it."

⟫⟩◈⟨⟪

A small house in the mountains of Colorado

Three men stared at the same Web page as a password flashed across the screen.

"He's just logged on."

Their leader rose, glanced at the screen, nodded. "Which means he's still alive. Now find him. Fast." He tapped his boot against the floor as if pacing out the seconds of life.

"Then get rid of him."

Coming Soon!

THE PERFECT MATCH
*Will fighting fires prevent Dan and Ellie
from striking the perfect match?*

LIKE A RIVER GLORIOUS
Rachel was an unwilling partner in deception. Now she finds herself losing her heart to Adam Burke—the man she must betray, unless she can find a way out.

MEASURES OF GRACE
Set free from her past, Corrine begins a new life—unaware she is being sought by a man bent on vengeance.

Visit **www.heartquest.com** today!